To

Ashley,

For What It's Worth

Printed in the United States of America.

For What It's Worth

A collection of Short Stories

Written by Roberto Scarlato

Stories included:

Failing Upwards

The 75th Last Meal

The Letters

Your Escape Plan Now

Alex Dujima's Book Code

Bring him back again

The Graveyard shifters

The Nature of a Secondhand

I.F.

Lighter

Pennies

Pus

Me and mine

Powerless

Gun Control

10 Days In The Extra Life

Regenerhate

The Aches

The Subtle Teachings of Mr. Rifa

Introduction

This collection of short stories may seem random but they are, in fact, very connected to one another. The majority of these stories focus on the internal turmoil that we all go through. Some are funny, weird, downright degenerate…and that is intentional. I'm really interested in people in general and have been introduced to some very interesting characters throughout my life. I like character studies and this collection was a way for me to branch out, to step into the shoes of people I've never met. It gave me a chance to figure out their motivations, their dreams, hopes, losses. It really is quite an experience to jump in and out of these characters. I hope their stories convey the repeating theme that we, as mere toddlers on this planet, are constantly searching for our place in life. We all want to know where we're headed, where we are going. For the people who found their worth in these stories, I'm happy for them. Others weren't that lucky. Such is life. But I hope that all of you kind readers find out how much you are worth in the eyes of another.

In loving memory of Ivano,

The man who never frowned.

Failing upwards

As I walk in, I can already see "Tex" sitting at the concierge desk. He's in his underpants and a greasy shirt and, for some reason, is wearing a bellhop hat crooked on his head. Perfect. The guy is over seventy years old, owns the place, and yet he will never admit to his outlandish eccentricities.

The door handle rips off as I enter, the wood breaking away from the brass knob as easily as a rusty nail through a foot. I hold it in my hand for a few seconds. My mouth cringes to the right in annoyance. It's like I was shaking a hand and the owner of it disappeared. I debate for a bit whether to put it back or not. But to put it back is like putting a bullet back in the wound. What's the point? I fumble to shove it back into thc gapping hole and, when I finally have it in, the handle to my briefcase breaks and the bag drops to the ground. I bring my other hand with the briefcase handle still clutched tightly in it to my face.

This place is starting to rub off on me.

This place is a broken, rundown, abandoned, no good, filthy, unorthodox pile of rubble.

So why do I still come here?

Easy answer.

Rent control.

The owner is senile and still charges ten bucks a night. How he lives on it I'll never know. But, geez, finding a place to stay is hard when you're a loner in Chicago.

The year is 1953.

And it only gets harder from here on out.

My name is Charles Avery. You can call me Charlie.

"Tex" calls me "Mr. Bills".

The dope.

It's so hard to find a decent hotel around these parts. And I have to work my bony butt off to find the most decrepit eyesore just to feel relaxed.

Every day is an adventure trying to get upstairs.

You'll join me in the madness, won't you?

Already, as I'm tossing the broken handle away with a grimace on my face, I can hear "Tex" put on the same dang song that he always plays on that heap of a record player of his. *In the Hall of the Mountain King*. He always does that when I show up. Aside from the lowlifes, the down-and-outers, the hobos sleeping around the place, I'm the only one who decides to take the adventure of sleeping in a room and trying to reach the top floor of the hotel in order to do it.

In case you can't find this hotel that I'm talking about, it's in the upper north side, wedged between two black buildings that are on their way to being abandoned as well. "The Rundown" is what we call it. But back in the old days this place was known as "The Riverbank Hotel."

Already the song starts. And the game begins.

Why is this the old man's only source of entertainment?

"Evening, Tex," I say out of the side of my mouth as I hook the briefcase under one arm and try not to crunch the rubble under my feet. All of it is from the ceiling. It started to go when the new water damage started. Already I can hear the creaking overhead and duck as a chunk about the size of a large portrait comes sailing down and crash-lands right at the point where I was standing.

I shake and quiver, holding my briefcase as if it were my soul ready to float away.

The old bat "Tex" begins to snicker so much that one of his teeth falls out. He picks it up, dusts it off, tries to put it back, fails, then ends it all with a "Shucks! That was a good one too."

Now I get my turn to laugh as I shake off the distress and start making my way as before.

"Bathing time!" someone shouts. And before I can get a grip on anything, the hobos go into their routine. Like excited children they gather and line up against the walls. Three or four on each side are carrying mop buckets. With glee they tip them, splashing the water at every angle on the floor.

My new shoes get splashed at all angles. The hobos, with their clothes still on, thank the Lord, are diving on the floor, slipping and sliding everywhere. Some crash into each other and laugh in a drunken stupor.

I try not to spin.

Then, miniature ships of green zizag past my feet.

"Rodney, over here," one of them shouts.

I see the man they call Rodney, and he seems more than happy to send the green ship on its way, flinging it across the slick ground as if it were a rock skipping ripples in a pond. But it doesn't skip me.

Nope.

The green bar of soap somehow wedges under my shoe and I am slipping all over myself.

This brings another chorus of laughter.

With a bar of soap stuck to your shoe, you'd be surprised how much that throws your walking abilities off. I am trying to keep myself calm, but many of the old tramps provoke the silliness even more. One slides over to me and proceeds to dance with me. The nerve.

The bunch of misfits put on a whole show. A mad bunch of hooligans is what they all are.

I shove him away, losing my balance, dropping my briefcase in the process. *Forget it*, I tell myself. Every man for himself.

I bend and scrap the large, molded chunk of soap of my shoe. Darting here and there, dodging the wistful winos who seem to be caught up in a dance number, I lurch myself to one of the four long staircases leading to upstairs, the stairways of my salvation, my rest.

Glancing behind myself, as I climb, with my hands as much as my feet, I can see below. Suds. Bubbles. Thousands of big and small, bubbles soiled by tramps. The dancing men are caked in them. But this does not stop them from drinking, Lord no. With the floor so slick, they slide the bottles back and forth, laughing to themselves as they make a sport of it. Some even crash into each other, erupting in laughter once again.

I, myself, oh, did you forget me?

Yes, sir, I'm the one trying to escape all this.

I'm halfway up, gaining distance.

Ker-crack!

Not for long, I see.

The sudden lurch brings me to my knees, clutching the railing.

Then, I glance up to see that the wood, old as it is, has finally given its last vow of support.

Confound the damn steps!

Now, as I hold on tight, they give at the top, which tells me that I'm going down in a big hurry. In mere seconds I'll tumble down, soap or no soap, give my leg a good break, then wonder if any of these buffoons will phone for a doctor.

The entire staircase tips sideways, veering to the left, leaving me no choice but to grab onto the enormous chandelier. Scurry and spinning, kicking my legs, unable to control my spin. If only Margery could see me now. She would not have believed it. Neither would I.

Thankfully, I conform into a sitting position in the chandelier itself, giving me a bird's-eye view of the chaos unfolding before me. Like dominoes, the staircases collapse and crack against one another, creating waves as pipes are bursting all over the place.

The chandelier can't seem to stop its spinning and I hold on for dear life. Funny as it may seem, I never had the stomach for merry-go-rounds at the fair, and this one seems to be going remarkably fast. It doesn't help matters much that the roof is now joining in with what I can only describe as the bubble bath mayhem below. Streams of roaring water come down and are just as solid as banisters. I should know, the chandelier keeps spinning me into them.

And in the midst of this fumble of fate, this theatrical night which grows worse with each desperate climb to the top, though I can't remember it going this sour this fast, I see, wiping the water from my face, one of the boys below has found my typewriter and is using it as a poor man's excuse for an umbrella. But as he brings it up to shield his head from the streams of water coming down, the ink has run and paints his entire abdomen in blue ink. He gags and whines as he tosses the devil of a thing out of his sight and, as well, out of mine.

Oh, did I not mention I'm a writer?

Soaked as I am, I can't help but laugh at his misfortune. In time he will get his laugh as well. The water starts to wane but that doesn't stop the chandelier from spinning or the chain from tightening, making the ceiling very unstable to handle both the weight of my soaking body and the chandelier.

Readily panicked, I try to change the trajectory of my fall or, by some slim chance, swing myself over to the banister to the floor I am trying to get to.

"Incoming!" I find myself shouting, practically grunting to get my swing to go in a straight line.

Chunks of the ceiling are giving, making the bums dart back and forth in the water.

The record skips, but still charges ahead.

Inch by inch.

Inch by inch I swing to get to my room, to get my rest.

Another large chunk falls, a man below narrowly avoids it and somehow it cracks something in the floor, allowing the few feet of water that has gathered to drain noisily into a long forgotten drainage system.

Victorious, I clutch onto the banister just as the chandelier gives, spins and crashes into the concierge's desk, destroying the floor, the desk, the register, the record player and rattling "Tex" something awful. I know what he will say. To hell with the rest of his furnishings. That is his only copy of that record.

Now fully tired, I lurch myself over the banister, breathing heavily and dizzy from fright. The buzz has died down and some of the bums below have themselves a nervous chuckle to lighten the mood.

My jacket, as I squeeze the coat tails, oozes a combination of water, soap, sweat and I don't know what.

Exhausted, I shuffle to the door marked 336, pull back the door to see a glowing white mattress awaiting me.

Rest.

All this work. Now rest.

Ding!

I freeze as I hear the sound. I wonder two things at this point. One would be how on earth could the service bell survive the crash, though I could imagine "Tex" carrying that around with him. He always does - sometimes wearing it as a cap. Second, who in their right mind, besides me, would want to check in here?

After hearing a small chorus of wolf whistles, I receive my answer and cringe as I shut my eyes and put my hand over them as well.

"Mr. Avery!" Tex calls out. "Seems you have a visitor!"

My back curls as I sniff a few drops of water up my nose and turn on my heel to make my way back toward the banister.

I look down and there she is, folks.

Margery.

Her mascara running, it could only mean one thing. She's sorry about the fight we had and wants me to come home. I turn back to the bed, it still glows, waiting for me to slop down and forget it all. And it has taken me so much just to make it up here, just to get some rest.

I turn back to my dearly, devoted, caring, loving wife of ten years, two children and a history of fine peach pies and I say, "Can it wait till the morning? I'm really tired."

She frowns at first, then smirks.

With that smirk, that famous smirk of hers, I know that tonight she's getting her way, and I'm certainly not getting mine. Not after all the tears she's just shed over our silly fight.

"Sorry, Charlie. Time to go."

Dripping wet, I nod my head.

How the hell am I going to get down?

The 75th Last Meal

Samuel hated this. He hated it all, when it came right down to it, the guards, the building, the parking (there was none. he had to park three blocks away and was now walking), the salt in the air, not to mention the killer he would be interviewing.

Samuel Tredmark was an honest, if not a little underpaid, reporter for the *Wing Bird*, a local newspaper. He was a concise writer and a drinker of scotch in times of stress. He wore brown slacks and had thick sideburns that accentuated his jaw line. His eyes were bright green, and they always turned brighter in the summer.

Of course, interviews with murderers did have it's perks; especially as the killer was on death row and would be executed that night. He wouldn't have to deal with him afterwards. It would be short and quick, or long and painfully grueling depending on the mood of the inmate.

Samuel, in his gut, knew that even though he despised this man, he needed him now.

Maybe, just maybe the killer would spill the beans on some higher-up crime bosses. Maybe he would tell of the location of the bodies. Or, as stunning as it might seem and regrettably was followed with doubt, possibly confide to him why he did it in the first place.

Some reporters, a few at that, had their name branded on everyone's forehead the minute they wrote an article that turned their scummy not-a-penny-to-my-name asses into the next journalist for hire. Maybe he would do a bit of freelance once this was over. That is if it did, in fact, have an end.

The bars clanged sideways with a loud and echoing boom. His steps made on the slick floor had been louder than the bars, making clicking sounds like the same ones his typewriter made.

It was summer now, which meant that all those who had an agenda to look presentable had better retire. Sweat stains gathered on his buttoned-down white shirt in the armpit areas. He hated sweating there. They were standing out like little miniature bull's-eyes for everyone to see. But, then again, why look good for murderers, rapists, pedophiles, and prostitutes? Oh my! What a dreadful thought to realize. Not the presentable part; the fact that he didn't care how they didn't care. That was enough for a laugh.

Licking his hand, he tried hard to slick back that one cowlick on the back of his head. Some called it a bald spot. That's right. It was a cowlick to begin with, but later on that year it would form into a bald spot with impending stress.

His arms were hairy as he rolled up his sleeves to avoid the heat. A ready, trusty, number two was wedged behind his right ear. It had significant nibble marks from all the times he tried to gnaw out a story with it.

"Tredmark," the man said. He was an obviously fat man, the warden, judging by his cleanly pressed blue suit. It was a damn near crime that *he* didn't sweat. It angered Samuel a little. "You must be here to see *him*."

Samuel straightened up a bit to shake the fat man's hand.

"Don't want to but, you know, had to grab this story before someone else did."

The fat man's chin quivered in a hardly audible laugh. It got lost inside the blubber. "Constantly searching for little pieces of meat to gnaw on, eh? Tell me, Sam, do you and your hounds fight over which one will write the columns?"

He continued to walk a long, brightly lit corridor, that anticipated his approach by blinding him with a beam of light every few seconds. "Peterson and James write the columns. If I'm lucky, the editor will find time to fetch me one."

"How is Daniel?"

"He's as pesky as ever. He told me that you knew him way back when."

"That little turd knew everyone back in college. I'm merely his chess buddy compared to the higher-up's that he's conversing with." The fat man sighed. Sighing signified that he was troubled at the thought of having no friends. After all, it took two of Samuel to make one balding, fat, warden.

"You brought the necessary papers?" He turned.

"I did," said Sam, shuffling through his briefcase and now pulling out the colored folders consisting of the necessary documents in order for him to see the prisoner.

"You are aware," the warden blubbered on, "that this is his last chance to talk to anyone of the living world?"

"Wait. You mean I'll be the last person he sees?"

"Yes."

"But surely he has family."

"No friends, no relatives."

"All dead?"

"All dead."

Samuel quivered a bit. His next question was last minute, he knew. "By him?"

"No, natural causes. Nope. He only murdered strangers."

"I see."

"Oddly enough, from their missing posters and their

background checks, they were all very crude people. Not much more than local street trash, I'd say."

He jingled his keys inside his pocket, found the right one and opened the last barred door.

"Everyone deserves a second chance. These were still people that he killed," Sam spoke up. "Just because they died with a not-so-sweet reputation doesn't mean that in the other life. We're *all* sinners walking around on a free ride, when you look at it."

The warden turned to him and tilted his head like a confused bulldog. "Religious?" he asked.

"No. Realist."

He opened the door and let Samuel in.

The room was dark except for the bars in front of him. There had been a strange power outage that had turned off the hall lights but not the prisoners' cell lights. His had been the brightest in the hall.

The fat man was heard blubbering his apologizes for the lack of light and assured the young man walking down to go see *him* that they would continue to try and fix it.

A gentle hand appeared through the bars. A perfectly manicured pair of fingernails glided their way up and down the bars.

The dead man waited for his prey. He waited for his audience. He waited for his amusement. He was always quite amused with himself and all things around him.

As Samuel passed a load of hollowed cells, he was surprised to find that it was hotter here even with the lights off.

In the cell next to the man who was waiting to die, there sat a decrepit old vagrant whose eyes were glazed. His clothes were a greenish brown and they had looked ancient with dust. A darkish green T-shirt was seen, stitched together at every possible rip. His cell was perfectly tidy except for himself. He looked to be some hobo they had plucked off the street. His cell smelled awfully sweet for a man who appeared to look like he should smell like something foul. Coincidentally, Samuel felt more relaxed passing this old man's cell the most. It was a puzzling, pleasing sensation.

"Do not be fooled," the old man said. "Looks are not the only things he holds dear."

Samuel paused for a brief moment. Could he be referring to the man he would speak to in just a few moments? Was he preparing him for something?

As Samuel slowly turned the corner, smoke was emanating from the gritty bars containing the prisoner. Everything was picture perfect.

Death row inmates don't usually get beds but, nevertheless, there was one pushed in front of the wall. Inside the cell there was nothing but crystal clear white paint and an almost blinding light from above.

Inside, the man stood in front of the bed. In his hand was a common cigarette, but he sucked on it joyously getting all the pleasure out of its poisoned skin. He was wearing a remarkably faded maroon robe and was quite tall for it. He was also quite slender for his age which probably racked in the thirties. The shoes planted on his feet were from only the finest Italian designer and they gleamed a reflective glow.

Not only were his hands astonishingly clean shaven with perfect fingernails, but his face was a gem of a structure. His features were handsome and cool. Not a care in the world. The perfection in his face was smooth and his thin toothpick-sized mustache came to points around the corner of his mouth. A single strand of black hair streaked down in front of his brownish eyes of scrutiny.

And there was something else. A calmness about him, as if Samuel was just a friend stopping by. The man had a calmness that was as rich as the king of England and even had the maturity and wit that would make even Vincent Price blush. In fact, he looked similar to the popular horror icon.

And then, when he spoke, the words were crisper than even the fattest bacon sizzling in a pan. There was a deep richness in his voice, as if he emphasized every word like it were gold. He wanted to be clear to his new guest.

"Ah, yes," he cooed, "a visitor to see me. How pleasant."

He took another gorge of his smoke.

"I'm Samuel."

"I know who you are, sir," said the prisoner. "I've read your pithy articles on birds. You have some sort of fascination with them?"

Samuel seemed out of place. The man seething in the cell was the most dangerous man he had ever encountered, but the man had also displayed an ease as if he had done nothing wrong. But, then again, all criminals think that way, so thought this one.

"I, uh, I have come here to do your last interview, sir."

The man looked increasingly annoyed, smoking still. "Yes. I realize that fact, young man."

"You know what date it is, don't you?"

"October sixth. My execution day," he stated.

"You don't seem at all upset."

"Me? Upset?" The man laughed. "I've got better things to do with my time, my boy."

"Such as?"

"Anticipate," he said dryly.

Samuel calmly looked around the grungy floor. If the man was indeed reading his mind, he was doing a pretty damn good job of it.

"Searching for something to sit down on?"

"Yes. They didn't give me a chair."

"What do you expect? This a prison built on coins, not dollars. They have to constantly make budget cuts here and there, you see."

Samuel tried to find a clean spot on the floor, but in his searching, he noticed something quite peculiar. The man standing in the middle of the cell cupped one hand and outstretched it.

"Care to sit in my palm?" the man gleefully asked.

"I'm not quite sure I'd fit?" Samuel joked.

"You'd be surprised how many people do," he said while

sucking another puff.

In the dark, Samuel bumped up against something. It was probably a chair that he had just found. Instead of telling the man he was crazy he decided to pull the chair up behind him and sit. The chair was incredibly comfortable and conformed to his body shape, perfectly supporting him. *It must be one of those new-age chairs*, Samuel thought

"I found a chair."

"Naturally," the man said, sitting down with a bow.

Papers seemed to get tangled in Samuel's fingers. He was trying to search for the right one. He found it, even in the dark. It was a long file, and he had fortunately brought a tape recorder along with him. He clicked it on with his thumb.

"I want to let you know that you don't have to tell me anything you don't want to. If you say, want your lawyer present, then I think that could be arranged."

"Young man, I have dealt with lawyers before. They have a certain knack for joining my side, but my lawyer doesn't represent *me*."

"Well, I'm sorry to hear that."

"I'm not. He was a coward," he said with a sinfully pleasing smile.

Not that the smoke was bothering him, but Samuel fanned a hand near his nose. A thick moldy smell was emanating from somewhere in the corridor. It reeked of burned toast and vile body odor. Samuel spotted a sewer drain near the bars in front of him. No wonder.

But now that he had looked up, he noticed that the man was continuing to smoke, legs crossed comfortably in front of him. He had smoked the thing past the filter! Did he not taste the change? Was he doing it intentionally to make Samuel feel even more awkward?

Trying not to gawk at him, Samuel continued.

"I've made a list of all the questions I've got for you."

"Have you? Tell me, what kind of simple list did you write up?"

"Yes. They are simple but…"

"Simple is not the word I would use, dear man, if I were to be in the presence of someone like myself. If I were you, I'd think of the questions that the others did not ask."

"Others? What others?"

"Why, the others like you."

"Like me?" he said puzzled, "But you've only just met me."

At this the man grinned again. He was becoming increasingly entertained by Samuel's interview and did not hesitate to be even more mysterious than before.

"Are you so sure of that?"

"Yes. Why?"

The man giggled in his throat. "You'll find out soon enough," he said, speaking like a father trying to teach a son.

"Well, let's get on with it," the man said as he swallowed the last of his cigarette. Why did he swallow his cigarette? Did he get a kick out of consuming disgusting things like that in front of Samuel?

"Very well. It says here that your birth name is Michael…"

"No," he interrupted. "That's not correct at all."

"So you go by a different name?"

"Yes."

"What is it, may I ask?"

"Oh, let's see what it is today," he said while turning his head to the ceiling and patting his chin. His head snapped back to Samuel, and he spoke with creative genius as he said, "Devious Lathrop."

"I see."

"Yes. Interesting name I chose, don't you think?"

"I think we better start."

"Please do."

"First, right off the bat, why did you do it?"

Devious petted his mustache. He looked like he had been through this routine before and had tried to come up with some other way of answering the question.

"I was lazily bored. I had to find some people to take. Even if it meant getting caught."

"Okay. Second, do you know where the bodies are?"

"Sadly, yes," he said, annoyed with that fact. He made it seem like he was repeating himself in the way he said it. It was all very confusing. "Some are up while others are below."

"Below? You mean underground?"

"Let's just say they didn't reach China. If that's what you're asking."

"What about up? You said that others were up?"

"Why, yes. Lots. I can't control where they all go."

"Up where?"

"Up there." He pointed childishly towards the ceiling.

"Oh, you think they've gone to heaven?"

"Sadly, yes."

"But where are the bodies specifically? I need specifics."

"I can't be any more specific than that."

Just then a guard approached carrying a tray of steamy buttermilk pancakes caked with butter and syrup with some scrumptious strawberries oozing from the giant mass. All of it was topped with whipped cream and a random pattern of sprinkles.

The guard placed the tray inside the slit for the prisoner to grab and left down the corridor. He seemed in a somewhat zombified state.

"Ahh," Devious smelled the delightful dish. "My last meal. I better slow down on these. I'm getting quite pudgy." This was true, from what Samuel had seen. There was a slight bump just below the man's rib cage. He must have consumed a lot of those pancakes before he was caught. It must have been his favorite dish or something.

Samuel looked about, confused. This was not the way a normal prisoner acted, and certainly not the staff. Was this a dream? Was he just realizing, just now, that it was a dream?

"I thought a prisoner wasn't allowed to have a last meal on death row until after the visitor left."

"On occasion, these gentlemen bend the rules for me," he

giggled. "Excuse me while I gorge myself."

As he was chowing, Samuel watched. The man slurped everything as if it were his life source. He really enjoyed his feast. So much so that he slowly took his time rolling the strawberries in his mouth from one cheek to the next, letting it dissolve perfectly in his mouth.

"May…may I continue?" Samuel asked confused. Confusion was like a thick hat that pulled itself firmly over Samuel's eyes. He hated that feeling—he had felt it before.

"Please do," Devious said, half of his strawberries juicing their way out of his mouth. It was a sickening sight.

"When did you feel this urge to destroy people?"

"Oh," he laughed, waving a hand. "That was ages ago. I couldn't specifically say what year."

Devious scooped up a giant mound of butter and shoved it into his mouth without even squinting. He swallowed it whole. Samuel cringed a bit.

"What would you say to the families of the people you murdered?"

"Mmmm," he said, holding up a strawberry with his fork. "That strawberries are back in season, my good fellow."

"I need you to answer my question."

"I just did."

Samuel was annoyed but continued on.

"I would like to know what instrument you used. The police can't seem to pin it down."

"Myself."

Now Samuel was feeling that they were going around in circles. Finally, he got fed up with this man, but their conversation ended just in time. Devious was finished eating and the guards had come to shackle him and haul him to the dead man's path.

Samuel stood and tried to push the chair back, but it had disappeared in the darkness. It seemed strange, but he shook it off in his fit of annoyance.

"Good luck," he told Devious on his way out. He tried to get out of there quick.

But as they were moving Devious out of his cell, he took one last disturbing look at Samuel and said with grinning lips, "I'll see you soon."

That night, Samuel dreamed. He dreamed of horrible things. Awful things.

The dream was always the same. It was a dream of him flying backwards down a corridor as if he were being pushed by a strong wind. The corridor was heavily lit and a string of jail cells were passing his sight.

But he always frightened himself by looking in one cell that passed him slowly instead of quickly. He would never forget that face. A face of a man laughing. But this was no ordinary laugh. It was a consuming laugh. It was a disturbing laugh that made the man in the dream's neck appear to have straining veins, displaying just how hard he was laughing.

The laughter cackled and got lost in the corridor of his mind. But the worst was to hear it echoing in the darkness until he finally woke up.

Drenched in sweat, he breathed heavily. The air from the window was cool and moist. Samuel shut it.

Samuel hated this. He hated it all when it came right down to it. The guards, the building, the parking (there was none—he had to park three blocks away and was now walking.), the salt in the air, not to mention the killer he would be interviewing.

Samuel Tredmark was an honest, if not a little underpaid, reporter for the *Wing Bird*, a local newspaper. He was a concise writer and an even better drinker of scotch. German with a little hint of Italian had been his nationality. He wore brown slacks and had shaved his sideburns to daggers that rested securely, like he would pluck them off at any second to use them as weapons, on his jaw line. His eyes were bright green because of the summer—they always turned brighter, of course.

Of course, interviews with murderers did have their perks. But something wasn't right.

Samuel stopped in his tracks outside. He looked around and even stole a glance at the gray sky above him. It was then that he realized that this had already happened.

There had to be some logical explanation. The day couldn't possibly be repeating itself. Normal days carried on like a clock; always moving forward and never moving back. No clock in the world had the ability to move backwards. Samuel knew this. But what he didn't know was what scared him the most.

He knew, for sure, that he hadn't dreamed up yesterday because everything was very physically vivid. The colors, senses, smells, especially the smells. But then again, dreams are very vivid in the mind of any writer.

Samuel grew impatient with his anxiety and galloped across the street to the prison.

Once in, he met up with the fat man who he had talked to before. He looked exactly the same in every aspect. A large blue suit covered his extremely wide frame, and his double chin bounced along with his steps.

Samuel grabbed him madly, the pencil dropping out from behind his ear as he did. "This isn't today, is it?" he asked in desperation.

The fat man was copious in his incoherent blubbering and tried to understand Samuel's question, even though it was a confusing one.

"Y...you're Samuel, aren't you? Y...you're here to see h...*him*?"

Samuel grew angry. He shook the man and shoved him up against the wall, forgetting that he was just a writer and not an action star.

"What are you talking about? I already saw him. He was

the most vile and ignorant man I've ever seen. His own cell reeked of dead fish. I remember it."

Fatty decided to shove Samuel's arms away. He ruffled his suit jacket and tried to straighten it. "Now I know you're crazy," he declared. "Not one person is admitted to see the prisoner without my permission. Such untidiness, really!"

It didn't happen often, but Samuel's hair was most ruffled. And now it stood on end with anxious fear. The fear was breathing hot pockets of breath down his neck, and his veins begun to contract in nervous fidgets.

"He…he's still here?"

Fat man sighed, rolled his eyes, glared at Samuel and shouted, "Of course he is!"

How is that possible? he wondered. *Has everyone gone mad? Did the fumes in this place produce any illusions or did they invoke amnesia? There had better be an explanation to all of this. There's got to be!*

"But not for long," the fat man replied, still wiping himself off. He then noticed that there were some rogue crumbs on his chin and proceeded to wipe those as well. "He's scheduled to be executed tonight. Not a moment too soon too. The families are sending me their angrily misspelled letters. So angry that they rush to write it to me, I suppose. I suppose everyone's in a rush in this day and age."

Only one way to handle this, Samuel thought. *I have to live out the day .exactly as before. Maybe it's a dream, but I'm going to control it this time. I've got to see him again. Maybe this time I'll wake up. Gotta wake up, Gotta Wake Up.*

"Ah, Here he is, my knight in shining armor, come to whisk me away to a life of exquisite melancholy," boasted the man in the white cell.

"Can it, Devious!" boomed Samuel.

Samuel was dressed in his normal clothes like before; only he was missing his trusty old number two. He didn't care anymore if he had a story to write, he wanted to hear it with his ears.

"What the hell are you still doing here?"

"Please, don't remind me of home," he said gloomily.

Another cigarette was clutched in his right hand in the utmost elegant position. He dragged it in gracefully and poured the smoke out of his mouth in a lasting, heavy, breath.

"You realize what date it is, don't you?"

"October sixth. What's my prize?" Devious laughed.

"You're supposed to be dead," Samuel said with a disgruntled fury in his voice. He pointed a finger at him. It was just too frustrating knowing that you were being toyed with by him.

"Since when were you the keeper of rules? You can't possibly hold all the keys. That somehow strikes me as too much of a responsibility for a man like you."

True, Samuel was a struggling reporter. He could barely keep any meat on the table without it being ripped from the plate. But he knew that the law and order of the natural world didn't apply to the man in the white cell for some reason. This angered him. Because in his heart he knew that all things, whether living or not, needed to find their order and place.

If there was no place for this man, then who was he? Could it possibly be a dream? Could it possibly be a continuation of the dream he had last night? Or was it *this* night?

Had he woken up, got up, closed the window, and fell right back asleep? It was a possibility. Not a firm one, but something to latch onto for a while. Even a mad man needs his little crumb of hope to nibble on. A lot of people wake up and fall back into the dream without realizing it at first, don't they?

This could, in Samuel's mind, very well be a continuing dream in which he knew he was truly dreaming. A lucid dream to keep him company.

"Thinking of impossibilities?" Devious asked. He also had a devious-looking smile plastered all over his face.

Samuel let the question hang into the dead air. Meanwhile, he searched the grounds for the familiar chair. He found it in the darkness behind him. Bending his back, he sat in its comfortable pose. As he backed into it, he noticed that the man's hand went back down again to its side. What was he doing before? Was he holding it up to Samuel?

He shoved the thought aside and paved the way for more important inquiries. Last time, he had wasted the moment by asking vague questions and had tried to move the time along quickly. This time, he hoped that time would slow down just a little bit for him. Enough to where he could use it wisely. It was better to be wise with the time he had rather than wastefully ignorant. So now, after much frowning of his brow, he began to churn his mind into a batter of smart questions. It was better to start off fresh with intelligence. After all, Samuel had no way of knowing just how far this man's intelligence reached. It was better not to know, but it was also best to be prepared for the worst. Prepared to tackle the pride and wrestle it down to the ground. It was just him, the man, and the mood, now. All other generations would have to wait.

Soon, the guard would be along with the prisoner's last meal. Buttermilk pancakes with strawberries and whipped cream, no doubt, if this was, in fact, the same dream - or a dream at all for that matter.

"It wasn't natural the way you were caught, was it?" Samuel asked through a lip full of nervous breath. He tried to contain it. He didn't want the prisoner to smell it on him, much like a dog and their sense of fear in a victim.

"'Caught' is such an over exaggerated word." Devious leaned back, putting his feet up on the bed and crossing them as if he were right at home. "Why don't you explain it to me? I'm sure you've done your homework. Quote it by page number if you so choose. Begin. I'm listening."

Hands clenched tightly, Samuel began. He stared through

the bars and tried to speak in the clearest voice as he retold the story that he had come across in other rival papers.

"It was a hot day, like this one, when you finally showed yourself in public. You were dressed in a perfectly tailored suit as well as those shoes you're wearing right now. I recognize them from the pictures.

"Officers at the desk recognized that you had a dead body in your arms. It was badly mutilated with wide gashes. It was a woman when it was alive. Your face was like a block of concrete. You showed no emotions, no facial gestures. You plopped the body on the counter of the front desk of the police station and lowered your hands.

"Everyone was screaming, some fainted. The chief questioned you right on the spot. He asked who killed her and you replied..."

"Naturally, me, chief," Devious said.

"You take...pride in this?"

"I try to put enough effort into pride as I can. I so relish chaos. When those people screamed, I tried very hard not to giggle. But even after I said it was me who did it, a smile shattered across my face."

This was not a normal conversation. It seemed that nothing bothered this man. It was an eerie confidence which came, also, with sweating fear. That kind of confidence was hard to break for Samuel. He wondered why he would even try at all, but he continued in the game. He continued on with his hope of revealing an answer.

"You take relish in what you eat as well?"

"Why of course, young man." He lifted himself up, almost sadly offended. "If we don't indulge, what have we to gain?"

"You could just learn to control yourself, pal!"

Ouch! That was stepping on too many toes that time, Sammy, he thought roughly. He'll be awfully pissed now.

Devious, with eyes built like torpedoes, calmly placed the cigarette on the cold floor while it was lit. Sitting up, he casually walked towards the bars, towards Samuel. It was only a ten-foot walk, but those ten feet seemed awfully long for Samuel. One instant, involving a surge in the overhead electricity, encompassed them both. Samuel never took his eyes off of Devious. A flash of darkness triggered something in the mood. A quick flash that ended as fast as it had come but still had the overlapping trigger effect of anxiety. In the darkness, Samuel could have sworn he saw Devious' eyes glow a silvery film. One that reminded him of night shoots at nocturnal creatures in the wild.

Devious finally reached the bars and clutched one of them in a firm hand. He gave off the very real appearance of towering over Samuel like a skyscraper does to an insignificant bush. His confidence was definitely looming now. It was not only in his body…it was circulating in the air. Samuel felt surrounded by it.

"Young man," Devious said, calm anger building in his throat. "When I see that same principle you just spoke of to me *reflected* in today's society, then - only *then* - will I spend a half of a second to consider stopping. Is that clear?"

Samuel felt as if he had just been reprimanded, which was surprising for a man of his age. This man obviously wasn't a normal good old psycho. He was something much scarier. Possibly a sociopath. Those were the worst.

But, for now, the beast was tamed when the guard arrived, dull as usual, with a tray of food for the inmate to consume.

Devious took the dish in one hand and placed it perfectly on his bed. But wait, it was something different. As the guard walked away, Samuel leaned in to the cell to have a closer look.

"Leg of lamb?" he questioned. This was wrong. Something had been changed in the dream. Was that possible? Had Devious changed it?

"That," Samuel pointed. "That wasn't there before. You had something different. You had pancakes with strawberries. I remember."

"Yes," said Devious, retiring to his bed to eat. "I was beginning to get bored so I gave you your memory back."

"My memory back? What are you saying?"

"Samuel Joseph Tredmark," Devious said with a mouthful

of meat in his teeth, spitting as he spoke. "Born of Elizabeth Tredmark, alcoholic, and a past of three jobs prior, you surprise me. Stupidity is not like you."

Samuel sat in puzzlement.

"I can control your mind as well as the time."

This, truly, was what scared Samuel the most. He felt his chest caving in, like an asthma attack. A shiver choked the back of his neck while a cold sweat trailed a waterfall down his knees. He was under some kind of control? How could this be?

But, alas, the magician in the bright cell did not reveal his tricks. He simply told him that they were there.

"Technically," he continued. "This is the 26th last meal that I have consumed. I always request different meals, and they always bring them to me."

A moment of silence transpired. Devious continued eating while Samuel sat in his own pondering pool of sweat. Now, his plan was torn to shreds, just like the man tearing his meals to shreds with his teeth. Samuel had tried to be smarter than the man but was ultimately dumbstruck.

What was he to do now? He had no plan. All he had were more questions.

For the first time in hours, the old geezer in the cell next to Devious spoke in a clear sweet tone. "Ha! He thinks that's an accomplishment! Believe me, son, his dribble comes out of his mouth constantly. Not just when he's eating."

Samuel turned towards the voice. He felt infused with a little piece of hope now. Maybe there was more to the iceberg. A possible head case for the papers, if anything at all. Or, like he thought, it could still all be a vivid dream.

Devious stood up in shock. Something had startled him. The meat was dangling from his mouth as he climbed up onto his bed like a women avoiding spiders. He looked positively comical as he looked, for the first time, terrified of something unseen.

"What was that?" he asked, the meat falling from his mouth.

"The man..." Samuel began.

But his words were cut short by Devious. He waved a hand at Samuel trying to silence him.

"No," he said. "I heard something…something like swords clanging together. Something indefinable. Something undeniable."

Samuel's mood began to brighten. For a brief moment, he enjoyed the prisoner's loss of words, of which he did have many. Now Devious was the man dumbfounded.

Now Samuel changed his view from sociopath to criminally insane.

The guards came soon enough and began their scheduled routine. They snapped on the shackles, pulled him out of the cell - which he didn't resist - and began the walk on his way to the dead man's path.

He turned towards Samuel and said a familiar, "See you soon."

Just like before, his chair had disappeared.

But the visit had not been like before. Now there was a mystery as well as a fear of the future. Also, the dialogue had been different. Everything seemed to shift in mood as well as control.

Because now Devious was walking stiffly down his path. He turned to one of the guards as he barked something to them. It sounded like a command in the distance but felt an awful lot like a worried comment.

"Somebody has got to find that sound that I heard. What was that sound?" he asked, then he disappeared as well into the darkness of the corridor.

Samuel decided to leave. To begin his day once more. Who knew how many of these there would be. But just before he left, he eyed the old hobo in the dingy cell next to the bright one.

That old geezer sure had more confidence than the other guy. Explosive amounts of it too. Samuel appreciated the boost of confidence he had gained when the old hobo had spoken up on his behalf.

He tapped on the bars with his finger, much like tapping a goblet for an ancient toast.

The old man looked up, smiling.

"Thanks, old man," said Samuel.

The window came unlatched again. He shut it ignorantly and tried to go back to sleep, but he couldn't. He knew what kind of day lay ahead of him.

He knew he hated it, but he was going to have to start the day all over again. There was nothing more aggravating than visiting a highly pompous person in the same situation. He wondered if this time he would be more confident. Or, better still, that the dream was over.

He pinched himself good and hard when he got up and realized that it was no dream. It was anything but.

This time, after his conversation with Lard Warden, he had walked down the corridor to the bright cell. This time, he sat and waited. Both parties did not speak to each other. The silence was a blessing as they both had nothing to say. It was like they were trying to anticipate what the other would say next.

This time, the last meal, which was the 27th by Samuel's count, had been a fresh plate of sushi. Twelve of the little suckers were lined up in a spiral across the huge plate. They were delivered by the same zombified guard as usual.

Finally, Devious spoke up as he sickeningly crunched into one and swallowed it whole. He made a grim face and then laced a smile across it.

"How utterly disgusting," he said with a delightful hum. "You must try one." He leaned the plate over for Samuel's viewing. This created a break in the ice.

But Samuel calmly declined. “I don’t eat from other’s plates.”

“Now seriously,” Devious sighed. A slight hint of annoyance and playful banter swiveled around him. “What could you possibly catch from me?”

“A bad habit,” Samuel remarked.

“Sharp as a whip, old boy!” Devious smiled.

Now, more than ever, the bulge appeared an inch bigger. Devious had to slow down his actions a little in order to catch up to his appetite. But why did this man have such a hungry appetite? And just how was he controlling the staff as well as their minds, let alone Samuel’s?

Devious popped a couple more sushi rolls into his mouth, downing them like they were candy. He was so amused by Samuel’s disgust that he actually, by accident, found a maggot that fell out of one of the rolls and played with it with his finger. It was no bigger than a sliver of a fingernail and probably weighed less than a needle.

He plucked it from the plate and held it up for Samuel to see. “Oh, look what I’ve found.”

The disturbed Samuel was sitting, not amused and apparently lost in thought. Constantly beating himself up over how to make the days normal again, but he couldn’t fathom a simple escape plan now. He knew that. But there were a couple things that Samuel didn’t know. And that was that his rather unbelievable host had fears as well. Devious had fears that were quite normal actually. Samuel struggled with fears and tried to pin one down that made sense.

In his mind, he began listing fears that seemed plausible. *Arachnophobia, could’ve been spiders that scared him onto the bed. Germ freak, clean freak, scared of loud noises, possibly. Scared of not being important. Scared of not being threatening enough. He could be…*

“Hey,” he was interrupted. “Look at this.”

Devious pulled the maggot, squirming for its life, and lowered it down into his teeth. Crunching sounds were heard as he chewed it vigorously. He gulped it down in no time and looked in Samuel's general direction.

"Whether it be cooked or uncooked," he said, picking his teeth, "there are always scrumptious things to behold."

Well, Samuel thought, depressed. *He's definitely not afraid of eating maggots. That scratches off germ freak. That at least narrows my choices down, but it does present a problem.*

This time, it had been a normal steak and eggs platter. The 38th last meal in the running of so-called 'last meals'. Lately, their conversations had drowned in boredom. There wasn't much to say, but that didn't disturb the creepy feeling underneath the skin.

"Why must you sit there in regret?" asked Devious.

Samuel, groggy and half-listening, raised his head above the fist he was nesting it on.

"W…what?" he asked tiredly.

Devious shook his head, almost displeased at his guest's lack of attention.

"You've been coming here every day trying to figure me out, I've noticed."

"Yeah. So?"

"So why trouble yourself with such thoughts? Let sleeping dogs lie, let the flowers bloom, and for once let the mystery be unsolvable."

"You can't just get away with this. I've already figured that you are not of this world. I just have to figure a way in which to beat you."

"Or at least classify what I am?"

"Yeah. That too, I suppose."

He shrugged his shoulders, using as little effort as possible. He was tired of this déjà vu circle. It positively bored him to come back here every single day, but he knew that he must. He even tried telling the guards and warden that the prisoner was supposed to be executed yesterday, but they wouldn't listen.

Another desperate attempt was to check if all the dates had been correct. He dialed the operator and confirmed it.

It was no dream. That is what aggravated him the most.

It was real. Real every day. Real Forever.

"I don't wanna spend eternity in this place," Samuel said.

"I know what you mean."

Samuel breathed in, then out, then in again. A little while longer of him watching this jerk eat his meal and he knew for sure that he would pass out.

He decided, after a long yawn which Devious noticed immediately, to leave. The apartment was only a couple blocks away, and he wanted to see his bed again. Maybe nap for a few hours and then start the stupid day all over again.

To his surprise, as he leaned against the weird chair for support while getting out of it, he noticed how soft it was. It definitely wasn't plastic. It wasn't cushions neither. It was soft and squishy.

He looked down at it in squinting perplexity. It was peach colored.

It was flesh.

Samuel backed away quickly as the giant hand that he had been sitting in melted into the wall behind him.

"I CAN'T BELIEVE! I CAN'T…" Samuel stuttered as he pointed to the grimy wall.

"Sure you can," Devious said, lowering his hand down to his plate.

It was then, at that moment, that Samuel realized the hand he was sitting in was somehow part of Devious. He had never noticed it before in the dark.

The 49th meal came and went. So did the 50th. Samuel had his doubts about number 50. He had some vague hope that the 50th meal would indeed be the last. But it wasn't. A nice round number like that could be easily passed.

Somehow, every day, something was drawing him back to the prison. Back to this living nightmare.

Every meal the prisoner downed made Samuel unhappy. After 50 last meals, Samuel was convinced that there was no limit to this man's power. It would go on forever if he so chose.

Victory seemed bleak. Hope was still churning though. It kept him warm, and it made him whole. He never knew where it was coming from, but he hoped that it would remain.

Until then, he would have to sit and wait for an answer to come.

Devious, his mouth messy with stains, scooped in his last bit of ice cream. Chocolate ice cream covered his wardrobe. Samuel couldn't imagine downing fifteen scoops of his favorite flavor, but Devious did it with such ease.

A loud belch escaped his lips and made him laugh. Then he stared at Samuel, who chose to sit on the ground this time like a little boy, and threw his head back in another laugh. His large belly, now the size of a beach ball, was jiggling in the process.

The guards carried Devious away to the electric chair after he downed his 66th last meal. They needed two men to lift him upright. He was getting quite thick. Stains trailed over his clothes as his stomach was now a tire of dangling fat.

Samuel felt disgusted as he got up to say goodbye and walk out of there.

"He's a glutton for punishment," said the old man.

Samuel stopped and gazed in. He had seen the old man countless times, but for once he decided to make small talk.

"Hello," Sam said childishly.

"Hello, sonny boy," said the old man.

"How they treatin' you?"

"Good. Good. Can't complain."

"Let me ask you something. How do you put up with this guy gorging himself right next to your cell?"

"Oh, not all of us have to put up with his ignorant attitude. I chose to ignore it a long time ago. I even had him kicked out of my house."

Sam blinked in amazement.

"You actually lived with that guy?"

"No. He lived with me. But he became arrogant and wasn't welcome in my eyes. He used to work for me until he became so selfish."

"What business you in?"

"People."

"Insurance?"

"Just people."

"Do you know how he's doing this?"

"Yeah. I know. But you just hang in there. That garbage that he's doing is nothing compared to what I can do."

"W…what can you do?"

"Trust me. He'll be finished soon."

Devious sucked in the last bit of crust from his jumbo pizza with every topping in the book. His 68th meal went down more slowly than the others. In fact, it took Devious a whole hour and a half to finish it. He took his time now and then, but he had grown slow with blubber.

A pepperoni was stuck to his cheek. Noticing it, he licked it back into his mouth and silently slobbered it in. Devious had now grown two men too thick.

Samuel eyed him curiously. He wondered if the madman would throw up.

"Done yet?" Samuel questioned.

"I am never done, good sir." Devious belched, losing all of his charm in the process.

Heat was in the air as Samuel Tredmark made his way into the prison. He made small chitchat with the fat warden and couldn't wait to see the prisoner. Sure, the warden was fat. But Devious was a whole other story altogether. Devious was beyond the normal weight of an average man. A monstrosity for all to see.

Samuel had a swing in his step on this, another repeated day, as he made his way down the darkly flickering corridor.

His coat was swung over his jacket, his hair was combed, his shirt was straight, despite the sweat stains on it, and his mood was chipper. Over the past couple of days he had grown quite pleased and even cheerful. It had been true that he could not define the man in the cell, but he knew one thing for sure. He didn't fear Devious anymore. It was very hard, Samuel thought, very hard to fear a fat man.

The obese man, rotting in his cage, was nowhere near the smooth, operatic, handsome man that he had once seen. This was a man that was sheer folds. Every wrinkle in his skin was lost in a never-ending map of flesh-colored stretch marks.

Somewhere along the way, Samuel had guessed, that the man must have ordered seconds. From his count, it was the 71st last meal he would be attending today.

As he approached the wide width of the man that was in the cage, he stopped short.

The sickly smell that he had sensed once before was back again with tremendous force.

"Now," Samuel said, slipping his jacket over his forearm and sitting on the ground in front of the bars, "where were we?"

The giant man bellowed his laughter and spewed up some soup. A grotesque man who barely contained his fluids.

The simplified guard arrived, right on time, with another 'last meal'. Setting it down, he was somewhat taken out of his trance, eyeing the foul man through the bars. He squinted in puzzlement as he turned towards Samuel in recognition.

"Has he…always been like that?" the guard asked, pointing

his finger at Devious.

Samuel smiled.

"Yeah. You were just never around to see it."

The guard straightened up, took one last look at the prisoner and walked off, mumbling as he made his way out of the light.

This last meal was a special treat. Four cherry pies stacked one on top of the other. Specially requested, of course.

Devious dug his huge cellulite hand into the top pie, extracting a chunk to eat. There were bags under his eyes and his hair was all stringy. The cherry crust was mere inches away from his mouth before he noticed that Samuel was doing something not to his satisfaction. He was smiling.

Devious turned away from his reddened hand.

"What are you gaping at?" he barked.

"Nothing. Just a whole lot of skin."

"You fool. This is mere covering. You have no idea who or what I am. This whole time you've been trying to figure me out. You have nothing! You are nothing! You're worth nothing!"

Samuel bent his head down a little. He may be the product of a pair of divorced parents, he may be a boozer at times, he may be a poor example for the modern hero, but he was still human.

He lifted his head a little and saw the smirk on Devious's wide face. He belched horribly here and there.

"Why are you even sticking around at all, Samuel?" Devious asked.

"That's a simple question. I answer it with a simple answer: I wanna see how the bad man dies."

Samuel hated this. He hated it all as a matter of fact. But still, he knew that he would have to see him again.

Everything happened as before. He got up, shut his window in the middle of the night and went back to sleep.

The morning came, and he made no hesitation to put his

clothes on in a hurry. His brown shoes were wedged near the door while his shirt was busy sitting over the arm of a chair. He arranged his briefcase and files and straightened his tie on the way out.

He drove to the prison where he found a parking spot immediately. The sky was gray, as usual.

The trees were swaying in the wind. A small, insignificant raindrop landed on the pavement. Samuel hadn't noticed.

He approached the desk and voiced his call for the warden as before.

As he waited, he looked briefly in his briefcase. The pages were littered with scribbles all over the place. Hundreds of papers were compiled of him visiting the 'Devious man'. He had thumbed through them nightly.

On the side, practically falling out of the briefcase, was his huge tape recorder, which had been filled with the same interview many times over. Now the tape, as well as the batteries, were wearing down.

"Tredmark," came the voice of the warden as he made his face known. "Happy to see you again."

He walked over to Samuel and shook his hand.

"I suppose you wanna document his death as well."

Samuel's eyes blinked their confusion. His arm felt weak as he was still shaking hands with the overweight warden. Was it possible? Did the fat man finally stop his game? Was everything flowing back to normal again?

"You mean," Samuel started. "You finally killed him?"

The warden removed his hand. "That's a rather cold question to ask. I thought you were the one gabbing my ear off about everyone deserving a second chance. After all, aren't you a realist?"

Samuel smirked at the warden as he looked around in overwhelming relief.

"No. Religious now."

And so it was on October seventh that Devious Lathrop, the man who refused his birth name and had been of another world, died before he reached the electric chair.

Now Samuel was standing in the brightly lit corridor staring in at the dark unoccupied cell of the former prisoner of the state.

Samuel felt victory in his veins as he pried himself away from the bars and smiled knowing that whatever that man was, he was not living now. The man was indeed human. He died of heart failure because of all the food that was weighing him down. Whatever magic that he had or whatever spell he had cast on the shadowy prison had now been lifted. The evil man had just finished his 75th last meal.

He flung his jacket over his shoulder once more and began to leave towards the exit of the corridor.

But before he could get a mere baby's breath out of range of the hollowed out cell, a familiar voice spoke as it had so many times before.

"Told you he would finish soon enough," said the old man.

Samuel leaned over to the bars.

"You still here? I thought you'd be gone by now."

"I am never gone. I'm always here. My son's picking me up today."

"Son? You have a son?"

The old man's eyes twinkled in the light. "Yes. The gentlemen in the prison were kind enough to let me sleep here for a while until my son could pick me up. Actually, I suggested it to them. I knew that what's his name was going to be here."

In no time at all, the gate slid back and a man appeared wearing simple sandals, jeans, and a suede jacket over a white shirt. His hair was up in a ponytail and his beard was thick.

"You ready to go, pops?" said the young man.

The young man looked at Samuel and gave him a reassuring smile.

The old man looked up and saw the two looking at each

other as he packed his bag.

"Oh," said the old man. "Let me introduce you two. Samuel this is my son Emmanuelle. Emmanuelle this is my friend Samuel."

They shook hands and smiled.

Once the old man was ready to go, both him and his son left the decrepit prison.

Samuel still stood there, holding one of the bars. He watched as the young man was carrying the old man on his way. Samuel starred down the dark pathway as he turned his gaze to the left. *One pathway to death*, he thought.

Then he turned his gaze back to the brightly lit pathway where the two men were headed. *One to life. And, why not? A stairway to heaven to wrap it all up.*

Y0UR ESCAPE PLAN N0W

Don't be alarmed, Allen! I know this may come as a shock but you have got to continue reading if you want to make it out of here.

But first, make sure that you are alone before reading further. Act quickly. There is no time for skepticism.

Thank God there are no cameras in that room. If anyone should come in, hide in the washroom beside the control panel.

If anyone should knock on the door, tell them that you are ill and that it must have been something contracted from the food that you have been eating here. This will, at least, give you enough stalling time. When they check the food, they will find no toxins. I'm sorry that I'm making you a liar on a clean-cut job record, but it is necessary for your survival.

I am Lexington Verbatim; we've met in level T.L.U.46 before. We briefly made conversation, but that is not what is important right now. This document, the one you hold in your hands, is important as of right now.

For the latter part of two years I have been conducting checks on the scientists of this facility. Corruption spreads like a plague through the walls of this underground lab. For five years, Allen, you have believed, like everyone else here, that you were working for a high-level company called R.A.D.A.R. (Research And Development of All Radiation), a separate branch of the government that researches all possible radiation threats, even manufacturing different types of radiation ectoplasm for global-warming testing.

You believed, as I did, that this place that housed us was built for the purposes of finding a solution to the global cooling that our planet has undergone. But know this, that there are some surviving cities out there. Cities where the blast was not able to reach. And slowly, each year, these men have been conducting a way to eradicate those survivors above by melting them with this facility's own reflective beam ECTO-Waves. At first, they were designed to keep the ABUSERS and the UNCLEAN TRESPASSERS out. But now, they've been enhancing them, Allen! Enhancing them to the point where they not only act as shields, but also as a fortress weapon! That's what this place has become, Allen! It's a giant fortress now. And the HIGH COUNT, who oversees all this intends to keep it that way. He will never give in and he will never love the world above enough to save it. He has grown mad with his icy palace that he thinks he's built and has not hesitated to persuade everyone except you and me. Just today, he was asking things that sounded very much like traitorous questions, and I played dumb. At least, that is one trait I'm sure he thinks I have.

As you must have come to realize by now, this document is your escape plan now.

Horrifying, I know. But, step-by-step, we can do it, Allen. We can get you out of here just before the charges blow. Again, don't be alarmed for you must be levelheaded and calm! But you must also read quickly.

I have discovered that the five hundred employees that work here are all corrupted on some level or another. But there is still you and me, Allen. And I'm confident that with this document you should be able to reach the surface in enough time to warn someone and steer clear of the blast that will soon engulf this underground lair.

Now listen closely, the reason why you and I are not corrupt is because they hired us outside of the major office's branch. We were the lucky few. But now it is left to one. You are that one, Allen!

In the lower level, I was able to sneak in and document the map to a definite way out of here. It is full of twists and turns and is of great danger, but I'm sure you can do it. YOU HAVE TO!

Unfortunately, given the restrictions to all tube messaging, I wasn't able to enclose the map that will lead you on your path. As you know, the tubings have scanners that will sound an alarm if they detect the coding within the map paper. I can't even scribble a crummy picture or a diagram because the scanners will also register the shape of the buildings through the paper. The only safe thing about tube messaging is that the scanners can only read and pick up maps, no typing. They think, however unlikely, that with written directions, if a document of this magnitude existed, that no human could possibly make it to the surface.

But know that there is always a way around the system, Allen! There are always ways to beat the system! The scanners may pick up coding as well as the shapes of the blueprints, but they can't stop me from telling you how to get out of here turn by turn through this document. I know it is rather lengthy, but it will have to do.

Right now, I am four levels under you. I am taking THE PROVIDERS, who keep us here, down to the lower level. I have made a false complaint to them about some of the reactors' wiring. Because of the technical jargon, they should be confused for a good long while. They may have kept us here and they may have fed us here, but they will never keep their secrets here.

They will kill us all if they so choose. But not you. You shall be my beacon that will reach the surface.

Right now, the charges are set to blow in a very secure hiding place. One that the scanners can't find. You'd be amazed at how many unbalanced corners I've found in this place. I developed the charges in the beginning of October 2073 and had them completed a little after 2076.

The destruction will be, in a word, extensive. But I have personally tailored your escape route for you.

You just need to pay close attention. That's one thing you have to do. YOU HAVE TO PAY CLOSE ATTENTION TO THIS DOCUMENT! Whatever you do; do not read the entire document while sitting in the control room or the washroom because then it will already be too late!

Take this document with you as you leave the bathroom. You may read ahead if you like, bit-by-bit, but only to know what you have to do next. I just pray to the Lord Jesus almighty that the ability to speed-read is one that you mastered long ago.

Here we go, Allen. You must be ready for this. And for goodness sake be careful out there.

First, I want you to get out of the bathroom - if you were in there this whole time - and walk over to the control panel with the four rotating screens. But when you exit, act as if this document is mere spreadsheets and nothing more. I hope you are a good actor as well.

What you'll need to do, once you've convinced the guard that the food poisoning has struck you, is disable the shield on level B6-D5KLB. This is the level right next to you. You, right now, have a medium-level security clearance so the shield blocking anyone from getting in will only be down for one minute - maximum. If you hurry, you can jog to that level! It isn't far away and the cameras in the corridors, and whoever is watching, will assume that from the papers in your hands you have a deadline on a group of irradiated samples. Everyone knows that those have to be under constant watch, and they will ask no questions.

After finally making it through, stay out of sight! Lord knows what these men are packing today.

Move quickly inside this room and stay low to the ground. There are head scanners above the ceiling that cover the entire area with their red misty gaze. They are similar to clouds that you would see if you were on the surface right now. But I have laid down a set of simple mirror shards to reflect the beams back at the wall should they come too close to you. ABOVE ALL, YOU MUST STAY ON THE MIRRORED TRAIL! It will be dark but this document should have illuminating capabilities. I designed it that way. You should not be concerned with light sensors since we have not entered that room yet.

If you've made it, well done! You can make it, Allen! I believe you can do it! Why, just the other day you were commenting on the rats in the maze that was in the main hall for decoration. You said it yourself! "A human intellect, given the right circumstances, could nibble his way out of his own prison. The walls appear to constrict him, but there are always ways of breaking through those walls."

Well, here is where it gets sticky. I hope you haven't cut yourself on the shards. I apologize for that. Use a bit of the emergency serum that's on the wall next to the door. It should cool the cut in case you're are bleeding. But now you must read even quicker if you haven't already.

Here you will find a long raised platform walkway. It is highly metallic and very rusty. There should be a doorway leading to an elevator about a mile up ahead. DON'T RACE DOWN THERE YET! You have to go about halfway. This document should flicker if over a hollow hole. There are no cameras on this pathway. Why should there be? They think the whole walkway is restricted and that there is no place else to go. But there is, Allen. There is.

Upon recent walks down this pathway, I have discovered a gap just below the midsection. I've marked a nearby railing. Do you see it? Do you see the purple glow? That's an experimental light-reactor gel. Any gel that I have placed within this facility will react to this document. That's the beauty of this escape. I've taken the liberty of hiding them throughout. If you are ever in doubt of where you have to go, wave the document around the area.

Right here, you're going to want to align your jump downward. I know that it seems crazy, but you have to do it. The cylinder walls may look like meat grinders, but you still have to do it. And for goodness sake, if one of the guards happens to come near you, make it look like a suicide. Trust me on this! You will not be hurt!

The pathway should be deserted so be a good sport and start moving over the railing and align yourself. Now, with both hands clasped on this document, after you have let go of the railing, be sure to jump feet first down through the hexagonal gap below. Be sure to hold this document above your head because this is the sticky part I told you about. You're going to be entering the water system. Unfortunately, the water has been processed through the funnel channel and been sucked for purity so it may stick to your clothes but it will not emit a smell. These people are so crude, they've been trying to find a way for us to eat our water substitute instead of drink it. It comes out in clear wobbly gobs. How revolting!

Read quicker! You must jump down! You must do it! Do it now! DO IT NOW!

By now, you have hopefully come to THE SCRAPING STATION. Or so I *hope* you have. I admit that the tubings can get rather rambunctious, but if you kept your head above the muck, you have traveled an easy road.

These machines that you should be seeing right now if you've made it are part of the solidifying water process. You should be able to maneuver yourself over to one.

Never fear, they are specially padded and magnetized in order to carefully but proficiently pick up all the solidified water.

Once you've been scraped off on the diagonal leaking tray, which is probably clear, you can begin to escape THE SCRAPING ROOM. But hold still. Unless this water that is on you goes straight to the CANNING DISTRIBUTION ROOM, it will eventually harden. DON'T FEAR! If you move too viciously, the chunks will be bigger and you'll probably knock yourself out cold. And that will do neither of us any good, Allen!

Once it hardens, it will then expand and start to crumble off of your clothes, leaving no sign of dampness to your appearance. That's the one negative side to solidifying water: if you wait too long to eat it, it will eventually crumble. But that one negative thing is saving your life right now, Allen! So shake off those greenish blobby pebbles and march forward.

There should be a CLEAN ROOM in front of you. Inside will, of course, be dark. But I've painted my purple trails on the walls to help you. They should be outlining a hidden room.

The room you enter will have green elegant wallpaper and a desk will be at the other end. It will already be lit. A nicely furnished polished desk. It will be made out of chestnut wood. Here you will do two things. First, lock the door behind you. Now, go to the desk and try to chip off a good piece of it about the length of your forearm. You should be able to find an instrument to cut it with. There are plenty of sharp letter openers and such. BUT YOU MUST MOVE AT A FAST PACE! HACK AT THE WOOD!

Once you've done that, hide the piece of wood in your sleeve then move over to the painting above the low bookshelf. It's the only painting in the room, and it has a tiny hidden swastika on President Lincoln's coat. If you have trouble finding it, I've dabbed that with the purple goop as well. But I doubt you will have trouble. I myself have been invited to this room many times and have been able to spot it from a good distance.

It's a button. You must prepare yourself when you press it though. NOT YET! First, take the end page of this document, which will be blank, and crumple it up. Now block the sprinkler overhead. It is actually a light-sensitive scanner that will react itself once you press the button. It will automatically turn the lights off and look for any illuminating presence. But, seeing as how the paper is right under it, it should conduct a bright enough glow that the sensor will be tricked into assuming that the lights have never shut off.

After you've done all this, walk through the now open wall. There is a door to your left. Open it!

Inside will be only enough space for one human to fit inside. Below you will find a container no bigger than a finger. It will glow, of course, with the purple goop. It is a sample for you to keep and to take with you when you reach the surface. When you get there, present it to THEIR government. You are my only hope in this! You must be my carrier pigeon, so to speak.

Now exit the room and make your way to the DISTRIBUTION ROOM. Now you must keep your head on or it will certainly be chopped off by the canning machines that will randomly lower themselves in your general direction.

To make your way through this, you have to time your steps every five seconds. There is a fritz in the mechanics that stalls the machines every five seconds. You'll be traveling via conveyer belt.

When you've reached the edge, there will be a lever that you can pull with your free hand that will increase the speed of the conveyer belt that you're on. You must lie flat for this! The flatter you are, the faster you'll go. You'll also be hidden on the conveyer belt in a room of about twenty hard workers!

BE WARNED: YOU'LL HAVE TO HOLD ONTO THE SMALL HANDLES UNDERNEATH THE FABRIC IN ORDER TO SURVIVE THIS WILD RIDE! ALSO, THE CONVEYOR BELT WAS NOT BUILT TO WITHSTAND THE SPEEDS THAT YOU WILL BE PUSHING IT TO, SO IT WILL EVENTUALLY COME OFF THE TRACK! KEEP STILL AND HOLD ON! YOU'VE JUST MANAGED TO SNEAK BY A FULLY POPULATED CANNING ROOM! HOW DOES IT FEEL?

Hopefully, you were able to land on a soft bed of sewage. Yes, sewage. It was the best I could do. But thankfully you've survived to read further.

Wait for the cleansing water to reach you. It is the same hardening water you saw before. This is how the facility gets rid of its trash. The water breaks up the pieces beneath you. And you will be cleaned by the rushing current.

After the current has hardened itself, it will expand like it always does, assisting you to be lifted up towards the open vent just near the ceiling. In such a narrow cylinder like that sewage pile, the current should be strong enough to hold your weight once it hardens. Just be sure to jump into the vent before the growing structure cracks and finally bursts into crumbles. It is hard to reach, but I'm sure you can manage it, Allen!

Next is the RADIATION SUIT TRANSFER MACHINE. Now, this is a very wide, very complicated, piece of machinery. Beyond the field of endless hooks above, you will be arriving precisely above the room. Climb into the light fixture and maneuver your way over to one of the hooks.

They will be moving at a relatively slow speed and should be within your reach. Since the light fixture is big enough and able to handle your weight, there should be no problem with you changing in it.

Reach out and snatch one of the radiation suits from one of the hooks. Bring it into the concave fixture and begin changing. You can leave your clothes here and no one will discover them.

Allen, you must remove the tracker chip that will be sewn into the belt of this radiation suit. There is probably a good chance that you will clip it off easily by lifting it out with your fingernail. Put this troublesome chip in the light fixture as well.

While changing into this wide green radiation suit, be sure to take that piece of wood and secure it tightly to your leg. Rip off a sleeve of your shirt if you so choose. But above all make sure that it will not gouge you. Blood is the last that that we want dripping from the ceilings, Allen!

Once you've finally slipped into your new suit, be sure that it is an extremely tight fit. It should be a one size fits all.

Now, listen closely, Allen, because there is no room for error in this! I want you to tuck this document securely into your pouch once you read the word 'go'. When you reach the end of the line, then you shall continue reading.

Be sure that once the hook reaches you that you can grab it.

All hooks will be occupied with a suit at this time of day.

You have to reach out, unhook the suit that will occupy your escape hook, attach yourself on the hook via the small ring on the back, then firmly toss the suit that you took off the hook down to the factory below.

You will be suspended in midair and will dangle for good a few minutes.

The suit, if you have dropped it as I have told you, will land in the factory, hopefully near another worker. When the worker looks up, he will see an unoccupied hook. This hook will be a good few hooks away from you and will cause the worker to believe that the hooks need to be replaced seeing as how the radiation suits are beginning to slip right off of them.

He will then pull a switch that will merge your track to a different one.

You must do this quickly! GO!

Now that you've reached the end of the line, with no problems I assume, you have to free yourself from the hook and drop down to the ground below you..

Now I know this may sound primitive, but do you remember that wood stake that you have? Well, I must admit that it is not a trusty weapon, but it is hard enough. And it's also the only thing that you'll be able to protect yourself with. Don't be so down! Look at it this way, more shady deals have taken place on that desk that you stole the piece of wood from than any other organization. At least you'll get a thrill whopping these guards left and right with their own corruption.

There will be guards, Allen! Oh yes, there will be guards! And not just a handful at that! They will be spread out throughout the exit shaft! But this is where you must grow strong. I trust you, Allen! You must not drop this document or get caught! This document has become your life! Guard it well!

If you need motivation, just remember the famous words of the poet Horace Wheelie of 2053: "Go now…for the future is waiting! It will not stop for stragglers!"

The first guard is sure to be Jenkins! He is a tall man that is too overconfident to be a guard. His weak point is in his right shoulder. Just recently he had an operation and it is very tender.

Whop him a good one on the shoulder blade!

Knock him out completely when he is down!

I know that your new suit is baggy and full of tugs here and there, but you must push on!

Thomas, Rorely, and Otto will have weak points too. They have been personally checked by me, since I am there only physician. Thomas has a bad heel. Rorely has back problems. Otto will have a sensitivity to light.

Knock down Thomas. Brain Rorely. Shove the document in Otto's face. The blinding light will give him a shock enough for you to knock him unconscious too.

No need to hide the bodies! There won't be enough time.

Now you must make your way to the ventilation shaft! I've marked the precise vent at the corner of the hallway. Refer to the document to expose the purple goop.

After you have climbed in and have sealed off the vent, you may now shimmy your way through the vent. But with every shimmy you take, count. It is a long way, and it is a very constricting vent pathway. I wasn't able to get into it, but you should be fine.

Once you've counted to a hundred, you should be able to lift a panel where there should be a shaft.

These are the ELEVATOR SHAFTS. Take the wood plank and firmly wrap it around a cable.

Move over to the control panel and rewire wire Blue7 to Red36. This will cause all elevators to arrive on the last floor, in turn lifting your cable to the very top of the facility!

You're going to make it, Allen! Don't stop! Keep going! Hold on tight!

The trip will be incredibly bad if you have a fear of heights. I'm sorry if you do.

But remember that height is the only thing standing in your way to freedom!

You will, by now, have reached the top. Sneak into the

lobby but dive into the office at the end of the hall. People gazing at your radiation suit will take a hint that you are transporting samples and need verification from the board. The board will not be present in the office, but there is an electronic call manager.

It will hold all the numbers of the facility only but you, being a wiz at reverse engineering, will be able to change the thing into a call receiver, or what the peasants of the past used to refer to as a 'telephone'.

Make the call to a Mr. Donald Wordoll. He will be your contact once you escape.

Now all you have to do is smash the window in the boardroom and walk free.

Upon smashing the glass, though, an incredibly fast freezing current will blow in and consume the entire lobby in ice. Your suit that you have stolen has been specially designed - by your enemies - to withstand the paralyzing conditions of the cold.

It is seventy below on the surface, but you will be able to move through it with no problem.

Say a final farewell to the facility as you pass the shields. By now, they have been disabled by the charges and now the explosion is working its way up to the surface. If my calculations are correct, you should be able to get a good enough distance away, which leaves you exactly twenty minutes of running time.

Now, a final word on this document if I may, even though I shall be dead, you must live on! Be sure to hand this document over to the THEIR authorities once you have contacted them. THEIR craft should be able to find you with the latitude/ longitude tracker.

Good luck with your new life above ground. And farewell. friend. I hope that you will have a warm and happy life, Allen Quixote.

Signed,
Lexington Verbatim.

Alex Dujima's Book Code

Alex Dujima stood hovered over the phone, sweating. The office was docile and hollow with loneliness. A small yellow pad of paper was kept next to the phone's base.

It was roughly two in the morning and all was well. Except for poor Alex, that is.

Alex was an extremely strong business associate type of a man. A very professional man. Mr. Alex Dujima was a man who answered to and no one else. But now came the drop of the final shoe, and a big cover up was in process.

As he dialed, he wiped his forehead clean with his free hand. His glasses were getting foggy and the desk lamp, which was the only light source, wasn't helping matters either with its melting gaze. It gave only a circle of light to the objects it was most interested in: the corner of the desk, the incredibly strong business-suited man clutching onto it, and a bookcase in the far corner from the man, directly behind him.

Long black threads of his hair kept getting wedged in between his glasses as he listened for the dial tone.

One ring.

Two Rings.

Three Rings.

Finally a voice came to life from the speaker.

"Alex," the voice called out. The connection was a bit scratchy, but it would have to do for now. The tone of voice sounded more reassuring than the greeting. Too busy to say hello probably. A professional man to the end. A man who tolerated no mistakes. "I take it you made it to the office."

Alex turned his blue steely eyes towards the door and gave a confirming nod, even though the man at the other end of the phone didn't see it.

30-2. The correct office, indeed. Now his lips grew dry with a sense of worry.

The bag next to him was pink with glimmering reflections. A plastic bag that held a key item.

"F…," Alex began.

But before he could add another letter to his speech, it was terminated immediately.

"Don't say my name, you oaf!" the man screamed. Now his voice was trembling with cautious words. "Don't you *dare* say my name! I don't want you to even think it. Have you any idea if this line is being traced?"

Alex stood, watching his own shadow move against the glass pane window. It was a starry night was out tonight, and it only got hotter here in Vegas.

"I guess…" Alex started. "I guess I didn't think of that."

"Damn right you didn't!"

Alex hated being yelled at. He had a great hatred for many things. Two of which dealt with overconfident people. But, in the end, he knew that he was a dog for this corporate fiend. A dog in a suit and tie to match. Mr. Go-fetch-this-fido-guy. This man was considered… a piece of corporate scum as well.

The bag ruffled beneath his feet as he gave it a sturdy

nudge to point his anger at the ground.

"Ah," said the voice. "That would be the bag in the background. Right?"

"Certainly."

"Well? Come on, come on. Open it up and place it on the desk."

Alex did what he was told. He had no choice otherwise. Not a lot of money was riding on, this but it still had its kinks. One of the kinks dealt with a very hard realization, that Alex had to be given one sentence of command. A simple command at first - that's what Alex thought. But after coming too close to his boss and too many people getting wise, he was forced to receive his next command in code.

His boss, a fairly new boss, had a job for him to do. A job that required no mess-ups and zero tolerance. This job was very strict and very precise, the boss said. And Alex never disagreed with his boss.

It was Alex's fault in the first place. If only he had concentrated more on discreetness and less on his next bit of information, he would have seen the cops roaming the strip.

Right now, his employer was in the midst of an investigation. Dirty files, tapped conversations, missing money galore. An empire built on lies and deceits. It all comes tumbling down sooner or later - but not without a fight.

That's why this new boss had hired Alex. But Alex was usually the dog that acted too quickly. He couldn't wait to see his master. But the master would not have it. Things would look too peculiar if this tall gentleman named Alex Dujima just happened to be at his boss's side. People would think he was a bodyguard or something. They would search up his files. Too many damn questions. That's what his new boss wanted to avoid. His new boss hated too many damn questions. And Vegas was full of them. Plenty of them. Let's just keep 'em at that.

The thick paperback book tumbled out of the pink plastic bag and landed with a mighty flop against the desk. It was the newest edition of the boss's favorite book. *Money is The Color of*

Blood was recently published by Township Express and had done well in many local bookstores. It was written by a man named Arthur Freely - the boss's favorite author as well.

The cover was a slick design, picturing a spread of a hundred dollars with blood splattered over it, and it had about six hundred pages. Or so it felt.

"Ready?" the voice called on the other end.

Actually, Alex was in the midst of getting ready. He searched for his lucky ink pen, which was crammed in his pocket next to his rattling keys.

He breathed heavily as he pulled up a chair and scrambled to sit straight. He was a worrier too. Under the desk, his leg repeatedly tapped up and down in a nervous rickety motion.

"Yeah. Ready," Alex said.

"Good."

"What page?"

"Turn to page 174."

On the other end, in the background, a loud jackpot was heard as well as a man flipping out over his lucky win. Another flipping sound was heard, which sounded like pages.

The boss must have been at a Casino. He probably had the book with him. He wouldn't dare say the title through the phone, but Alex already knew it was the same book that he had bought.

Alex looked out the window, out across the starry, lit-up strip as well. There were a chorus line of casinos in the area, and he tired to guess which one the boss was at. But did it really matter? Alex already knew the boss would most likely pick the farthest one from his office. It was all part of his plan, really.

"You there?"

"Yes, I'm here," Alex said, returning from his unneeded thought.

"You do understand how this book code, works right?"

"Simple. It's the first letter of every word on the page. But there are many lines and…that you have to give me the line number as well as the number of letters that the important ones are near."

Silence. Another jackpot. Alex grew nervous. Had he said something wrong?

"Sorry," the voice came back. "Guard was passing. You understand? Good. Now just remember to write these numbers down and decipher the codes. I won't have time to repeat them. Understood?"

"Yeah, boss. No problem, boss."

Alex did as he was told. He copied down nineteen different lines. Each line told him the page number, which were all the same, the numbered line, and the correct letter.

After he was done, he felt like cheering. The boss had spoken in a clear and simple tone and the connection hadn't gone out once.

"Done?"

"Done, boss."

"Good. Now decipher the damn code already."

Alex concentrated all his vision on the code now. Carefully he counted, and carefully he underlined. He kept a notepad, ready to be burnt. The first letter of the hidden message was definitely a '**K**'. That much was for certain.

He heard his boss tapping his fingers on the other line. An impatient man to the last.

Then, after a couple of minutes of work, Alex finally arrived at an answer. But it was a weird one. Alex checked it twice. Then he checked it again. It was absolute ludicrous. It had read:

K.I.E.L.L. M.I. A.S.S.I.T.U.N.T.A.N.T.

Alex was stupefied at first. But that soon passed as he mouthed the words without making a sound. He then crossed out the unnecessary letters. The ones that didn't make sense. Then he made a minor adjustment until the sentence finally fell together. His message had read:

KILL MY ASSISTANT

It wasn't an easy request. Alex had never killed anyone before. Sure he had roughed up a few people, but this was more important than all that. A lot more important.

But still, he couldn't get his mind around the unused letters E, I, U, and N.

Rapid tapping was still heard over the line. Alex groaned. That explained it all. An impatient man to the last. The boss had been so hasty in his book code that he had used four extra letters that were either misspellings in the sentence or were completely useless.

Mark that up on the chalkboard of the many things that angered Alex Dujima.

Alex was now burning the scrap of paper with his lighter and the ashtray housed the ashes.

This was a difficult task ahead of him. But he didn't question it at this time. He had no time to be the question man. He had only enough time to become his boss's answer man.

The only thing he needed now was a strategy.

"It'll be done," Alex said.

"I want the place to be spick and span."

"Not a problem. Are you sure you want this done tonight?"

"Are you sure you can handle this?"

"It's not a lot."

"To me it is."

"Understood."

That's all he needed to hear. The phone hung in his hand as he quickly placed it on the base and…

"Ouch!"

He stubbed his toe on the paper shredder as he was just rising out of his chair. Another mark on the chalkboard of his mind. That chalkboard would be full soon if he didn't hurry up.

"Stupid shredder," he thundered.

He gave it a swift kick to show it who the boss was and it tilted over. Then he panicked.

He knelt down to where the shredder was. Yep. He had definitely kicked it a little bit too hard. There was now a football-sized dent which spread across it. A few glistening pieces were also on the floor.

It was definitely broken.

At this, Alex giggled. It was a silly thing to do. Now he would have to take the damn thing with him. He couldn't leave any trace of being in that particular office at that particular time.

Perhaps it would fit in the plastic bag, but he would have to stretch it.

He stood up quickly with a jolt and wiped the receiver down as well as the desk and the lamp. No fingerprints. He couldn't leave any fingerprints. That was one thing that the boss was clear on.

But it was hard to imagine that he could kill someone. He didn't even know how he was going to do it.

Although…he did have a faint memory, further back when he had met his new boss, that emphasized that the assistant did have a habit of stopping by his office on the weekends to tidy up.

Maybe that's why the boss was so urgent in his request. It all made perfect sense.

Now it all came down to Alex. He was either a coward or a brute, and he chose to be a brute with intent to kill. But no fingerprints? How could he do it with no fingerprints? How could it be possible?

And the boss had mentioned the office, wanting it to be spick and span, so he knew he couldn't use any sharp instruments. There would be too much blood. Just too much damn blood on the damn carpet.

At this, Alex giggled again. It was exciting and brain racking at the same instant. He had never killed anyone before.

He never thought that he would be choosing the method to do it, but it was still a job that needed to be done.

Which way would be the cleanest?

It was tough. It was brutal. It was a decision that needed planning.

Strangulation would be too much. Too much choking and gagging and flailing limbs. Everything would get knocked off the desk for sure. Then he would never be able to pick everything up after that.

He rubbed his chin as he felt the mole at the bottom of it. He tapped it as though it were a magic button that would shoot an answer right into his lap.

As he was thinking, his eyes wondered over to the tall glass windows as he continued to press. *Which casino could he be in? What would you do, boss? What would you do?*

Decisions, decisions. It all gave him a headache. A big headache. A headache that made him turn from the window and his useless day dreaming of…

The Window…the window…wait a minute.

Alex saw the latch just in the middle of the crease of the frame. It was sticking out like a lever - a death lever. Winner takes all and walks out with the pot.

Jackpot, that is!

Alex hurried to the window and undid the latch. The massive window lurched open, giving Alex a start. Had he not been able to grab hold of himself, he might have been the next thing to fly into the steamy Vegas air.

Don't get killed on the job now.

"I know," he said to himself. He felt annoyed.

There was only one thing left to do now, and that was to wait.

Alex hated waiting as well.

He held his position and made a brief guess.

Thirty-five…forty-four stories up. Yep, that oughta do the trick. Unless a stool pigeon is out here on one of the ledges…I don't see any problem here.

He could have bent further but didn't feel as though he wanted to risk it.

Silently he picked up the bag along with the paperback book. He stuffed the shredder in a nearby large draw and eased it shut. Then, making quite sure that the bag was securely fastened, he knelt toward the corner of the room, next to the window, pulled a cabinet door in front of him and waited.

The black door covered him perfectly in the wedged corner. It was almost too perfect.

As he waited, he thought silently to keep his mind occupied.

So many jobs he had been on and not one of them involved killing. But it needed to be done. It was absolutely imperative to his boss's orders. He would not disobey.

Plus, he was sure that the boss would give him extra if he was satisfied with the job. A perfect little scheme that he could consider a fool's exit. He had grown tired with his dirty dealing and had expressed thoroughly that this was his last job. His very last job ever. After that, it was anyone's guess.

Maybe a few quick pulls of the slot machines...Maybe a couple rounds of black jack...Could go for a nice cold drink... better not be that stuffy cocktail mess they serve down at The Ritz.

A sound. Not a very loud sound, but it was heard nonetheless.

It sounded like walnuts cracking or possibly...

...a lock being opened by a key.

Yes. The time had finally come. The time to kill this little pipsqueak and still make it in time to go and get a seat at one of the famous poker tables. He would have to beat the dealer but he knew well how do break a man with confidence down. He had done it all his life. That was the beauty part about his work. He was just so damn intimidating. That's why he hadn't needed to kill anybody in his line of work...until now.

Now he was ready. But his mind floated a bit. He was forgetting something. The pink plastic bag below his feet! And the desk lamp!

Quickly, like a child trying to sneak a cookie out of a jar, he dashed to the desk and pressed the lamp off. He could see a pair of shoes coming across the corner underneath the cubicles.

He rushed quickly back to his hiding spot and made his way into a crouching position. Lifting the bag up, he pressed the door firmly against himself as tight as he could squeeze. Even tighter as a matter of fact.

His shoes would be no problem in the dark. Apart from the massive open window overlooking the strip, the office looked quite normal. Everything was swallowed in a curve of covering shadow. The only open or disrupted thing in the office was the window which looked incredibly like a box-shaped mouth once you walked in.

The entire fragrance of the air was circulating in foreboding awe. And there was something else.

Everything was silent. Everything was calm.

But something in Alex's mind stirred. The shoes. The shoes he had seen before he rushed back to his hiding place. *Were they women's shoes? Stiletto heels?*

Perish the thought. Alex did not want to know. He was now sweating, holding that flimsy-looking bag with him in his triangular prison.

It doesn't matter! It doesn't matter! he told himself inside his own head. But somehow it did. He had never killed anyone before, but he especially didn't want to kill a woman. It was against his whole view of life. Only corrupted men deserve to fall to a corrupted death. That was his motto.

But maybe this woman needed to die. Didn't she? The boss had made that perfectly clear in the code.

Perfume. It was definitely a woman. That was the scent he was smelling. His nostrils made a slight squeak, sniffing it in, but he stifled it immediately.

Had she heard?

No. She was just now unlocking the office doors. She came in. That fragrance filled up the room. It was in his lungs.

Alex peeked a little from his hiding spot while the woman made a move to close the door. She was a thin woman with brown pulled-up hair and a suit skirt that was all black and professional. Her creamy white skin was so pale that Alex thought it would light up the room. When she turned, he turned. But he did catch a glimpse of her face.

There was no time for love at first sight, but she was so damned attractive. It gave him a silent disliking for his position.

Who knows? They could have hooked up somewhere in Vegas had it not been for their mutual boss.

She was wearing glasses like him too. Light from the window revealed more of her attractive face. Her blue eyes were like diamonds cutting into the air with laser beam anal retentiveness.

He couldn't control anything anymore. He wanted to scream! He wanted to shout out where he was, throw his hands up in the air and whimper a pathetic 'Let's be friends, kid.'

But that was simply out of the question. He had to get this done. He had to convince himself that she was the enemy in this. She was the job and nothing more. It could have been any reason. Blackmail, drug trafficking, or good old intent to cause mischief. In any case, he had to make up something to make his mind feel better about this.

He had to do it. He had to psyche himself up to do it...but he did it.

As soon as she placed her files on the desk, turned on the lamp, and walked over to the window, he tensed up.

"What's this?" she asked as she reached for the latch of the window, obviously annoyed. Leaning over, with her butt sticking out, she noticed a hand creeping around the black cabinet door that was wedged next to the window.

He charged at her, wasting no time to drop the pink bag, which made him resemble a somewhat disgruntled grocer that she had a run in with the other day. The glasses flew and the stilettos dropped.

Alex was dangling from the strong latch which he held. In his furious bull-charging motion, he had lost his footing and was almost out of the window himself.

He dangled by his fingers from the latch and slithered his way back into the office.

A long shallow scream trailed all the way down the windows followed by a sickening SNAP-POP!

Alex didn't even want to look. He didn't want to know.

Then, the phone rang. The boss said that he would call

sooner or later.

Alex picked it up in an exhausted excited breath.

"It's okay," the voice said. "I've got you on a secure line. You can talk."

Alex took a couple moments to catch his breath. A near-death experience of this sort was nothing to be taken lightly. It had never happened to him before.

"What the hell are you all huffing and puffing about?"

"Bo…boss…" he panted, making a sick belch of air as he did. A nervous trapped air belch that disgusted his current boss. "I did it. I …did…whew…it."

"Well good. No mess?"

"Yeah. There's one outside right now. I kept it spick and span, no mess in the office," Alex said while grinning, pretty pleased with himself - feeling proud and liberated for the first time.

"What? You mean you threw the papers out the window?!"

"Huh? No! No stupid papers went out the window!"

"Well, then! What's the mess?"

"There's no mess. It was done clean!"

"Then what's the mess outside? What are you talking about?"

Silence.

It was awfully loud.

Then, a repeated bang-bang-bang came from the window tapping against the latch. He had never locked it. His eyes rolled back and forth in a confused wishy-washy moment.

"Boss. It was clean. I got rid of her!"

"Rid of who?"

"The assistant. Your assistant!" he said. It was aggravating enough to have a man like this question his own request. "Don't you remember? You told me with the book code."

"Alex! I never told you to kill anyone."

Now Alex felt, for the first time in his life, a cold sweat that was collecting under his armpits, and it was now stinging his soul. Somehow the aching soul seeped into his heart, which made it rumble loudly and then began to pulsate and pound like a revving engine.

"B...but...but...boss?"

"I gave you the book code line for line. What did you do?"

"I...I pushed her out the window."

"Sylvia?! You killed Sylvia?!"

"Boss...please stop...you're scaring me."

"No, no, no. You got that the other way around. You're scaring me. I've never talked to a killer before."

"I ain't no killer!"

"You just told me you were."

"Yeah...but..."

Alex scrambled for sanity which couldn't be found. He could have mistaken it banging at the door, but that had been his own heart that was beating in his inner ear.

"Alex. Listen to me. Leave Vegas. There's no time for the papers now."

"Papers? What papers?"

"Alex! You're not listening to me! I gave you the book code to the le...oh God...what have I done?"

"You didn't do anything boss...I kinda did it for you." Alex said nervously, now choking on his words.

"Alex," the voice pleaded. There was a fathering tone in the voice now. One that Alex had never heard before. "Please, for my own benefit, you...please..."

"What, boss? What?!"

"Just please tell me that you didn't buy the paperback edition of *Money Is The Color of Blood?"*

Everything inside Alex froze. A stiffening freeze. It made him cling to the phone even closer in desperate angst.

"Why?" he asked.

"The paperback edition of a novel is different from the hard cover copy. While the paperback copy holds six hundred pages, the hardcover holds only four hundred or so. The reason is the much bigger font. You fumbled the book code! You must have."

Tears were now streaming down this lost soul's face. He knew he was dead. He could already hear the guard coming up the stairs, searching for the room from which the splattered woman supposedly jumped from.

"I guess I did," was all he could say at the moment. "Just out of curiosity, what was the message that you intended to give me?"

The voice read it from a paper that was obviously heard ruffling on the other end of the line. He read:

"SHRED MY FILES NOW ALEX."

Alex did the math in his head. The sentence was exactly ninteen letters long. Exactly.

Now it all swarmed together and finally made a thud in the pit of his stomach. The boss had never used the wrong letters. It was Alex that used the wrong edition of the book. What were the odds of that happening, That a simple mistake in page number could ultimately be the downfall of an unknown businessman?

"Maybe you can still shred the papers!" the voice pleaded.

The shredder was broke. The woman was dead. The office window was open. The guard was increasing his speed. There was no hope. Chalk up a new one on the blackboard: only label this one 'Stupidity' instead. But it would be the last stupid mistake of Alex Dujima's life.

"Just jokin' boss. I can shred the papers."

The silence was unbearable, but it was short. The voice seemed a little ruffled as well as baffled.

"Well….good. What are you going to do after that?"

"I figured I'd meet a new woman," Alex said, holding his head in his hands.

"Glad to here it, Alex. Alex? Alex?ALEX?!"

There was no more Alex. The window flew open and Alex had left. He didn't fly away, but he sure as hell didn't reach heaven.

The Letters

The first thing I truly realized was that I was in deep shit. I was suspended in mid-air. I felt a slight dizziness as I warped out of my nightmare only to be hanging in a brand-new one. The floorboards were three feet away from my toes. As I continued to look down, I realized that I was stark naked. I couldn't see my damn dick over my beer gut. I was so ashamed.

I challenged my neck to crane my head up. My wrists were bound too, leading up, wrapped around a hook to a rope that disappeared into the darkness.

The solitary light source was hung solitarily overhead. It created a spotlight around me. It burned like the sun against my sweating flesh.

Then it all started to come back to me. My forearm brushed

against my temple, which reminded me of the tremendous headache that welcomed my rude awakening. Somebody had hit me from behind.

Not hard enough to make me forget who I was though.

My name is Mickey Voslo. I've worked for several shops, but that was just a cover. My real trade was money laundering. I was good. Damn good come to think of it.

Shit, my head! Even thinking hurt.

My temples throbbed, giving my brain a rough massage as if it were dough.

Then, more good news, somewhere along the way I began to get all high and mighty and decided to scrape off some dough for myself. Nothing big, a twenty-dollar bill at a time. After all, what were the bean counters going to do? Report stolen money from stolen money? Not likely.

But that's not what got me here.

What got me here was the fact that even though I was making more than my share, I wanted more. And in doing so, I attempted to rob my bosses' safe. Next thing I know, I'm strung up like a turkey waiting to be hacksawed.

My shoulders ached.

There was something quite unpleasant about this lair, this hideaway. It seemed empty, except for me. But then again, I couldn't see that well in the darkness that stretched on into another universe. Where the hell was I?

I didn't bother calling out or saying hello. That shit was too damn stereotypical. Plus, the fucker who took his time to hold me up for the night obviously went to some trouble to make me panic. It was working, but I pretended that it wasn't.

Moments passed until finally a person walked into my beam of light. His approach was so silent that I hardly noticed him. I had to do a double take just to make sure he was there.

From what I could see, he was a slender man with a sunken-in face. He wore a derby hat that came down to his eyebrows, giving the rest of his face a snarled look. He held a suitcase in his right hand and was trying hard to look like a businessman.

He didn't say a word.

He just nodded.

He reached to his right and pulled a rickety wooden table with bad legs closer to the light. He carefully placed his suitcase on top, like a lawyer preparing to stand before the judge.

Something didn't sit well in my stomach. I could sense trouble, I could smell pain coming.

He walked up to me and looked up into my eyes while I stared down at him. Casually, he took off his hat and crossed his arms behind him, tapping his hat behind his ass as if he were making smoke signals.

"Do I frighten you?" he asked.

I didn't know what to say or do. Which was the right answer and which was the wrong answer? What do I get for each?

I twitched in response.

"Good," he said.

He proceeded to get weirder.

But as he was walking over to the small table, some of the tumblers clicked in my brain. His accent. His accent was German. It was very distinctive. And if this man was German, he was hired by Big Louie. Louie always made a point of hiring foreign muscle to get his point across. But he only did that when he wanted someone dead.

I should have never touched that damn safe.

Already, I knew that my pitiful, naked, dangling life was in the hands of something foul. Now it was just a matter of time before I would come to know how bad this death stench would become. I could smell many kills that this man had performed even though the past bloodstains had been wiped clean. And something inside me coiled. The tense feeling pulsed through my fingertips and made me grip my fingers around the already chaffing rope that was cutting into my wrists.

The nameless man stepped over to the table. With great care, and a touch of tidiness, he wiped a finger along the table. It was dusty. He pulled a rag from his coat pocket and flicked it. He undid his bottom coat button to reveal a perfect line from his shirt to his belt. He wiped down the filthy table, the dust particles making spurts of dust galaxies in the cold night air as they refracted the light.

Once that was done, he placed the suitcase at the far edge of the rectangular table. He pulled his chair closer and sat, facing me. He scooted once. The sound of the chair legs echoed three times throughout the huge room. That made me cringe. I could feel the vast emptiness of the place. And even though I was never a whiz kid and was only able to pass eighth grade, I knew that this place was a factory.

A cold…abandoned…factory.

Perfect for killing.

I guess my captor already knew that.

This bastard *did* have it all figured out. He smiled as he heard the sound of the chair scraping throughout the factory.

It lasted for ages.

He turned back to me, eerily saying, "Good acoustics."

He unclicked the briefcase and opened the top. Without looking at me, he pulled out something shiny - something long and slim. The sharp object grinned at me. It was a knife. The damn guy was going to cut me up after all. For all I knew, he must have had an arsenal of tinker torture toys in that little case of mysteries.

But, as I squinted harder, I saw that it was a letter opener.

My brain sprouted a field of question marks.

Then he uncloaked some more little goodies. A glass cube paperweight, a package of already sharpened pencils, a fresh stack of paper (I was guessing maybe four hundred sheets), and an even fresher stack of long manila envelopes. He produced a second stack of these. Afterwards, he counted everything, made sure nothing was missing, then closed the suitcase and slid it under his chair. Now his table had all the makings of an office. Simple, yes, but an office nonetheless, minus the walls. All he needed now was a little bobble-head and a nameplate at the front of it.

For some reason, hanging there, staring at this oddball while my penis shrank in fear, I got the feeling this was an interview. It felt like it. I was really put on the spot with this.

He didn't say a word.

It made me think that he wanted me to break the ice first. Then, the tumblers did their work again. The papers, the table, the envelopes, the stamps. My head leaned back as I felt my eyes roll. I finally realized that I was not only in deep shit, I was drowning in a monsoon of it.

"Damn," I said out of the side of my mouth. "I didn't think that Big Lou would have the big brass ones to hire *Il Postino*."

"The Postman, if you please."

It all came together. I nodded as I tongued something out of my teeth. I knew I would be here a while. I might as well get comfortable.

From old paranoid lore, it is said that The Postman was a fiendishly long-winded hit man - a man who brought regular post-office-like equipment and supposedly talked his victim's to death. But that was just one version. Another, that I heard from Bruno, said that one shouldn't be fooled by this crackpot's appearance. He was really a swift and gruesome man, capable of making torture last. But the last thing that I ever heard about The Postman was that he enjoyed the biz. Got into it when his family was taken from him in a political bombing. He wanted to be a journalist, a writer for his country. Instead he wrote death warrants to the men and women he was hired to kill. No one has ever escaped from The Postman. But that was due to the fact that no bodies were ever found. What did he do with the bodies? More importantly, what did he *do* to the bodies?

"From this moment on, I will teach you fear."

Something floated up inside my chest. I think it might have been cockiness. Somehow I felt superior to this fraud, this girlish man posing as a viscious unrelenting killer. It looked like I could knock him down with just one good blow to the head. I had dealt with weaker.

And I had heard that this old and crusty windbag liked to be paid in euros. Five hundred — no more, no less.

"Forgive me if I seem non-enthusiastic, but you're The

Postman. Not the teacher. Teaching is not your forte."

He picked up the letter opener.

My mouth, if it was still open, closed shut.

His right eye twitched as he used the opener as a low-grade pencil sharpener. He ignored my statement and went on to sharpen four more pencils.

"Just in case," he said.

The glare of the opener blinded me and I started to imagine all the things he would do with that thing. He'd be able to carve me six ways from Sunday and no one would know…except him. I couldn't get the damn thing out of my mind. It was obviously his weapon of choice. Why wouldn't he use it?

"Oh," he said, blowing the shavings of his pencil and eyeing my line of sight. He picked up the opener and looked at it. "This is a nasty little instrument if used improperly. Somebody could get hurt with one of these things. I've seen it happen before."

He grinned, and in the far back of his mouth, my eyes registered a gold tooth. At least the prick had some amount of worth in that foul mouth of his. I would love to punch him until that little beauty jiggled loose.

"Does this little thing worry you?" He gave the opener a tick-tock motion. "Well, by all means…let's get rid of it, shall we?"

The Postman grabbed the edge of the blade with the tips of his fingers and jerked his wrist. Before I could respond, the opener went sailing towards me and crunched into the floorboards directly underneath my feet. My knees jerked up in reflex, and they nearly hammered my stomach. When I first saw it airborne, I could have sworn he was aiming for my crouch. Maybe he was.

I jerked and wiggled, a naked worm on a very uncomfortable hook.

"Stay with me, Mickey. That was just to get your attention. I want you to know that I will not pick that thing up again. I promise you that. It will remain there for the duration."

I couldn't take this game he was playing. I knew he meant business. There was nothing else I could do but pay attention, or at least pretend to and formulate a plan.

"Since, we're going to be here for quite some time, I may as well tell you what I'm going to do. You're going to be tortured, Mickey. And nothing and no one can stop it. Accept that now."

I nodded my head; maybe I could grab the opener with my feet.

"What I need is your cooperation to make sure this goes smoothly. Tell me, Mickey, how many relatives do you have?"

"Why in the hell should I tell you?"

Shit, the knife wasn't close enough even when I stretched.

"Because if you don't, I'll kill you quickly. Then I'll find out in my own little way and go after them one by one. I'll find them. And I'll hang them right next to your useless maggot-infested corpse. However, if you tell me who your relatives are, I give you my word that I will not pursue them."

"You're a man of many promises tonight, you know that, donthca?"

"Look around. Who controls your fate at this moment? I do. Who else would you trust?"

"You can turn on a promise any time."

"Not this one. This one is ironclad. I'd rather wade through sewage than to go back on my own word. Sticking to your promises is what generates respect. And I am well connected, if you understand."

"Why do you need to know?"

"Because I think all of your relatives need a little closure."

"What do you mean?"

"The way I see it, your death is inescapable. The only thing left is to warn your relatives. I'm going to write a letter to each one describing to them, in detail, the manner in which you will die. It may take a while, depending on how many relatives you have. Then, after I'm finished with one letter, I'll seal it away in one of these manila envelopes. Each one will be mailed tomorrow. I hope I have everything covered."

"You can't send them! They'll be terrified! You'll cause heart attacks with those letters!"

"There's no definite proof of that. Knowing you and your dirty dealings, the letters might give them nothing more than a little uncomfortable indigestion."

I bowed my head in shame. This was so fucked.

Then I could hear the little bastard snickering. I looked up.

The Postman cleared his throat and hocked up a big nasty lougie. He spat it on the floor two feet away from him.

Evidence.

DNA.

That was all I could hope for.

"Oh I see," he said finally. "They don't know what you really do. This is splendid."

I was on the edge, damn near ready to go unconscious just to get away from it all. But I couldn't go anywhere.

"Now, on with it and out with it. How many *living* relatives do you have?"

"Does that include cousins, nephews, married-in family?"

"I would say not. Little children shouldn't be exposed to letters of an extreme nature. Through marriage doesn't count at all. I'm talking blood relatives. Aunts, uncles, grandfathers, grandmothers, the works."

I backtracked in my head. I climbed, in my mind, up my family tree and glanced at every relative sitting on a branch, occupied by their own trivial hobbies. When I finally reached the top, I knew that this twerp had more than enough pencils, paper, and envelopes.

"Fifty," I said. "Fifty in all. At least."

The Postman made a tsk, tsk sound with his mouth as if to say '*That's too bad, sport.*'

"So be it," he said. "Who's first?"

I quivered. "My aunt Tilly. She has a stronger heart."

"So be it," he repeated.

The pencil scribbled as he began to write a personal letter to my aunt. From what I could see, with my limited vision, he had excellent cursive writing. It disturbed me how he decided to write so professionally, even to my aunt. A simple quick note would have sufficed. No, he had a lot to say. He filled a full three pages before he was done.

I couldn't see what he wrote.

God help my aunt.

I hope I was right.

I hope she had a strong heart like some of my uncles had said.

Whatever he wrote, I know that it was a lot. And that, in turn, meant that he was going to do a lot of stuff to me. And that did not bode well. I hope my aunt had a strong stomach as well.

My stomach was already curdled.

I guess that says a lot about me.

After he finished, he folded the letter into three parts, slid it in the long manila envelope and sat up.

Pushing his chair in, I could tell that he was going to come over to me. What he wanted, I didn't know. Maybe he was the type to stick the pencil in my mouth so I could sign the letter myself, confirming to my relatives that I was as good as dead.

But he didn't.

Instead, he came over, held the wide envelope up to his crusty teeth and hung out his tongue. And when he licked the pasted part of the envelope, I could swear he was looking at me in…well…you know…the sexual way.

I was too far away to kick him for that.

You would think that all of this would settle down after that, but you would be wrong.

Before I could even hint at giving a face of disgust, he quickly griped the envelope by the edges, and with a twisted speed that was almost super human, he winged the sharp pasted side of the envelope at my fragile skin. The side of the envelope swished right past me, right under my right nipple.

I had a slight moment of shock followed by the shrillest scream I ever belted out. I grunted and grinded my teeth as I looked down at my nipple. I felt it as the envelope went in and already I could feel the blood trickling down. A sweat bead, at the wrong time, found its way into the wound and made that sucker seer like nothing you would believe.

I didn't want to cry, but my eyes were crowded with juice.

The sick bastard cackled, then sealed the envelope shut. While his back was turned, my head felt too heavy to lift but I was able to faintly say, "What the fuck is your deal?"

He turned, pivoting on one foot. "Only forty-nine more to go."

And that's when it really struck me - he was too good at this. He knew how to make a person crack.

The Postman sat back down and shuffled back into his chair. He placed the finished letter to the side and pulled out a fresh sheet of paper.

He licked the tip of the pencil. I have no idea why people do that. I hoped he would get lead poisoning, the crusty fuck.

The pencil tip-tapped the paper. To anyone not in this situation it would seem like a normal sound, but to me, in this atmosphere, it sounded like a hammer coming down and echoed just as much as all the sounds in this place.

I didn't wanna die here.

"Who's next?"

I anchored my chin on my chest; I wriggled and shook the sweat off my face. "I d...I don't know."

"Come on, Mickey," he taunted. "I'm an impatient man."

"M...my uncle Charles."

"Strong heart as well?"

"No. He just doesn't care what happens to me."

"Such a caring family, Mickey. You'll have to invite me to a dinner sometime soon."

Then he chuckled, probably realizing that I'd be dead soon and that his invitation was pretty much gone.

Big Lou was a bastard. He went overboard with this. This was something I would wish on my worst enemy. And I was just a simple thief. I didn't expect a slap on the wrist, but, damn, this was way out into left field.

Already he was writing up a storm, and I knew what was coming right after. So, mentally, I prepared myself for the next slice.

Everyone wants a slice of me. Lou. This dipshit, and now even my relatives would own a little sliver of me when they opened their envelopes to find dried blood.

I lifted my head and his smiling face was right there. He sliced another chunk out of me. This time it was just above my left nipple. He caught me off-guard, writing barely a paragraph for my uncle's letter. I bit my lip as I felt the sharp, tingling pain and sighed as the blood cooled my nipple.

"What the fuck did you do that for?"

"You said he didn't care about you, remember? I figured on giving him a break."

I wiggled even more. I wanted off this merry-go-round. I twirled in protest.

The Postman slid his finger across my new blood trail. He eyed it for a moment on his finger, held it up to me, then he licked the blood clean off his fingertip.

I grimaced. "Oh you sick…"

"Ugh. Too sour. You've got sour blood for a thief, but I guess that's natural."

I was ready to have it out with him right here and now. I tried to kick, but it was useless, he knew exactly how far to stand away from me.

The methodical prick.

This was awful. This was no way to go. Didn't the Chinese do something similar to this. Well, no matter who did it they were all sick bastards.

"Forty-eight to go," he said, making his way to the table.

"My mother!" I screamed.

He looked up in surprise. "I beg your pardon?"

"That's what you want, isn't it? The next one. My mother's next. Write the letter and get it over with."

He put the pencil down and eyed me curiously, almost as if I was the first one to toughen up after all these times. Then he cocked his head to the side. For a straight hour he just sat there. I screamed and shouted, psyching myself up for the next slice.

Eventually, I tired out and that's when he picked up the pencil to write another death notice. I didn't wanna close my eyes or take my eyes off of him for fear that he'd surprise me again.

My mind tried to squeeze out a plan as my wounds were busy squeezing out blood. The letter opener was too far away, we were in the middle of nowhere, he wouldn't get close enough for me enough to kick him a good one, my hands were tied tight in a knot. He was the one who tied it, I was sure of it. What was this guy, a fucking boy scout?

The only thing left for me to do was to wait for some lucky break which would never come. That or I could try to lift myself up and try to hop off the hook. But I wasn't strong enough.

I saw the pencil go down. This letter was a good five pages long. What was the bastard doing? Being sympathetic? Telling my mother that is was just business and nothing personal? No, when a man gave you paper cuts and licked the blood that came out, it was personal. It was very fucking personal. Too personal for me, and I had enough of it. I tightened my grip against the hook.

He slid the letter in the envelope, licked it while he was at the table and made his way over to me.

My half-assed plan jumped into my noggin, waiting for a test drive. I was so excited about the idea that I attacked at exactly the wrong moment. I kicked my legs behind me and tried to swing over to him. At the last moment, he dodged the blow and grabbed me by the neck.

"For that," he began…but he didn't finish.

While holding a tight grip on my neck he looked down and sliced below me. I didn't see where he cut, but I felt where it was. I wailed like there was no tomorrow, trying not to bite my tongue.

He had sliced me where the sun didn't shine - right on the shaft of my dick. I felt my body somehow jerk up. There was a stabbing pain in my wrists, more tension for some reason. I felt the blood pulsing its way out. He unleashed my neck and let me twirl.

He made it back to the table once again.

I was coughing, wanted to throw up.

"Ffffucker! You fucking bitch!"

For some reason, it didn't upset him.

I'd enough. I couldn't handle forty-seven more of these. I should have lied about my relatives. Now I hated all of them, hated every single one. I wanted to knock each one off their stupid branches and watch them come crashing to the ground.

"Please…no more…not this."

"You should have thought of that before money decide to grow wings and flutter away."

"I won't do it. No more. No more."

The Postman stiffened up, his head held high. "There will be more. Always more."

I looked up, crying to God for mercy. And I found it. I stared at what was my salvation. As he was slicing up my goodfella, my body jumped and now the knot was swaying over the very tip of the hook. Before, I was screwed. The knot was right in the curve, the weight of my body holding me down. Now, with the knot teetering on the hook, I had a chance to swing free.

But no, there was a risk that if I swung, I'd swing myself right back into the big screw.

More bad news.

I could feel acid in my throat, the oncoming vomit fest. I only wanted to vomit because I could feel the blood trickling just over my piss hole. And that, my friends, is a feeling no one should ever experience in their entire life.

It's remarkably unclean and earth shattering.

So were my screams.

Without hesitation I gave him another name. "Uncle Vincenzo."

"You're one tough cookie, aren't you?"

I was tired, exhausted by the pains that shackled me here. This room was going to be my tomb if I didn't do something soon.

I just wished he would hurry up and write the letter. The pencil did its cursive writing, by the order of The Postman, and I sighed. Soon, he'd finish another letter. Maybe forty-seven wasn't so bad. Maybe it would be over before I knew it.

The pencil broke.

There was no eraser on the end of it.

"Oh dear," he said.

He picked up the sheet of paper as if it were addressed to him, as if one of *his* relatives had died. "I messed up. I'll need a new pencil and a new sheet of paper. Oh, this is not good. Not good at all."

He jumped up from his chair, ran up to me and sliced the thin paper across my piss hole. I cringed, practically snapping my own neck with the way I was flailing up and down. I growled and spat. And I knew this would never end. He smiled once again and turned, about to walk back to his table, but then, mercy smiled upon me. I found myself sliding down.

The rope snapped, severed by the tip of the hook it was resting on. And when my feet landed on the floor, I could see The Postman's neck crink up.

You better believe I tore the letter opener out of the floor and raised it high as I leaped for him. Fuck trying to cut the extra pieces of rope from my skin. That didn't matter.

The only thing that mattered was revenge.

Only revenge.

The nice, sharp, friendly blade sunk into his right shoulder blade. He gasped.

Quickly he pulled a one-eighty turn and was upon me. We struggled furiously in the shadows. Finally, because I was filled with oozing hatred, I was able to pin him against the table. The letter flew out of his hands.

I twisted the blade and then pulled it out with a swift jerk. The blood splattered across my face, cooling my fever. Now he was the one that was screaming. He grabbed at his wound, only making it worse.

I did my best to make it hurt. I sunk the blade down into his other shoulder, pinning him to the table. While I pushed it down, I borrowed the glass paperweight and brought it down on his nose, which, I'm proud to say, crumbled easily and noisily.

Blood squirted out.

I could see the gold tooth lying on the desk with a

bloodstain on it.

Victory! But not enough.

The bastard was still squirming, trying to pull the blade out of himself. If I had the time, and I didn't, I would have happily bestowed the same torture he did on me. I would have loved to make little paper-thin slices out of him. But, now, I was forced to take my revenge on the fly, to play it by ear.

I grabbed a handful of stamps and shoved them into his mouth. Maybe the glue would poison him. I remember snatching up the pencil and driving it straight into the skin above his collarbone.

He coughed and gurgled, but never begged. I saw his eyes roll up into his head.

"No!" I screamed. "No! You can't die yet!" I shook him with my uncontrollable fists. "I'm not done with you yet!"

Desperately I scooped the stamps out of his gagging throat. He took in a brief long sigh of relief.

Good. Get him.

I pulled the pencil out of him. He screamed and gave me a look that made my heart skip a beat. That look I will never be able to erase from my memories.

I wanted the look to go away, so I picked up an envelope and sliced him clear across his eyeball. Before I could see the wound, which I'm sure was horrific, he clutched it with his aged hand.

I pulled him off the desk, the blade popped out.

Then, when I had him on the ground, I repeatedly kneed him in the groin so that no children would ever spew themselves out of this beast. Then, I cried and gasped for air as I wrapped both hands around his neck and pushed with both thumbs. His neck made these weird popping sounds, almost like twigs snapping in the forest.

"Stay with me, Postman! Stay with me!"

But he didn't. Instead, he gave out one final gurgle, then came a crack…and he was gone.

"No!" I shouted, ruining his clothes with the snot that was

dripping out of my nose. "Don't leave me! You have to come back! Come back!"

But he didn't.

He was dead.

That's what I wanted.

So why did I feel unsatisfied?

Because he didn't suffer like me?

As I stared at his white and mangled face and contorted limbs, I realized that I had made him suffer enough. I also noticed that I broke his leg when I gotten him down on the ground. I didn't hear it snap because I was too busy howling with a lust to cause pain.

Now it was over.

Il Postino was dead.

I cried into my hands, drowning myself in my own sweat and mucus. I didn't stop until I ran out of juice. That really took it out of me.

I ached.

My skin, my wounds, it felt like they weren't there. I had my due.

But my curiosity was still explosive.

I saw the paper that flew out of his hand. It was under him; a little corner was popping out.

My hand crept toward it. I don't know what I was expecting; maybe some crazy symbols, a repeated sentence, a grocery list. My mind couldn't wrap around the fact that he was writing letters of intent right in front of me. I hoped that he was crazy.

To my surprise, as I knelt there, reading the letter, I found that he *was* writing to them. In fact, he worded everything rather delicately, knowing exactly what to say. Telling my uncle that his nephew ran out of lucky breaks and found his end. Told him that he shouldn't worry about the body because it was already cremated and spread in a place of my choosing.

I didn't wanna read anymore. This guy was a friggin' poet when it came to writing.

I crumpled the letter in my hands and tossed it into the darkness. I ended up walking thirty yards in the dark before I finally reached an elevator.

I was tired, thirsty, moaning with pain.

But I was alive, damn it.

I am alive.

Alive. Period.

Pennies

Horace Grant was one ridiculously hotheaded son of a bitch. But he wasn't always that way. He told me so. When I was a kid I used to spend my days on the hot porch sitting outside my parents' apartment. We were poor but still breathing and that was the important thing, I was told.

The first time I met Horace, he walked up to the building next to mine and shouted up at the top floor. Something about payments due. It's hard to remember, it was so long ago.

Next thing I knew, a window opens, an arm comes out, and down drops something shiny and hurtful. Halfway down, Horace gets a glimpse of what it is after shading his eyes from the unforgiving sun.

A butcher's cleaver.

The damn thing was coming down faster than anything I'd ever seen.

Horace was a little too late in ducking. The blade, I

thought, bounced off his shoe and twanged to the right, clattering on the sidewalk. But in reality, the blade was sharp enough to pierce Horace's penny loafers, and it chopped off two toes. It was the little piggy that had no roast beef and the one that cried wee-wee all the way home. At least, that was the stupid rhyme that my parents would do right before I would go to bed. I never understood it. I mean, seriously, why in the hell would hogs eat roast beef? Secondly, all the childishness went out of the rhyme after I saw the cold-blooded bastard shout like his voice would crumble the heavens.

As I was sitting there watching all this, I think I was more shocked and in awe rather than scared.

Horace banged on the lid of the trashcan, spitting curses and watching as the blood was practically jumping into the hot steamy air.

His face was a complicated, sweaty mess.

In a moment of rage, Horace scrambled to pick up the same cleaver that had gotten the better of him, climbed up the steps and began hacking away at the door.

"I'm coming," he said, a deranged smile on his face. "And nothin' and no one is going to stop me!"

I could see that a splotch of blood was still on the blade. And he was driving it in the door harder than anything you can imagine.

This was before men could take samples of DNA and match it to the killer. Way before.

Finally, he busted through.

I remained on the porch while he ran in, taking the stairs two at a time despite his foot.

Horace, as others will tell you, was never a hot-tempered man per se. He was, years back, a calm, yet forgiving loan shark.

Not to make you laugh here, but all that went out the window as easily as that cleaver did. That's when something in Horace's mind snapped that bright summer's day.

I ran in as soon as I heard the screams. I wasn't phoning the cops. I went into the kitchen and found a soda bottle untouched. I popped the cap open and went outside to sit in the exact same spot on the steps. How do I know it was exact same spot? I could still see the ass sweat stain, that's how.

By the time I lifted that thing to my salty lips and closed my eyes to take a chug, Horace was already walking down the steps of the building next to me.

My eyes snapped open.

Without turning my head, I leaned my eyes over and saw him.

On his white shirt and suspenders were shades of red, pink, and, strangely enough, purple. His face was sweating and it was making the blood specks run down his bristly chin. He turned towards me, cleaver still in hand.

Instead of attacking me next, which is what I thought he would do, he merely breathed a sigh of relief and tipped his fedora at me.

He pointed the cleaver in my direction.

"Boy. You haven't seen anything here, am I right?"

I nodded, bottle still in mouth, like a dumb baby who couldn't talk, while drinking extremely expired milk.

"Boy, you're just sittin' out in the sun. Didn't see anyone walk by, am I right?"

I nodded again, the carbon fizzing against my gums.

He was pleased. I saw him smile. He sniffed in a bit, he must have been sick a little.

Then he choked up a laugh as he saw his two toes still cooking on the baked asphalt. He scooped them up with his free hand and placed them in his pocket right around the same time he looked back up at me.

"And you haven't seen any of my toes lying around out here either, am I right?"

I nodded for the final time.

Still with a smile on his face, he was able to stumble and walk off with a limp. I spotted a dishtowel wrapped around his foot as he left.

By now I had spat out my soda because it was stinging my

teeth. Like I said, I was still in shock.

The police came from someone else's phone call and the area swarmed with trench coats and flashing lights.

I was still on the porch. The sóda in my hand was flat a long while ago.

They tried to ask me questions.

I only gave them the run around.

They asked who was here, I asked who was here.

They asked who did this, I asked who did this.

They must have thought I wasn't all there. But I was and I am. I wasn't going to give Horace away. If a man had the grit to chuck a cleaver at me, I'd most likely do the same thing that Horace did without thinking. But, then again, I really didn't know who Horace was those days.

Can you believe that the eight-toed son of a bitch would live to be 102? That's one tough bastard if you ask me.

My mom would smack me whenever I said 'tough bastard' around the house those days. First of all, it's a compliment so I don't know what her problem was. When I refer to someone as a 'tough bastard', I admire their plight. My mother would tell me to use cookie instead of bastard. Can you imagine that? That someone is a 'tough cookie'. No. That's bullshit. Cookies can crumble. Bastards can't.

Even when they placed Horace under arrest, at the age of 63 no less, he was never surprised and never begging for an appeal. It seems that all those unsolved cases finally caught up with him all because someone preserved his blood samples and were able to place him at the scene of the crime with the help of DNA. Who would have thought that technology would be so advanced in the coming years?

His lawyer got him a reduced sentence, but still, it was pretty long. But not in the court's or family's eyes. It wasn't confirmed, but his death toll was rumored to be over a hundred. Can you believe that?

He finished his sentence and got out when he was a startling 82 years old. Even then, he looked as young as 50. He was even able to shiv someone in prison on his seventieth birthday.

One tough bastard.

I was curious about his business, so, like any stupid kid looking for a quick buck, I joined the mob, although I wasn't part of the crew that Horace was a part of. And I was lucky to find that both the mob I was a part of and the mob he was a part of weren't enemies. We were small time.

The life I lived was unusually long. It feels like that every time you walk out the door expecting to get your head blown clean off and it never happens. Yep, life is long when you're waiting for death. I'm not sure that death was ever in Horace's plan. Shit, if Mr. Reaper wanted to ever come to Horace's house, and made the mistake of ringing his bell, he would be greeted with a whiskey slurpin', no second chances, big, broad, intimidating son of a bitch. And that's no lie.

At this point, I'm certain that Horace Grant scared the undertaker off his porch. Later, down in hell, the reaper would tell Mr. Devil not to piss off the man who lives on 236 Maple Avenue.

It was times like these that made me wonder what he was like before he turned that new leaf.

In the time it took me to screw up my life royally with mob ties, I had witnessed 24 deals that went down between 24 unlucky souls and Horace Grant. And every single one of those deals, Horace won.

I met up with him round the same time that I was thinking of quitting the business. It was the moment when I had a chance to work alongside him. It made me think that we were linked.

One day I got a call from his mob saying that they needed to quit this fellow for seeing a murder but he also owed them a debt. They knew they didn't wanna pay him off because that would cancel his debt. It's almost as if this guy was so desperate to get out of his loan that he purposely stuck his nose where it didn't belong.

They told me that they wanted me as back up, that it would only be a two-man job. In and out, they said.

I discussed it with my group, and they all agreed that it was an all-right deal.

I picked up Horace in my great green jalopy. When he entered my car, bigger than life, he made the car tip on one side. He slammed the door and pointed forward for my cue to drive.

We took off.

Here he was, the mythical man himself. The man who was tougher than nails and could even hammer them in with his rock-like fists.

All this time I was tracking him, collecting articles of the jobs I knew he had done. I still have them.

Don't go thinking I'm all into death and murder and stuff like that. I was interested in the man. He seemed to have an impenetrable field around him, something freaky.

My mom used to say that he didn't sell his soul, he muscled the devil until the red man was convinced that this man would live a damn long time.

When we got there, he asked me to come along. The whole time he hadn't recognized me. Who would? Would you really connect the baby sitting on the steps with the young man in a trench coat with a Tommy gun under it?

We walked in, taking Mr. Brewster completely by surprise. Horace motioned for me to stay back. Horace walked up to the man and slapped him in the face before he could say a word. The man collapsed. But that wasn't the end of it. Horace took out his gun and fired, at close range, at Mr. Brewster's knee. The chunks of bone and cartilage and muscles stunk up the room. Then, with his bare hand, Horace squeezed the juice out of the poor guy's wound.

"I'm having a hard time thinking this over," Horace said, raising his voice to talk over the screaming. "On the one hand your debt would be gone and we'd pay you. Now, as you can see that doesn't sit well with me. That's backwards business. On the other hand, you can pay me whatever you have right now and beg me to take it as a bribe to let you live."

The man gave in, crying like his whole family had died on Friday the 13th. He directed us to a safe that was under his kitchen sink. He told me the combination as Horace continued their talk together.

When I looked in, I thought we had hit the mother lode. It was wall-to-wall green. Horace asked how much it was. From what I saw, and counted, there was a total of three thousand dollars. As soon as the word 'thousand' exited my mouth, Horace blew the guy's head off. The shot was so blunt that the man cracked his head against the plaster.

I was completely scared at this point.

Horace tucked in his gun and gathered the money from the safe. Afterwards, he insisted that we go down to Lucky Lill's bar to knock a couple back.

We sat in a booth all the way in a dark corner in the back. He had whiskey while I took a watered-down scotch: after all, I was the driver.

We talked about some things. He wasn't that big of a talker. I knew that he didn't like people all that much, except for me. I was the exception. He had taken quite a liking to me.

I asked him if he knew who I was.

"Boy," he said.

He was perceptive.

When I asked him how he knew and when, he simply said that good people aren't hard to find. And if you remember what they look like when they're young, you can certainly spot them when they're older.

It certainly was a surprise to see how human he was. But when he killed that man right in front of me, I saw the cold-blooded man on that hot day one summer long ago.

Then he got into his bad people speech. He said that bad people deserve to be put in their place, to be humbled. He said that bad people weren't worth that much to the world.

So I asked him.

"What is our worth?"

"You mean you and me?"

"Yes."

"When it comes to you, boy, you're all right. Me, on the

other hand, I'm a rat bastard."

Then he shuffled in his pocket and pulled out something dirty. He smacked it on the table. I leaned forward and saw that it was a penny.

"That's what amounts to a no good, sneaky, slippery little bad person. They're not worth nothing but one red cent."

I guess that's why it was so easy for him to knock people off. I guess, when you thought about it, all together, to him, he caused at least a dollar fifty worth of deaths.

He ordered another round, not even wincing at each shot he took. I decided to order water to dilute myself.

"I've had my share of ruthless people, or pennies, as I like to call them." He sat and started at the penny sitting idly on the table. "Man, it seems like so long ago when I got into this biz. You wouldn't believe some of the people that I've met. Never in my life was I so naïve when I started out.

"I came to believe that if people didn't have the cash for me, they just didn't have it, and that was that. I'd visit them frequently, but it seemed that I always ended up extending their time to come up with the dough. You could say that they took advantage of my forgiving nature.

"One man, who will remain nameless, took it one step too far. That man you saw chuck a cleaver at me, everything I did to him, he had it coming. He was one of my regulars. Always 'borrowing' a grand here and there from me. He would never pay all of it back. As a matter of fact, the last grand he borrowed from me, he only paid me the dollars but he left out the cents - three cents to be exact.

"Now, I'm not one to pull grudges but those three lousy cents kept me up at night. After all, what's the point of running a business exchange when you don't get all your money back?

"I took it upon myself to get those three cents I had coming to me no matter how ridiculous it seemed. And wouldn't you know it, when I walked up to his house, he took two of my toes. I had to sew myself up after that. After I hacked into him, the same man I'd been doing business with for a long time, my supposed friend, I spotted some change on the kitchen counter and took my three pennies. But, my boy, it wasn't just about the money. It was a matter of principle. That's all."

That explained a fraction of his nature; the rest was a mystery to me. Later, he told me that the man whose knee he had shot off was 500 dollars short on his debt.

Horace wasn't one to be shortchanged.

Ever.

I drove him home, even watched him walk up to his door. After I saw him go in, I drove back to the bar, wanting to check on something. It had been hours since we had left the bar, and yet the penny was still there, untouched. I guess he was right. Pennies don't add up to much in this world, and neither do ruthless men. To the natural world, we discard both and hope for the best. But me, personally, I never killed anybody. Never wanted to, actually. I never pictured myself pulling off heists or knocking off local business owners. I was just a common street thief, a numbers man. I don't think I could do the business that Horace was into.

I pulled out of the business two days later. It was for the best.

I'd like to tell you that I learned my lesson and never put myself in the company of dangerous men ever again. But that would be me trying to play the harp when really I was a piano man. I lived long enough to attend Horace's funeral. There were many people that attended. Many of them just wanted to witness being amazed by the fact that Horace Grant actually departed the realm of the living.

All through the funeral, I didn't leave until they kicked me out.

I loved a good woman, had four children and raised them to the best of my abilities. Whenever I would come across loose change or a penny sitting on the table, I'd throw it out. Pennies weren't allowed in my house.

I visited Horace's grave many times, still strangely envious of his misunderstood ways.

<u>Bring Him Back Again</u>

Never in her life had she felt this kind of abandonment. There was no possible cure that she knew of. Others would try to make her forget, but they didn't know what it was like to carry this woe. But someday they would.

"*Now…Now…*"

That's what he said to her before he left her that day.

That was all Selma could think about.

It was a warm morning, not a cloud in the sky. This should have tipped her off that nothing was ever that perfect.

Ever.

Now…Now…

Now she sputtered and cried all over the wall, huddled in the corner of her very spacious bedroom. Four months. Four months to the day and not one bit of her felt better about it.

Stupid friends, she thought. *They've never felt true pain.*

Somewhere, in the back of her mind, she felt that snide little monster clawing at her emotions. That snide little monster, which was called hatred, tried to comfort her.

She clawed at the wall, exploding another wave of tears and mucus.

To her, she felt lost in an ever-winding pit. And in that pit was nothing but shame - loathing. It swallowed her up. It never let go. And why would it? Lord knows it was the devil's work, her feeling this kind of anger, carrying on like this.

But she felt like it wasn't her choice. The events of that day always repeated in her mind, like an old annoying song you just can't get out of your head. And it always began the same way.

"Why do you have to go?" she said dreamily, holding him tight.

A light breeze tickled her as she stood there in her garage, glowing in her light blue bathrobe, her dark hair still wet. The garage door was open, the jeep all fired up and rearing to scoot. Lately there had been a few noises coming from the engine. Possible erosion, but she couldn't be too sure. It was usually Jeffery who fixed her car.

She lingered and swayed in her bathrobe, cradling his wide chest, her chin nestled in his sternum, wetting his shirt and tie. Then, as always, she turned her head and listened to his heavenly heartbeat. Such a beautiful sound to her. It made her more docile.

"The funny thing is," he began, "they pay me money to do what I do, babe."

She cuddled him. Squeezing him more.

"They can get someone else."

"For this job? I don't think so."

"Your fortunes lie with me, dear Jeffery."

"True as that may be, fair queen, the humble servant must be off before he finds himself a rather lowly king's jester."

He looked into her eyes and cradled her chin in his right

hand. Selma loved it when he did that. It always made her smile.

They had known each other for seven years. It seemed like such a long time ago. They met in a diner and love carried them the rest of the way. But this whole time they had remained girlfriend and boyfriend - couldn't afford to get married.

She had inherited the house that her dad left her before he walked out on the whole family. He was the first man to ever leave her.

Jeffery had an apartment that was four blocks down.

The only thing she could afford was supporting herself while still scraping along with financial aid. Jeffery, on his end, worked every day of the week, didn't make enough, but still performed a miracle in keeping himself fed. Today would be the day to turn that all around. Today, he would welcome his awaiting promotion.

The person, whoever they were, knocked once and rang the bell twice.

Selma leapt from her carpeted bedroom floor, bolted past the kitchen and clawed the locks away on her front door. Selma, without looking, screamed at the person standing on her stoop.

"FUCK OFF! JUST LEAVE ME ALONE, YOU BASTARDS!"

Selma had never sworn in her life. She didn't like to use profanity in any situation - felt that it wasn't needed. But in this case, so many people had been visiting her, it had repulsed her to no end.

Didn't these people have jobs?

Didn't they have lives of their own?

I had a life once, she thought.

She opened her eyes, leaking tears. Jordan, her older sister stood defiantly. Selma recognized her glistening red hair immediately. Jordan did not tremble at her sister's outburst and she felt no pity for her. Which was remarkably cold for a sister. But

Jordan and Selma had always had a shaky past, constantly competing with each other. As Selma stood there, hiccupping from crying so much, she felt satisfied in cursing her sibling out when she knew full well that Jordan, even though she didn't not say it out loud, was comforted by her sister's misery.

"Lovely day," she said cynically.

"Every day is a nightmare."

"You can't hole yourself up in dad's house all the time, Selma. Sooner or later you're going to have to come out. Face the world."

"You mean face everybody in front of you for your viewing pleasure? That's what you meant, right?"

Jordan didn't not deny it. She plowed on, ignoring Selma's questions. "It happens to everyone, doll."

"Not like this, and you know it!"

"Not like what? You keep saying that as if you're the only one who has ever felt real pain!"

It was true. That much had been true. There were details of that day that she did not share with anyone. She didn't want to. Only more pain would follow with the shock that everyone would feel after she told them. This was her secret and no one else's, and it was going to stay that damn way.

While Jordan was rattling on, Selma placed her right hand in her pocket, holding the tiny object as if to let a little sanity escape from it.

In the end, Selma bowed her head and shut the door right in the middle of Jordan's speech.

If she only knew…

Jeffery knew that he loved Selma with all his heart. Every time he left for work after spending the night at her place, he felt enormously regretful for showing up to work on time. It would have been nice to just call off one day just to spend the day with her. Just once. Just one more extra day. After all, she was all alone in that house, had nothing to do but watch cable and work on her pathetic garden in the back of the house, which bore little or no fruit.

He lifted her chin up to his. Their noses connected. And without a word, they both connected lips. Their lips softly pressed each other. Time got lost in their moment.

And when their lips parted, she ran her fingers through his hair and whispered in his ear, "Call off."

"Can't," he whispered back.

"I love you."

"I love you too, babe."

And after he had straightened his tie, kissed her once more, and rubbed her hand gently, he picked up his bag and tossed it in the backseat. On the door, he noticed a piece of dark green paint missing. It was chipped off, and for some peculiar reason he was drawn to it, picking at it. It was something he'd have to deal with later. He enjoyed stalling his time.

He opened the door, got in, and rolled the window down.

"Okay, one more," he smiled.

Selma quit her puppy-dog look, which included a large pouting bottom lip, and pressed herself against the door while they tenderly kissed again. She hugged him and then stepped back.

She loved him so much.

On mornings as bright as this one, she would watch him leave. Always the same way. He'd back out the car, turn the corner and disappear behind her neighbors' house, the Alabasters.

Giggling, she waved.

It seemed perfectly normal to do so. After all, today was just like any other day, right? He was just going to work.

She pounded her fists against the weak closet doors. After a while splinters were being driven into her fragile wrists and she found that she was breaking the wood.

He said he was just going to work.

But he never did.

And he would never come back.

That killed her inside.

Again, she crumbled onto the carpet, where another river was forming from her tears. This was the worst of it. Selma's activity these past four months varied. On a good day, she didn't do anything. She just sat on the couch and stared at the blank screen of the TV, not moving. Just thinking. For hours on end.

There were times were she hated the blank screen because that's what she felt herself - blank.

She'd pick up the remote, dully click the button and the blue screen came up. It painted her with a dull blue. Great, now she was blue. Depression incarnate. It was mocking her.

Eventually, this dull routine wore thin. She smashed the remote in frustration. The TV would be on for days at a time. She didn't care.

Her most fragile days, she wouldn't eat. Or, if she did eat, she'd strictly stick to condiments. She could afford food, but she didn't want to.

There were days that she'd watch the kitchen faucet drip.

There were days where she'd check the garage, only to find it an empty cavern, now heavy with dust.

Over this fourth month, Selma was convinced that her heart did not retain any color anymore. No delightful pinks or hopeful reds. That it had become tar from the inside out - an oozing, pus-filled sac that was barely recognizable from the former. And every once in a while, she felt it curdle, almost as if she were having mini-heart attacks. She wondered if it was possible to die from depression.

Even though it was terrible to think, she hoped so. She hoped that something would give, and that she didn't have to deal with everyone's faces. She couldn't *feel* anymore. And she didn't want to anymore. She was all used up, dried out, barely holding on to a distant memory that would not help her in recovering from when he left her.

Today, she battled the house, went everywhere in it tearing up a storm. Clothes became ripped and objects were smashed. All except the little object that resided in her pocket. The last little trinket that he ever gave her.

She found herself in the garage again, giggling.

Waving.

He waved back.

Not paying attention.

When he made it to the street, another jeep blared its horn.

In horror, she watched as the screech of tires left strips of black marks on the road. The car collided with Jeffery. Inside, she could see his body rock as the unbelievable force shook him like a rag doll, his head bouncing in all directions.

Her hands reached her mouth and she wanted to bite her own fingers off. She couldn't believe what was happening…what she was seeing.

This jeep, which was much bigger than Jeffery's, plowed over the roof and flipped forward. Jeffery's jeep rolled out of sight.

Selma trotted quickly out of the garage and onto the driveway into the hot sun. Her slippers came loose, but she ignored them. Her feet were burning on the asphalt. That wasn't important right now. What was important was Jeffery.

As she followed, with her eyes, she could see Jeffery's car still rolling near the cul-de-sac. It was unimaginable. The car that hit him finally toppled over onto its own hood and slid out of the way, hitting a parked car and setting off the alarm in the process.

Jeffery's jeep was still rolling on its side until it finally came to a stop right on its tires, right in the middle of the cul de sac. The top part of the car was bent at an angle, the hood was smoking, liquids were dripping.

She saw the wreck that was her boyfriend's car.

She heard the car alarm going off repeatedly, but slowing down in her mind.

She saw it.

She saw everything.

Ding!

"Order up," came the chef's voice as he tapped the bell with his kitchen knife. With a flick of the wrist, he spun the carousel of orders waiting to be made. *Heatwave* was blaring on the two-year- old radio.

It was a busy day for Selma. Only one more hour and she'd be off the clock. She anchored the plate in the nook of her elbow, balancing two other plates in her hands and holding a check under her chin. Why didn't they hire more people? It was a small, family-owned diner and could easily take on four or five more hands. Instead, only two waitresses were working. And Lord knew that the owner, Mr. Patscoucci, would not be closing up to a tiny inconvenience like that.

From his office, he eyed Selma, always wondering what she was wearing under that uniform. A pale, balding, dirty old man. And she was working for him.

Selma's father left her. And it was still fresh in her mind. Left without saying anything. Not a word. And neither did she. Selma was quiet these days. What was the point of conversation while she was this miserable?

After she unloaded the two plates, she remembered the third. - an order of pastrami on rye with some seasoned fries. She looked at the number on the check and remembered where the young man was sitting. It was *him* again. Part of her loosened up a bit. She made her way past some glaring looks and slid the steamy plate onto the table of the booth where the man was sitting. Before she could take her hand back, he encapsulated it with his. Normally, Selma didn't like people touching her. But, instead of having an initial reaction of anger, she felt comforted by his warm, manly hands.

She looked right into his eyes.

Dark brown planets, a slight hint of a nurturing nature.

Trust.

"I'm going to get you out of here," he said.

She clawed at the door, trying to pry it open. The twisted metal jammed the door. The impact had shattered the glass in the windshield and on the driver's side, which was where she was standing, yanking at the handle with all of her grit.

Inside, through the tangle of spider-webbed cracks, she could see his shaking figure. Through the cobwebs of shattered glass, she saw him turn to her. She could barely see his face but automatically registered a cut on the left of his forehead. He also had a black left eye. His right one was wide open. A lonely dark brown planet, searching for her. As soon as he saw her face through the scattered lines, he moaned, trying pathetically to raise his arm for her.

"I'm going to get you out of here!" she screamed. "Everything's going to be all right! It's all right!"

His warming hand distracted her, made her feel safe. Nobody was this close with her. This was a first.

"What do you mean?" she asked, placing her notepad under her belt.

"Selma, every time I come in here, ordering the same thing, looking at you, just waiting. You never make conversation with me. Why?"

She wiggled her fingers in his grip. "Somebody should have told you, it's impolite to grab people."

He released her hand as gently as when he reached for it.

"I hope you're not offended. It was the only way to get your attention.

"Miss, miss!" someone called from the corner of the diner. They no doubt wanted more ketchup. There seemed to be a shortage of it in ol' Dullsville.

"I've got to get back to work."

The man with brown eyes looked over his shoulder. "For that mug? That's Sanderson. I know him. Now, he would have grabbed you impolitely. He likes to pinch women on the butt. It's his thing."

"Thing or no thing, he's a paying customer. So I've got to go."

"One hour," he said.

"What?"

"One hour of your time. That's all I ask."

"My boss won't…"

"…let you do anything except serve. He works you like a dog, Selma."

"Arf."

"C'mon. Please? I want to get to know you better."

"No one can know me better in the span of one hour."

"Fine. Rephrased. I want to hear your story for one hour."

"What's so good about my story?"

"It's the one that I want to hear."

She blinked. "Really?"

"Really."

"I've…"

"I'll give you a big tip."

He lay a hundred dollars on the counter in front of her. "I just want to hear your story. I'm interested in you. You make me curious."

"Curiosity killed the cat."

"Meow, baby."

She tried not to laugh. "What makes you so interested in me?"

"Because there's more to your story than meets the eye. And I want to know more of that story. My name's Jeffery, nice to meet you." He reached out his hand for a shake…

She pulled him, grunting, out of the car. She anchored his weight on her shoulder. With effort she pulled him into the shade of a big tree in a neighbor's lawn.

"Now…now…" he whispered.

"Call the police! Call an ambulance! Anybody!" she screamed.

Her heart curdled again. She scratched at the wall, ruining the paint. Her hell was coming alive. In the living room, the TV curdled as well and then pathetically fizzled out. It had been on for so long.

Water.

Water dripped in the sink and everywhere all around her. She could hear it everywhere. It was driving her mad. Her hands trailed up to her ears, pressing her lobes into her head. If she'd had had more strength, she'd have rip them off.

She closed her eyes. It didn't matter. More tears were cutting through as she nestled her head into the corner of the room.

It felt like the devil kicked her into this spot. It wasn't fair. Life…never is.

"Now…now…"

She cradled his head. Ripping away part of her robe to clean the blood off his forehead. He just continued gulping air and looking at the sky. She waited with him as the neighbor's called for the ambulance.

She waited with him.

Carefully she searched him, looked closely at his skin, being delicate, and gentle, just as he always was with her. No deep gashes, no gouges. The only thing that looked discomforting was the fact the left side of his chest looked bruised. Selma was no doctor, but she began expecting the worst. Was it a bruised rib? A broken one? Or, God no, internal bleeding?

"Now…now…" he coughed. His breathing was shallow. That's all he kept on saying.

"No. Baby, please! Don't talk! Don't talk! You'll only make it worse. Please, please! Stay! I'm right here. I'm right here. I'm right here. Keep your eyes open, Jeffery. Look at me. Look at me, Jeffery!"

She tired herself out, she thought. But nothing like this was ever done - only stalled.

Her sniffles felt cold to her warm cheeks.

Water, water everywhere.

Dripping from the sink, dripping from the pipes, dripping from her eyes.

The car might as well have hit her. The reoccurring nightmare was painful but, without watching TV and without reading books, it was the only thing she could think of. It was the only thing she wanted to turn to. She didn't want to forget it now. It had become a part of her. And it was her last moment to spend with Jeffery.

"Now…now…" Jeffery repeated. His breathing still felt hoarse. And, Selma wasn't sure, but she thought she heard an underlying breathing, possibly a sucking sound. Air escaping a wound? Maybe it was a punctured lung.

She shouldn't have moved him.

Now she regretted it.

His bloody fingers drifted to her face. Little shards of glass were still in them. The thumb and index finger caressed her chin. Tiny glass particles were scraping her chin as he did that but she didn't care. It still felt as fresh and as loving as when he did it a mere fifteen minutes before.

"Now…now…" he breathed.

He wasn't scared.

Strange as it may seem, she knew this.

It was almost as if this were the best time of his life. Like he had never been hit with the car and that he was simply lazing about under the shade of a tree with his girl - a soft summer picnic just for them.

His eyes, the dark brown planets that she had come to know and love, were calm. For the first time in Selma's life, she saw what it was to block out everything and devote her entire attention to him and nothing else.

"Now…" he said again. " …is as good…a time…"

"Honey," she cried. "Don't leave me. You have to breathe slowly."

"…as any…" he finished.

His other hand, she saw, reached into the pocket of his dark dress pants, which were terribly torn.

She finally stopped attacking her house. With excruciating tears that followed, she reached into her robe and produced the tiny trinket.

In his bloody hand he held a box. A small cube of a box that hadn't fully registered in Selma's mind because she thought what was happening was damn near impossible. Jeffery let his other hand drift to the box, leaving two bloody fingerprints on his girlfriend's tear-soaked chin. With great strength, he opened the tiny box. Inside was a ring. One fragile, little, golden ring.

Jeffery choked on his own blood, trying so desperately to muster up a voice beyond all that drowning blood and phlegm.

"Selma…" he hissed. At this point his voice was sounding like he was losing his it.

Or losing his soul when you took in the heavy circumstances.

"Will…you…will…you…please…take…me…Please…ma rry…me…Please…I…"

At that moment, her body generated a shaking fit and she could not contain the dam of tears that busted wide open. She had turned white from the shock, and she could feel her hands trembling as she brought them up to her face.

"Please…be with me…help me…"

She could. And she would.

She rubbed the ring between her fingers. It still felt as slick as the day he gave it to her. She held out her finger and slipped the wedding band carefully onto it. "I do."

How could she cry so much in just four months? It felt to her, at this point, that there would be nothing left of her, that she would be all dried up by now. How funny, she thought, if she wound up as a small dust pile on her own bedroom carpet.

Her fragile, trembling hands received the ring. And what a lovely one it was.

"Please…"

It all felt too real - or possibly unreal…surreal.

Nothing like this had ever happened to her, her friends, her relatives, her acquaintances, possibly anyone in the world she ruled out.

It happened to her.

And him.

Both shared the most heart-twisting experience of their natural lives.

This was the secret that she held onto so dearly. Not because she was embarrassed by it, but because it was truly the most darkly romantic moment she had ever witnessed. And something like that would not convey well with others. Other people wouldn't be able to understand the uniqueness of this atrocity. What do you say when listening to something like this? It was Selma's guess that there was no reply. There was no way to relate or comfort someone in this position. And to fake it was a sinful insult to Jeffery's memory.

This whole time her family had begged her to come out into the open. They all assured her that they would have open ears and an understanding for her simple loss. But it wasn't that simple. It wasn't simple at all. It was a first.

She regained her awareness of the moment. Jeffery kept blinking quizzically almost as if he was trying to see her more clearly. And that meant only one thing. He was on his way out. He was leaving her.

"Jeffery! I do! I...please! Be here! I need you! I want you, I want you, I want you!" she screamed.

Sirens added their input into the mix.

Again, his hand caressed her chin. The other dropped the box. "I heard you...I heard you...the first time...Love..."

When he finally made his way into that gentle sleep, she stayed with him. She nestled her ear close to his chest but did not hear his beautiful, rhythmically infatuating heartbeat. It had grown cold.

The doctors said that the cause of death was internal bleeding. Selma thought for sure that it had been a collapsed lung. Somehow, bleeding slowly on the inside sounded like the most painful way to go that she had ever heard of. The doctors claimed that he would feel no pain, but there was always the assumption that they were lying just to make her feel better. Not even they knew of her secret. When the paramedics arrived, she scooped the tiny box up and slipped it inside her robe along with the ring he had bestowed on her.

Richard Stevens, the drunk driver who ended her man's life so abruptly, had the gigantic unbelievable arrogance to claim that he wasn't heavily intoxicated while driving. Somehow he had survived the wreckage and had been reported to have had a .5 blood alcohol level - the highest you could get without passing out. The creep pled innocent till the day that they put him away. Jeffery was the first life he ever took on the road.

Without thinking, with rage guiding her, she flung herself at the kitchen drawer and seized the butcher's knife. She plopped herself to the clod and slick tile floor and breathed heavily.

The last couple of weeks she had been thinking of suicide. Anything to be reconnected with him. She didn't give a shit whether she would be damned or not. This agony was greater than the afterlife in her eyes.

Carefully she anchored the blade on her wrist. She was close to puncturing the skin. What else could she do? She couldn't bring him back, so this was the next eventual step. It was something waiting for her. She knew that if he saw her right now, he wouldn't approve of this one bit. But her mind was set.

Her eyes moistened once more. She closed her eyes. This was really going to hurt.

Before the knife could make the plunge…

…she felt a hand caress hers.

She opened her eyes and witnessed a bright light and a warm sensation. Her hair fluttered in a gentle breeze.

The Graveyard Shifters

It was the beginning of a nice new spring day. The birds were chirping harmoniously, a mother cardinal was feeding her young in the nest above. The gigantic tree gave an otherworldly shade that was comforting to any and all who would sit underneath it. It was a perfect, pleasant morning. A good morning for the dead to rise.

Underneath the tree, Joshua was working hard with the shovel. What he was doing was wrong. But, in the daylight hours, no one so much as came close to him. The cemetery had few visitors. Joshua knew, when he entered the cemetery, that it was the perfect day to dig.

It was the perfect day to be mischievous.

Sweat was coming from Joshua's brow and he wiped it away. His plaid shirtsleeves were rolled up and his jeans were already showing significant wear. How many times had they done this? Twenty? Forty times? And each time it never got old.

The plot that he was near wasn't a fresh one. This one was at least one month old. Green grass was waving until Joshua pierced it with his trusty rust-covered shovel.

Now he was packing the dirt back in. He tried to be quick

in doing this, but after a while his wrists started to hurt. No matter. He needed to be quick. That was all part of the game. Only a couple more shovelfuls and everything would be set.

That was it.

Plop!

The last one.

Thank God for that, he thought.

With a look of satisfaction on his face, he stabbed the shovel into the ground a couple inches away from the tombstone, which read

Here Lies:
Arthur Vance
A truly creative and gentle soul

Joshua read the words again as he tried, and failed, to slick his long blonde hair out of his face. This guy was a fresh one. One of the freshest they had ever come across and thought to try.

On the other side of the tree was a fresh, crudely dug plot that Joshua had worked on. Instead of being a distinctive rectangle, it was an oddly shaped circle. Just enough for a person to fit straight down into. It wasn't part of the game, but it was easier to fish the body out of it.

Oliver had advised against this, but Joshua knew he was always difficult like that. It didn't matter. This game was still fun despite the trivial rituals.

Joshua kneeled over Mr. Vance's grave. Eagerly he listened, waiting for something. He turned to look at the fresh soil, which, as before, shifted and every particle of dirt glittered like green dust, which gave off a particle gust until it finally fizzled out.

Joshua waited.

He glanced at his watch.

Nothing moved for a good ten minutes.

Never took this long.

Something was wrong.

Before, when they had gotten a knack for this, the times

varied. But this was stretching it a bit thin. The event, even as horrendous as it was, still held some type of timetable.

Joshua didn't know if that was a good or bad thing to consider.

He leaned over once again and dug his ear into the soft soil.

Meanwhile, on the other side of the tree, in the circular plot, two fingers started through the soil. They twisted and turned, almost stirring themselves out of the shifting soil like spider legs. The skin clinging to them was noticeably green. In no time at all, the hand emerged and clutched the grass above, ripping it from its roots. The body knew that it had made it above ground.

The hand had made it.

Then the entire left arm.

The head emerged, leaking dust and dirt, gasping for breath. Part of the skull was visible over the top portion of the cranium. The left eye was completely gone; the right was shriveled to the size of a prune. The teeth and gums were very pale and the dead, rotting skin of the lips opened and closed, remembering how to breathe.

The torso unloaded a big heap of dirt because it was hollow. The only things inside were pale white ribs. The suit that the body wore was fashionable for a heavyset man, and pieces were missing. It was tattered, loose and reeked.

Orange sludge, like pumpkin seeds, littered the once gleaming grass. Strings of orange muck were still clinging to the frame of the dried-up corpse.

The corpse found the grass and stood on his own two rickety feet, balancing was a difficult job for him.

He sneezed dust and farted a rat. The rat scurried away, afraid of the person he had been nesting in.

The corpse moaned quietly, looking down at himself, recognizing the graffiti that was his deteriorating body.

He smiled a big one.

A tooth popped out.

The corpse crouched low, careful not to break his fragile knees, to peer around the thick tree separating him from his unsuspecting little friend engaged in a bow to the plot in front of him.

Carefully the corpse of Arthur Vance tiptoed around the base of the tree, finding it remarkably easy to dish out the element of surprise.

Now Arthur was hovered directly over Joshua, casting a shadow of impending doom.

Joshua was not ready for this unexpected attack and his eyes were not open. He was still listening intently to the ground.

This was sure to be a hoot.

The corpse smiled and cupped his hands over what was left of his mouth and whispered, "Ooooiiilllll caaaaaaan…"

Joshua opened his eyes. He also grinned.

He hoisted himself up, turned to stare directly at the zombie and, while looking up at him, chuckled confidently. "Oil can what, huh?"

The corpse coughed a laugh, trying to hold his stomach to keep it from bursting, but it appeared that that little mishap had already been done long ago.

"This one's joints are a little bit firmer than the others," the corpse said, bouncing on his legs to test their durability.

"Hey," warned Joshua. "Don't move too much. You'll break him."

"Always worried about the bag of bones, eh? What about me, huh, I'm doing all the legwork. I'm the one buried six feet under."

"There you go again, acting like an ungrateful tailiwacker. You know that I've got the good sense to pull you out in time, Oliver."

"Last time you flinched a bit. You pulled me out whilst I was still coughing up mud."

"Okay, olive head."

Joshua bent down by the tree and picked up an aerosol can that promised a heavenly peach aroma. Without hesitation he gave the can a couple of shakes, plugged his nose with his fingers and unloaded the can on the foul-smelling beast. Oliver, using Mr.

Vance's arms, lifted them to form a T as he let his friend spray him down from head to toe. He didn't need to close his eyes for this. Hell, he couldn't anyway. Being dead wasn't all that bad. There was no pain, no aching. No nothing. The whole experience was numbing, feeling similar to when you sat on your leg too long, only the tingle that was the numbness was all over.

Oliver said, "That stuff's bad for the environment, you know."

Joshua stopped spraying for a moment and released his nose from the titan grip. "So is your breath."

He wasn't sure, but it almost appeared as if Oliver, behind Arthur's face, was trying to give him a dirty look. Joshua ignored him, making his way to the tree to set the can down.

"Least I'm biodegradable," Oliver said under his peach breath.

Now came the fun part.

* * *

George Stiles was not one to mope. As a matter of fact, in his younger days he had been the toughest nut to crack. When he crashed his bicycle into a fountain, he didn't cry. The time that he dislocated his finger trying to shut the door of his room, not a drop. Nothing ever really got to him enough to make him squirt some sobby juice. That's what his mom called it. She was a real bitch when he was younger, spanked him good ones even when he didn't deserve it, and even then he didn't cry.

But when his brother, Liam Stiles, 38, died of a coronary, it struck him like a sledgehammer tearing though a glass window. All that sobby juice came pouring out.

Now, after putting aside his plans to catch a flick, he decided to visit his brother at the cemetery. With him, he carried flowers. Nothing special, just white carnations. White was Liam's favorite color.

He got out of his car, holding his head low, walking to his

sibling's grave as if it were his own death march playing in the background. Him and his brother had some good times. All the curious troublemaking they had gotten into seemed endless, except for now. Now, troublemaking was at an end for both of them mainly because Liam was the provoker of the two. Always riling up trouble just to have fun.

George leaned forward and dropped the flowers heavily. With great woe he stood there, trying to convince himself that George was in a better place, a place where the souls roamed free in green pastures, playing endless childhood games, recapturing the innocence that gets drained out of them as they became adults.

He thought about all that and cried.

George lifted his hand to his face, pouting in it, careful not to let the sobby juice leak all over his brother's grave. His brother wouldn't want to see him crying. He'd want to see him happy.

And he was, genuinely, for a couple of moments.

But then he removed his hand and couldn't help smelling a sinful excess of peaches.

* * *

From a distance, Joshua was ready with his binoculars. He could see Mr. Stiles, whom he had no prior acquaintance with, adjusting his tie and wiping his eyes, unaware of the trouble heading his way.

* * *

George tried to maintain his composure and act normal. Even though there was someone in the vicinity who totally blasphemed with the peach cologne, he didn't want to cry in front of them. That would have been in bad taste.

But so was what he saw when he turned around.

The corpse of Arthur Vance, possessed by Oliver, leaned an arm on George's shoulder, ruining his charcoal black suit. George's eyes went wide as he saw this corpse grin at him.

"Hold it there, bud. Right there," Arthur's raspy voice said. "That's good."

Arthur was balancing on him while he was using some kind of branch to scratch his back. But upon closer inspection, it wasn't a branch at all. It was a skeletal leg with pieces of cloth still clinging to it. The toes were pointy and just right for back scratching. George, eyes still bugged, looked down and saw that the reason this dead gentlemen was balancing on him was because it was his own leg that he was scratching his back with.

After many grunts, groans, and oohs, Arthur finally got the phantom itch.

He smiled, slapping George a good pat on the shoulder while he still stood frozen. Dust floated into the air, and even then George did not cough. He didn't move a muscle. He just stared at this animated corpse in awe.

"Much appreciated, padre," said the smiling corpse. "Don't worry, gov'nor. I'm not one to be selfish. You know the old saying, 'you scratch my back and I'll scratch…'"

George wailed wildly, throwing his hands up in the air as he made a break for his car, stabbed the key into the ignition, plummeted his foot to the gas pedal and took off doing over ninety miles an hour.

The corpse chuckled loudly, dropping his jaw to the ground yet again.

After picking it up and putting it back on, he glanced seven rows down to the little hill with the massive tree that Joshua was perched in. He could tell that Joshua was laughing so hard he damn near fell out of the tree.

Arthur bent down and reattached his leg at the knee, a funny grin sliding across his face.

Then, without warning, Arthur Vance's body fidgeted and rocked all over the place, looking similar to what a live man would look like if he was having a seizure while standing up.

"Uh oh!" Joshua swung the binoculars around his neck and tried to descend the tree fast.

Arthur, meanwhile, tried his best to make it back to the tree where Joshua was, taking fidgety steps left and right, falling apart bit by bit. He wasn't quick enough. Not with his dead legs.

By the time Joshua landed on the grass, the corpse was already on the ground, limbs all over the place and twitching. And that could only mean one thing.

"Oliver!" Joshua yelled.

Quickly he released the shovel from its resting place and, with a firm grip, stabbed the dirt in front of the tombstone. With his arms already sore he strived to regain more strength, he kept digging hard and digging fast.

Already he could hear muffled cries.

This was good.

This meant he was getting closer to his friend.

The last bit of dirt he shoveled, he saw movement. A hand rocketed out of the dirt, one that was healthy and tanned.

The head poked out, greasy black hair, blue eyes and a beard. With both hands, Oliver hoisted himself out of the ground, spitting pebbles of dirt, and crawled over the mouth of the hole. The strange apparatus across his chest was weighing him down but eventually he was able to conquer gravity with no problem.

He lay sprawled out on his back, gasping for air, letting his eyes dart around as he was looking up into the sky.

The metallic monstrosity latched to his chest hummed, flashed light green dust and was silent. That meant that it was powered down. Oliver breathed heavily, patting the machine, it was very much like a creature; it had six very large metallic buckles, three on each side that would fasten around the back. Two legs over the shoulders and two on either side of the ribs. There was a green orb in the middle that could be activated by touch alone. The spider-like contraption was now off and still.

But Oliver wouldn't be.

It took him a few tries, but he was able to get up, snatch the shovel from its resting place against the tree and swung it at Joshua. Joshua, panicked but with catlike reflexes, ducked out of the way.

"C'mon!" shouted Oliver, inching forward.

"Oh, I see! Is that how it is, rich boy?" Joshua was still backing away slowly, but rolled up his sleeves in anticipation. "You fancy a tussle? Well go on! Have a go at me then!"

"You were supposed to pull me out faster than that!"

"Now look, Oliver, there's no need to be sore. How the hell was I supposed to know it would conk out? Once you press that magic button, there's no telling how long you have."

"How shall the burial rite be read, man?" came a raspy but ever lengthy voice from beside them.

They both turned simultaneously.

The long black hood.

The outstretched and incredibly rusty sickle.

The bone-like fingers, one hand firmly on the sickle and the other holding an hourglass filled with pouring sand.

It was Death.

Oliver let out a brief gasp as he reacted without thinking. With one full swing he was able to shatter the hourglass to bits. It emitted a bright golden spark before all the sand faded in the grass.

"Whoa, man!" yelled the hooded figure.

Oliver wasted no time in bringing the shovel back around to slice into the midsection of the one they call Death. Once the edge of the shovel made contact with the dark mass, the fabric took the full force of the slash, wrapping around the shovel blade itself. And in its place was nothing - nothing but air.

Oliver glanced around him as he saw the hooded figure behind him, clutching onto the handle, smoke rising from his white bony fingertips. "Cool, man. Be cool."

Oliver yanked the shovel away from the beast and looked at the handle. Handprint burn marks. This was Death all right, the sealer of every man's fate.

By now, Death held up his hands, his hood still covering his face. It looked nothing more than a dark hollow inside that void of a hood. It could be endless for all Oliver knew.

"I'm just here to rest, man. Saw you two fightin' and I just wanted to stop the noise is all. You were ruining my high, man."

Oliver was still in defense mode, shovel poised in front of

him like a spear, though he dared not touch the burn marks higher up on the shovel. "Your high? High? What the hell you playing at?"

"I'm just passing through, Mr. High strung. Just passing. It's getting dark and I figured on camping out here for the night. If you haven't noticed, the cemetery is closing in a bit. You're more than welcome to join me. Once you get your head on straight, that is."

Death turned and walked away, stumbling here and there, but giggling as he did.

Oliver lowered the shovel a little; his limbs were jittery and tense. His mind was like fresh Jell-O; thick and goopy and of little use to anybody. He looked around to see the sky take on a mahogany darkness. It was late, and it didn't look like anyone was around. Time sure did fly.

Oliver tiredly walked up to the tree and balanced the shovel against it, still keeping on eye on the hooded figure who looked to be heading for the mausoleum.

"Is…is he gone?"

Oliver looked up.

Joshua had a few scrapes and cuts from flying up the tree as fast as he did. He was a good thirty feet in the air, wrapped around a branch for dear life, eyes firmly closed.

"Yeah," said Oliver. "He's away now."

"Oliver, Oliver, I think I messed myself."

"Who cares, nancy boy? Clean yourself up. I need a closer look at this."

"What?" Joshua's eyes snapped open. "What for?"

Oliver was now carrying the shovel with him, pivoting on his foot as he looked back up at his friend in the tree. "Can't you hear? He said we were ruining his high. You're not at all curious about what he was getting high from?"

* * *

"A toasty fire, some age-old drink. What telltale signs would the misfits think?" Death mumbled to himself as he poked the fire with a branch, reveling in the hypnotic glow of the blaze.

Oliver came into the light.

"Ah," Death saw him. "Care to delight in misery's company, my main man?"

"You for real?"

"Yeah, I'm him."

"Can I...?"

"Yes. Always on 108. Big man sets his at 50."

"Beg pardon?"

"Figured you would ask the same three questions everyone asks. Are all the dictators in hell? How hot is hell? How cool is heaven?"

"Those are the three questions most asked?"

"In my employ, yes they are."

"Bollocks."

The not so grim reaper looked up at him. In the darkness, Oliver thought he saw two beady specks of lights somewhere in the depths of the hood. Could those be his eyes?

"British, eh? Hmph. Had to be Brits, didn't it?"

"And what do you mean by that?"

"Not a thing, gov'nor."

Without pause, Death went back to his business - sharpening his sickle with a stone. When he was satisfied, he laid it down in front of him, giving him a border all his own. Inside his right sleeve he produced a wad of rolled-up papers.

By this time, Joshua had come into the glow of the light beside Oliver. Before building up the courage to sit at the campfire, both men cleared their throats.

Death looked up.

"What are you doing here, dressed up like that?" asked Oliver.

"Got business to attend to," Death replied. "And you two? What do you guys do when you're not messin' around on sacred ground?"

Joshua dusted himself off, keeping himself behind his

friend. "Name's Josh. I work for the city. I drive those street sweepers. This here's Oliver. He doesn't work. Selfish bastard is what you call rich blood. All he ever does is carry me along whenever he wants to egg houses, shoplift, that sort of thing just to prove his worth."

Oliver nodded appreciatively.

"Hmph," Death said.

He never gave them permission to sit down, but they did, curious to what he was rolling between his bony fingers.

From his other sleeve, he dug out what looked to be a tuft of grass, and it was in some respect. It was that happy grass that Oliver and Joshua were no strangers to.

Death carefully rolled the blunt to the length of a pencil, pulled it into his hood, supposedly to seal it with his tongue, then stuck it into the void of his hood. Extending his finger, he brought it to the fire, where it caught a tiny flame. He brought the lit finger up to the end of the blunt and lit it. He puff-puffed away as both men were becoming calmer, looser more easily amused as they sat still, watching this so-called guru of misfortune.

"Can't believe it," Oliver snickered.

"What?" Death asked.

"That the grim reaper would be puffing on the grim reaper. Thought I'd never live to see the day."

Both boys let out furious laughter as death chuckled a bit and passed the doobie down to them. They each took a hit, small to start out, Lord knew where this herb originated from.

"Death," Joshua coughed violently. "You said you were here on business. What business?"

With this question, Death took his time in answering, taking the blunt back as Oliver passed it to him. He took a long, engaging hit, then blew a puff at the fire, which turned it emerald green.

"Meeting an old friend here."

"A friend?" they both asked.

"Yeah, man. Maybe you've heard of him. Good old Edgar We had some sweet times. He was a good bud. This was before I was really big into the whole sixties thing. Way before. We'd hang out, talk shop, write stories."

"How'd you meet him?" Oliver asked.

"Oh, like everyone else, he found me. Took him a swig of laudanum to do it, but he met me. Didn't die though, went back to his life and I kept visiting him, checking up on him, helping him out whenever I could."

"Bollocks," Oliver said. "How can you meet someone when they're doing laudanum? It doesn't make sense."

"He was trying to kill himself," Death insisted. "He was having a rough time with writer's block. He found me, we hung out, he threw up the laudanum and was alive again. He wrote while I told him stories. Poe was never one to sleep."

Joshua coughed, his throat swelling as he stared at Death, amazed. "Wait a tick. We talkin' about Poe? The Poe? Mr. Edgar Allan Poe himself? Blimey, you met him?"

"Isn't that what I been saying? Clean out your ears, man."

"Sheesh, I've read all his stuff. *Murders in the Rue Morgue, The Pit and the Pendulum . . .*"

"*The Raven*," Oliver piped in. "Always liked that one."

"Yep," Death said. "All from little old me. I wasn't sore that he took the credit. I was plum happy for him. Got dealt a sour hand, that guy. In the meantime, we'd visit each other here and there. I gave him a pass."

"A pass?" they both asked.

"Yes, in return for writing his stories, he'd have to come down to the underworld with me and make inventions. The underworld is filled with inventors, everyone trying to improve the castle."

"There's a castle in the underworld?" Joshua inched in closer.

"Of course. It's surrounded by a moat of white fire. Can't miss it."

"Wait just a minute," Oliver scooted forward, closer to the blazing green fire, which mysteriously made him calmer than before. "You said something about inventions. What could you possibly invent in the underworld?"

"Many things," Death mused. "Non-flammable books, faster growing crops, and, thanks to Poe, a more reliable form of transportation."

Both Oliver and Joshua exchanged glances.

Oliver squinted at death, trying to hard to understand. "You mean to tell us, Poe was responsible for creating transportation in the underworld? What'd he do? Make bus routes? Lay down tracks?"

"No, nothing like that. He came up with a way for transportation not by buses or trains or even airplanes. He used people as a form of transportation."

The men sat still, confused as to how this was possible. Death clarified, "You see, Poe realized, while spending time in the underworld, that no matter what, people were always everywhere. So, instead of relying on manmade machines, he created, using some scraps in underworld, a machine that transports you from one person to another, wherever they may be. He even tested it out in the real world. And it worked. From the 1830's to the 1840's, everyone, whether it be a second's worth or several days, were possessed by Edgar Allan Poe at any given time."

"Man, that's a trip," Oliver said.

"Millions of trips, actually," Death said. "Poe loved to travel. You had to admit, he was depressing but infinitely creative. I even let him keep the contraption, that famed *Poe Transporter* of his."

Joshua nodded, fully enraptured in Death's story. Oliver was busy looking down at his chest, looking down at the contraption that he and Joshua had been having fun with this whole time. Now he knew that he was wearing the famous Poe Transporter. He remembered how He and Joshua met in Arbuckle's Graveyard, how they drank heavily, pouring what they call 'sips' to every fresh grave - one last drink to tide them over. Then came the hum, Oliver discovered the six spikes protruding out of the ground. The drunkard that he was, he fell in the grass between them, passing out. Joshua witnessed, with wide eyes, that the spikes encompassed Oliver and buckled him right in. Oliver was pulled through the ground and without warning appeared behind Joshua as a newly risen corpse. That was the first time the artifact worked its magic on them.

Now Oliver felt a tinge of disappointment. This device was his, no question. It picked him, he found it. Possession is nine tenths of the law, the way he saw it. No one would take his beauty away from him. Not even Death.

Oliver looked up, unsure if Death was staring at him or not.

"Well," Death perked up. "I have to go visit him now, care to join me, gents?"

* * *

Joshua and Oliver couldn't believe their own eyes. Who would have thought, through the countless times they had spent possessing dead bodies at several well-known cemeteries, lucky not to get caught, that they wind up talking to Death and staring at the gravestone of Poe himself:

Edgar Allan Poe

Born
January 19, 1809

Died
October 7, 1849

There he was. Both men were awestruck. Death pulled something out of his sleeve. It was a brown unlabeled bottle with a wide base. He pulled the cork from the top and poured a sliver of the amber liquid onto the grass of the dead man's grave.

"What's that?" asked Joshua.

"Cognac," Death replied. "He loved the stuff. Ever since

1849, I come to bring it back to him."

He pressed the cork back in and set it down next to the headstone. Next, he pulled from the same sleeve a bouquet of white roses. He took great care to set them down fast, as if they were aflame.

Death held his hand over what could have been his heart. "No man like him. Was glad to help him with his third book and the others that followed. At first, people were disgusted or didn't understand his new direction. I told him not to get too disheartened. 'Such is death,' I told him. 'Disgusting now, beautiful later.' And, just like I said, by the early 1830's, people started getting interested in me and the afterlife. 'Give the people what they want, Poe.' I told him. Imagine it, boys. For the payment of drink and good company, I gave him another story which he in turn gave to his publisher. Fair trade, I say. Him and I were linked. Even the magazine he published with was called *The Casket*. Funny, right?"

"Oh, it's a killer," Oliver said, sarcastically.

"To think that he and I inspired Sir Arthur Conan Doyle to write. Man, that takes me back."

"Were you there when he died?" Joshua asked, sitting at the base of Edgar's grave.

"Yeah. 1849, that's the year he started going crazy. The year of the great cholera epidemic. Drank a lot more. Used the machine too much. Couldn't get his bearings. On the third of October he was picked up behind an alley, wearing clothes that were four sizes too small for him. Poor man."

"That would choke a man to death. How'd he fit into them?" Oliver asked.

"The machine was on the fritz back then, being used so much. He wanted to travel one last time, but the machine messed up and sent him back to the alley with different clothes. He didn't know that he was transporting to a midget."

Oliver looked skeptic. "Come off it now. That can't be true."

"Sure as I'm here, he got the wrong clothes. Somewhere in

Cleveland there was a little person walking around in clothes four sizes too big, unaware of what had happened. By the time they rushed him to the hospital, his mind was already slipping. I was there with him. Throughout our friendship, he'd always given me a nickname. He'd call me 'Reynolds'. 'Reynolds,' he'd say, 'where am I? Reynolds, am I here, there, everywhere, nowhere?' He worried me. But it was his fate. The doctors just as well assumed he was imagining things, talking to objects in the room. But he was looking right at me when he said it. Finally, on the sixth he was raving, damn near on the edge of his bed asking me to help him. But I had no play. When the big man says it's time, you better believe it's time."

Death took a moment of silence.

Joshua was now standing, stared at the gravestone once more. "What were his last words?"

"'Lord help my poor soul.' Forty years old and just like that, he was out like a light. Damn man was a genius."

* * *

Dawn was rapidly approaching just as Joshua, Oliver and Death headed back up the hill to the coliseum where the gigantic tree stood. They were sloshed on grass and cognac, singing childhood tunes as they walked back.

Eventually, they wound up holding hands and singing and swinging in circles. They were merry.

But they also couldn't stop.

Faster and faster they spun.

Like *Ring Around The Rosey,* they spun.

But even with that rhyme, they would fall.

Both men were coming out of it now, seeing that they were moving in such a fast twirl that the very dirt they were spinning on was beginning to crumble. Their feet ached as they held hands with Death and as their feet dug hurriedly through layers upon layers of earth.

When they came to, they spotted, off in the crummy distance, a castle with a moat of white fire. Death was in front of them, cradling the Poe Transporter to his chest as if it were his precious infant. Through the void of the hood, they could see a gleaming yellow smile.

"What is this?" Joshua screamed, holding on to Oliver for support.

"It can't be! IT CANNOT BE!" Oliver shouted.

"Oh," said Death. "Believe me, it is. Edgar was my dear friend, gentlemen." His voice took on a harsher tone now, no longer the friendly, soothing stoner dialect it once was. "A very dear friend of mine. With you two hooligans making such a ruckus upstairs, you had to have known that sooner or later a dog of the underworld would come for you. That dog happened to be me. This invention belongs here, not in the real world. And no more shall it be used, especially not by you two fiends."

"BUT WHY?" Joshua shouted still, he couldn't help but shout, you had to make yourself heard above the screams.

"Because, boys," Death smiled vehemently. "Whether you're a king, a thief, or even a street sweeper, sooner or later, you will dance with me - Mr. Reynolds Reaper."

The Nature of a Secondhand

I

Taking the stairs two at a time was dangerous business. I had more sense than that. I nearly killed myself trying to close my robe and trot down the steps at the same time. But something decided to give. The wrinkles of my face eased themselves for once to let the cascading smile break through my age.

Abel and Lambert were here.

They stressed energetically to me to be patient, that my order would take a while, but I suspected that my two grandsons would try to surprise me with this visitation.

Unbeknownst to them, I hadn't slept a wink, even with several glasses of warm milk, churning the night away reading some of my various mystery story collections in front of a roaring fire. Any other man the same age, with such poor ligaments and with blood that felt clotted every time he stood still, the warmth of the inferno would lull them to sleep.

But not me.

No rest for the wicked.

The sky through the windows emphasized a blinding blue tint. No doubt, the weather was immaculately beautiful to behold. The flowers across the street at Ms. Peak's house were lovely and full, even while catching brief glimpses of them through my dusty windows.

I knew they came bearing my gift that I had bought for myself. I spotted them through the attic window as I was searching for my duster which, coincidentally, was hopelessly packed with dust itself.

I would need a duster for my duster soon.

Shaking it, of course, ignorant of the enormous soot-like cloud it would make, I shifted to the window, cracking it open a pinch and witnessing, with my own eyes, them carrying the long box that would hold my timely gift; the thing that I so desperately longed for.

II

The front door cracked and groaned just as I was covering the final stairway. The door was old - older than me. With another shove I could hear it budge as if a giant were kicking it with his big toe, mistaking it for a rough boulder of dirt.

"Abel, please!" I heard from the other side.

On the last two steps I fell forward, arms out to protect myself, and managed to fall on all fours without any injuries.

The door gave way.

It was a shocking thing to behold, a large wooden corner coming straight for my face. Luckily for me, the corner gouged into the planks without hitting me at all. After the dust settled, I looked up to see both Abel and Lambert chewing on their fists in awe.

"Grandfather!" they both shouted.

Both young men hurried for me to help me up. I noticed, while they expressed deep regret for an aging old man, that the shape of the box the object arrived in was not unlike that of a coffin. Not a fancied up one but of the lowest common denominator one. And if I were…

Good Lord, I thought.

It was a coffin.

The wooden cross at the top was worn but I have eyes and those eyes were sharp in focus at this moment.

I turned to both of them.

"It must be time," I said, already tasting the rising bile. "Coming for me already. Had I known the pitchfork man acquired two apprentice reapers and disguised them as my grandsons, I would have made a break for the chimney and kept on going till I was able to scale the pearly gates."

"Isn't like that," Abel said.

"Not at all," Lambert patted the dust off me. "You wanted the item right away and, grim as it may be, this pine box was all they had to carry it in."

"A fine business," I carried on, "making their customers feel like the departed."

At this, they sprung into laughter.

Right away, I knew it was the seed of Abel's idea.

"May we have a better lark in store come April," Lambert stated.

I should have known. Whoever heard of an establishment pawning off ready-made caskets to their loyal customers? Lord knew where the two vandals had acquired it. Quietly, I tried not to picture the image, but there it was. A few months prior there was a massive rainstorm which produced some flooding on the streets. Being that the graveyard three streets down was fairly new, the soil was loose and the few bodies that were buried in that seminal plot of land floated to the surface and coasted down the road to scare Mr. and Mrs. Taxpayer into their houses to be shut-in's. For days they tried to recover as many as they could. All but three were accounted for. Reasoning told me that if these two did find this pine box in a ditch on the side of the road, where it most likely would be, that whatever remains that were inside floated out.

Where that body went, only God knew.

"This is childish, degenerate and above all downright dreadful!" I stamped my foot.

"Calm down, grandfather. It was unoccupied."

"Recently!" my voice screeched. "Recently unoccupied, you two dolts!"

I'm all for fun and games…but some boundaries, even unmarked ones, were not to be crossed.

But all that does not amount to much in the eyes of younger folk. All they see is a crippled old codger throwing a tantrum when that's exactly what they came to see. Such disrespect in them.

Thinking only of myself, and not wanting my prize to be tainted by this level of dilapidation, I told them to pry the nails back and to stand my gift on out of the box, and in a hurried fashion, shaking my fist at them.

III

They propped it against the wall near the entrance, where two life-size stacks of newspapers framed it perfectly. The newspapers themselves were nearly ten years old and yellowed, but it gave me a chill in my spine to toss them out. My boy Daniel has frequently referred to me as 'the shut-in pack rat with his head in the clouds and his feet in the past.' I never reread them. Didn't need to. I had all but committed them to memory.

With a dirty rag from his pocket, Lambert walked up to the face of the old grandfather clock, spit into the rag and wiped the face of the glass casing.

Remarkably, the tall clock had not one drop of water to sag it. It was something of a miracle. I noticed, as Abel slid the casket across the floor, a sound to shake your soul, that the base was dripping. Pulling my robe closer to my chin, I turned back to my gift.

The clock stood six feet tall with a long statuesque body and with cherry wood color even underneath the dust.

It was mine.

All mine.

During my childhood - it plagues me now to see how far back I can remember - my father was poor. The only solace was the promise of more bread. All I would ever own during those precious years were a roll of twine, a frog which died three weeks after I had found him, and a discarded ticket stub to a play entitled *Our American Cousin,* the only play my father ever took me to. The only time we ever visited Washington D.C. I was a lad of ten. My father, some could say void of humor, carried me out of there in the middle of the second act. I hated him for a brief period, but then felt relief years later after finding out that a deranged actor murdered the president at that exact same theatre the night we were there. That's one scar of childhood my father inadvertently avoided for me.

When I turned twenty, father left. The startling event encouraged me to leave the nest since everyone else had left it. I traveled from city to city with the clothes on my back growing tighter as the years passed. I was able to acquire a brief job as a census taker, to which I enjoyed immediately.

The mansion of Herman Molt was as grand as it was epic. Just standing on the porch gave me a feeling that I was under washed and would need to return when I had money for a proper bath.

Inside was a deluxe collection of rugs, tapestry, cats and…

Cook-coo.

The clocks. The clocks shook me out of my concentration right as I was jotting down Mr. Molt's business venture. But none could hold a candle to the grandfather clock I spotted in his hall. He was in the middle of answering when I peered around him to see the majestic, hypnotizing pendulum of his grandfather clock. The hour was three in the afternoon. I'll never forget it.

"Did you get all of that, lad?"

"Sorry?"

"I said," his brows furrowed. "did you get all of that?"

"Oh. Of what?"

He set down his tea to follow my gaze behind him. When his face returned, it came with boastful pride.

"Young man?"

"Yes, sir?"

"Tell me your name."

"Am I in trouble?"

"No, I just wish to hear your name aloud."

"I assure you, sir, my mind wandered. I was not looking at anything."

"Son, that piece is my most prized possession. I'm delighted to see that you noticed it. I simply want to know what your name is to further congratulate your taste."

He held out his hand to me.

I cringed at first, thinking he may strike me for my stupidity. Instead, I welcomed his palm into my own and shook it.

"Cecil Weet the second, sir."

"Well, my new good friend Cecil Weet, let me give you some advice. A man of wealth needs only three things in life; enough food on his plate, a love for the written word, and a clock to pass the time."

"No need for money?"

He shook his head adamantly. "Man has no need for a gathered flimsy paper empire. Wealth is born by those who nurture the idea of time working for them rather than against them."

It was a profound notion. One that I stuck to with vigor.

Herman Molt died a year later, hunched over in his chair, nose buried in a copy of *Great Expectations*. Not a glorious exit to the Lord's grand plan, but still, immortalized in his favorite book. That alone is all anyone could hope for.

IV

Snapping me out of my reservoir of thoughts, Lambert held his hand out to me. He held the brass instrument up to my face. It was too close, so, naturally, I gripped his arm and furthered it from myself.

It was small. Sturdy. It reminded me of pepper grinders, the ones my father used to manufacture.

"Now you can turn it," Lambert smiled.

"Turn?"

"Old fellow, do you not know what this is? It is a winder. You open the glass face of the clock, stick it in the porthole in front of the three and twist clockwise until you feel the hard, stiff click."

Lambert unclenched the fingers of my right hand and dropped the winder into it. Gradually, I looked down at the winder then up at the clock's face. Everything seemed in order. Looked in order. I counted the numbers. All twelve were there, flaunting their roman numerals. But in my intestines I felt shunned by my own shimmering possession.

It was the case of unwound time.

An ancient relic of frozen history.

"Yes, yes," I said, more to myself than to my two demented grandsons. "You'll leave me now, vagrants. I want some time alone."

And the time, surprisingly, I would receive.

They turned a quarter between themselves, clapping the dust away as forcefully as they could. I was rid of them already, but would they ever truly be rid of me? Would I fade in time, like dust in the wind?

"Ungrateful," Lambert mumbled. Abel followed him out the doorway.

It was just me, the silence, and the uneven mystery of the grandfather clock.

"A treasure, no less," I assured my trophy.

V

The hour was nigh and never. In my chair of ruby coloring, with a blanket coiled around me, I sat in front of the unwound clock.

Through the windows, night.

In the fire, burning wood.

But the hour was still unknown.

A powerful hour that tingled my dull, brittle spine with new fluid of life.

The hands, all three, would move at my touch - when I so commanded.

I unclenched my hand, rubbed the winder between my fingertips. "It is time," I murmured. "And time so it shall be."

With a jolt, I stood. I opened the case, fed the winder into the hole and cranked. Now, I know that age and loneliness plays tricks on the mind. Also burgundy, which I admit was beside my chair. But in that moment, cranking out the new birthing hours from my clock, the brass grew brighter. The wood hummed lightly in acceptance of giving it a breath of life. The dings and dongs grew louder, booming. I dared to wind on. My eyes stayed open against my will, my stance was unmoved. But my breath was growing short, struggling to find precious oxygen between me and the clock itself. The pendulum ticked to life.

Oh, the constant booming. I felt God knocking on my door, I swear by it.

It clicked. Once it clicked, the booming settled, thereby giving my ears deserved rest. It was here. The hour spun into place. Four past six, I remember.

Pulling the winder out, I received a shock that stunned my crippled hand. Under inspection, I found no burn nor any singed hairs, but my palm was warm. I gazed at the face of him.

"Never bite the hand that feeds," I spoke to it. Then carried on, watching the secondhand tick my life away.

VI

I awoke, crouched in the chair, feeling hot and cold flashes. A constant spinning had me pinned to my chair, but not one that I could see clearly. The room stayed intact, yet aged rapidly, rotting in the corners, growing small ponds of dust and plants.

The hair on my chin grew and trailed down to my knees, which were turning to bone, then ash. The need to scream was long since dead. Or was I?

Somehow, still able to gaze around my surroundings, the clock was in a fury, the hands spun so violently, two poor gnats found their way into the whirling vortex and were sliced to tiny ribbons. The sun rose and set in blinks.

The clock's hands finally slowed, then rewound.

Back they went.

Faster, then faster.

Faster, faster, faster.

My ashes turned to bone, then skin.

The walls that surrounded me and the clock breathed in all the dust out of existence.

My burgundy, the bottle had overturned during the night, splashed back into the bottle. The bottle, feeling bold, stood upright and leapt into my hand.

And then, when the hands finally ceased, I screamed. I whimpered. I patted at myself to make sure I was there.

Tick, tick, tick.

The time was steady. The hour was four past seven in the morning. My fear subsided. I knew I hadn't been dreaming. I was, I swear, awake.

That was my first day with the grandfather clock.

Though, now, as I see it, I had spent 269,200 days frontward as well as backward with it.

VII

Every day held a promise of absurdity. Fearful of the clock, I chose to sleep in my bed on the third floor. But even a change in location did not stop the clock's madness. The clock would be normal for days then weeks, then it would choose an hour by which to flourish its demented desires.

On one such morning, I awoke to waterfalls filling up my house. Four past eight.

On another, dunes of sand spread and fell from holes in the roof as well as the chimney. Four past nine. I was in the kitchen at the time when the faucet saw fit to shower my hands in pebbles. I navigated sluggishly through the sand to the safety of my bedroom. I had stacked several books on my bed, as the sand was filling the room quickly, to preserve the one pocket of air I had left. The sand later reversed its order and sifted away into the cracks of the house.

When I collected myself mentally, I did research in my library. In ancient times, the most primitive form of the clock was a sundial. Then, right there on the page were the two other forms of keeping track of time - a water clock and an hourglass of sand. Now I creep, candle in hand, searching the cracks for a spurt or a light powder of dust to emerge. I expected it around every corner.

I did not trust this house.

More importantly, I did not trust the clock.

VIII

Again the clock tormented me with this madness. In my sleep, I heard the hands of the clock downstairs growing loud. They thumped hard and firm, much louder than normal ticking. They thumped louder as if they were getting closer, coming up the stairs to my very room.

I awoke in the dark, hearing the thumps in my room. Then I felt seized by hands. The cold darkness that surrounded me shocked me back to sleep.

I awoke yet again, only this time within the clock itself! Huddled in a corner, I pressed my back against the wall, for I was only two inches tall, and, with great fear, I was dodging the oncoming pendulum from slicing me in two. Twas a sight to be seen. Edgar Allan Poe must have held this nightmare before me, no doubt to write *The Pit and the Pendulum.* But, to see that swinging mass of metal, swaying back and forth, seeming to come closer with each swing, I felt the very breath within grow short until I fainted dead away.

I awoke once more, this time to morning.

IX

The clock was not mine, I knew. And it never would be. I did not own the clock, my friends. The Chronos of time owned me. It held me. It made my dwelling its playground. But for what reason? I questioned how I should trudge on.

There was no defeating time. Time owned me, no matter what I did. At the hour of nine on a humid night in July, I chose to stand in front of the clock.

I promise, I had no Burgundy or bourbon or whiskey, nothing to cloud my eyes. As I stood closer, standing on my frail toes to get a better look at the face of the clock, I noticed its captors. The long minute hand was not a stem, but a man. A man fully clothed, but still a man clothed in a suit, blackened by age, frozen with his eyes closed. The hour hand, about half the length of the minute hand… or man, I think I should say, was more portly and just as blackened, his tiny mouth frozen in a frown. His eyes, closed as well, thank the heavens, were drooped like those of a crying clown.

But, and this was indeed odd, the secondhand held no man. It was just a slender stem.

Why was there a man missing? I pondered.

And how long before he would take his rightful place between the two?

X

Today, the men disappeared. But I desperately wanted them back, my friends lost in time. What would it take to appease the beast of this house?

Did it crave another man?

Did it want me?

A sacrifice?

XI

I prepared my will to the letter. Cleared the entrance hall of everything except my comfortable chair. The clock struck eleven on that night…I remember. Good Lord, I remember to the hour the time I got up from my chair, opened the hatch to the pendulum and walked inside the clock.

XII

From the time I merged with the clock, strangers have been in and out of my house. Some were foolishly concerned that I was lost, never to be found. I was not lost. I was home, right where I should be. Regardless, I overheard them preparing a funeral in my honor. A grand one at that.

I caught glimpses of my son, Daniel, sobbing as he held onto the side of my cherry wood side for support. I felt guilty about that. But he still held me without ever realizing it.

And what of my two grandsons and the house? Well, as I've said before, I prepared my will to the letter, making absolutely sure these two misfits inherited the house and I.

They rejoiced for a time, ignorant to what I, Hower and Minnel had in store for them. I had become a third generation of timekeepers, able to bend time to my will. My friends followed suit. Yes, they were entertaining, to say the least. Hower would thrill me for hours with his stories of houses he haunted. Minnel only took but a minute or two to chime in. And as for me, Cecil Second as the two called me, I discussed things with them. We talked of wine, women, our long love of books and music. Then, at night, we would render my two grandsons helpless, toying with their perceptions. We made sure to only do this when they were full with drink but still awake and lively.

Yes, we filled the house with water and sand. We rifled through time faster than anything you could imagine. We had them, you see. And such a fantastic lark it was. One that no one would believe, even when the two drunkards invited friends over to look at us, hoping that we would turn the tables again. But we did not. We were gentlemen, you see. Not in front of company, goodness no. The two grew mad in the time they spent with us. But, no matter, we would rewind the time and do it all over again. My friends thought for sure we would be kindle for the fire. But my grandsons were too frightened by us, too scared to even touch us anymore. The cold, mischievous realm of time is very different from the forgiving nature of mankind. And one should never fool or predict the nature of a secondhand.

Pus

If you had lived next to apartment 2B, in a rundown seedy motel by the name of Buck's Getaway, you would have known the horror that became of Scott Hammond.

It all began with a simple bug bite. Scott Hammond, the tenant of 2b, endlessly studied insects. Every day, he would come back from his job at the grocery store, which he hated on an unhealthy level, to be greeted by a chorus of chirps, bleats, squeals and buzzes. The harmonic sound of all the creatures he captured was serene.

The back wall alone held six wide shelves with five fish tanks on each, full of flying, jumping, squirming, slithering bugs. Sitting on top of the television was a small fishbowl with tin foil strapped to the rim with multiple rubber bands. Inside were two luna moths. He was trying to breed them. Then there was a section in his kitchen with three separate tanks devoted entirely to mosquitoes. Those little bloodsuckers were fierce. Whenever the owner of the motel would come for his latest rent check, mocking Scott for his untidy bum wear, Scott would get his revenge by bottling two or three of the little devils in a test tube and then emptying them into Mr. Fryers' mail slot.

Scott had no prerogatives to dress to impress. The only company he had were his bugs. The only ones who would listen to him were his bugs.

In return for their kindness and their acceptance of him, he took care of them. He fed them all their mandatory diets, some of them with his own blood kept in storage plastic bags in his freezer, he watched them, and he read them various selections from Robert Frost.

What he had was a happy, but small, place inside their kingdom.

Unchanged.

Until the day he noticed one nasty little sucker feasting on his arm. He felt the twinge of pain running up his arm while he was bagging food. At first, arthritis was the only possible explanation. But as he looked down his arm, firmly attached to his elbow was a bug measuring the size of a half dollar. Not only were three of its stingers embedded into his arm, but the legs were too. And Scott could feel the prickly little things running deeper, as if searching for something.

Normally, whenever one of his regular bugs at his apartment would get loose, he'd get stung a couple of times until he bottled them back up. But never like this. And it was never this painful either.

"Shit," he said. A mother covered her baby girl's ears as she was resting comfortably in the child seat of the shopping cart, her feet playfully tapping her mom in the stomach. The manager came over and told Scott in a reprimanding way that that kind of language would not be tolerated in his store.

Scared to reveal the beast on his arm, he covered it with his hand, excusing himself to the bathroom. On the way he snatched a pickle jar off the shelf, emptied it in the toilet of the stall he was in and sat down on the seat. With a pair of nail clippers that he kept in his pocket, he carefully tried to remove the stingers from his arm. At first he tried to pull the bug off, stingers and all. But the dedication of this bug to his flesh was unwavering. Scott's skin could stretch no more. So, regretfully, and it pained him to do it, he clipped all three stingers off, the creature squealing in pitiful protests. Scott was sorry to do it, but it was a must.

When it was done, he placed the bug inside the jar, sealed it, pulled down his sleeve, flushed the toilet (which made it overflow because of the pickles) and left the bathroom. He told the manager he was sick, apologized quickly and left quietly.

Experiments began when he arrived home to his family of bugs. The speckled bug that bit him wasn't in any of his books. There were no pictures of it or a classification for it. Scott was simply amazed and overjoyed that he'd possibly stumbled upon a rare species of bug. Night and day he researched, digging, probing to find a name for this bug. But there was none to be found.

At the same time he so piously searched, strange things were happening to him.

The stingers seeped into his skin, making it soft and mushy. When he finally had enough guts to check it out in the mirror, it didn't look that bad. It looked like a simple boil.

However, when he popped it, it would not stop leaking. He leaned over the toilet and let the ooze drip and stretch into the bowel. He went through one full roll of toilet paper to stuff into the gaping wound.

Pus.

Thick, yellow pus everywhere.

The stingers, frighteningly, had disappeared, hidden somewhere in his skin. And that little mystery caused him two whole weeks of misery. Every night, he'd barely make it to the bathroom in time to puke up a good liter of pus.

He sneezed pus.

He shat pus.

Pus leaked from his gums when he brushed his teeth.

Pus was seeping out around the corners of his eyes.

There was even a moment where he had a really bad headache, but that could have been a pus-filled congestion in his brain.

New wounds appeared and they were getting bigger. All these wounds made him cranky. And in that heated moment, he tossed out his glorious collection of bugs, killing more than half of them as he chucked the tanks out the window to shatter in the garbage dump below.

All his attention was now devoted to the one bug. Each book he went through that didn't have a record of this thing, he tore to shreds. And with the papers, he clogged his dripping wounds. The stench of this stuff was unbelievable.

The bug wasn't helping matters much, even though it was hypnotizing to look at. Every night, at three a.m., it squealed a retched sound that Scott was sure made a baby cry four doors down from him. Just being in the same room with the little shit as it made that sound was enough to make someone jump out the window. Many times, Scott contemplated this.

But Scott was not one to go down without a fight. Classifying this thing was out of the equation. The only thing to do now was to find a cure.

It took him three more weeks.

He was reduced to almost nothing.

The sickness, whatever he had, made him lose over sixty pounds, clocking him at somewhere between 118 and 117. His weight changed every day now. The pus did not stop its flow though. Scott was convinced from the dramatic weight loss that he was leaking himself out this whole time. He didn't want to find out that one day the marrow in his bones was now infected with pus. They probably were right now and he didn't know it.

That impending fear kept him up twenty hours out of every day. And every waking moment was dedicated to his salvation.

Finally, one glorious day, it struck him, as all life-changing miracles usually do. He still had the sealed bags of his uninfected blood in the freezer. Maybe there was a way to use the pus from the wounds, the insect's blood and other different fluids he had extracted from various bugs in order to get him back to a fit state.

Many combinations later, he arrived at the cure. And when he exposed the sample of his infected blood to the serum, the yellowy pus just faded away.

Excitedly, he was able to perfect an injection.

The soothing serum entered his vein and replenished his life again.

The pus did not flow anymore.

Before he knew what he was doing, he was making trips to the store, stocking up on goods. He ate like a king for the next three days, beefing back up again. He was now back to a reasonable weight.

In all honesty, he should have thrown the bug away when he got stung. But, even though it was grueling, these past few weeks, him and the bug had formed a connection. Even with its hour-long squeals in the middle of the night that kept him up. Hell, it was a damned miracle that the neighbors did not complain, but they were drugged out hippies and crack whores anyway. They were probably too baked to notice.

Now, on a bright summer day, Scott stroked the glass of the jar, smiling at his quarry. He had finally conquered this little shit. He had called it that a lot lately. As a matter of fact, on the jar was a label that displayed the initials L.S.

The motto of science was to keep your discoveries and share them with the world. In time, Scott would make his serum public. But only after he released his little buddy L.S. out into the world. With this rare bug out there, there was more than a chance that he would sting several people, since he had just grown some new stingers. When those people begged for a cure, Scott would be their genius savoir.

He was never able to figure out just what L.S. was, but that was okay. His best guess was that it started out as a normal mosquito but was then altered by today's gaseous pollution. Oh well, he thought.

He picked up the jar with his wide grip, careful to be as gentle as could be. He carried it with him to the door, a funny-looking smirk dancing across his face. The bug was tweeting its little bleat-bleat as it was nestled in the nook of Scott Hammond's arm.

His hand met the door and he looked down at his unique find. “Go get ’em, tiger.”

His hand twisted the knob while his other released the lid. He was looking down into the jar the whole time, not noticing the high-pitched buzzing that came when he opened the door. He figured that those buzzing noises were distant and were probably normal cicadas.

But to his horror, as he thrust the jar forward, releasing the little beast into what he thought was the open world, he really only released the thing into a cloud of moving blackness.

When he focused his eyes, he realized that the cloud of blackness outside his door was a massive grouping of bugs just like L.S. And just like that, the treacherous conclusion was formed. The whole time this little insect had been squealing all those nights, he wasn’t doing it for tradition. He was doing it because he was calling out to his brothers and sisters. Calling them back here to the man who had captured him.

Scott could see their bulging, black eyes, their fuzzy insect legs, their firm backs and pointy stingers. At a brief guess, there must have been fifty of them, holding their spot in the air, staring at poor Scott Hammond.

“Oh shit,” he said, sweating. “It’s got friends.”

His hand released the jar and it shattered to the ground.

Together, as one, they swarmed Scott Hammond.

Me and Mine

I'm left here standing alone and afraid in the heat. Standing is all I can do. I'm concentrating all my weight on my right leg, sweating my face off all over my toes. And as I'm standing, panicking, I'm thinking about all the lucky bastards who die in regular-class accidents. A lawyer driving down a major street in downtown New York, talking on his cell, gets slammed head on from a bus that had the forceful right of way. I think about an old war veteran, on his way to grab a two-pill Viagra high and get back to his highly paid eighteen-year-old hooker for one last ride, falling to the ground right before he even makes it to the cabinet. Believe it or not, these statistics, although disturbing to think about, are comforting in the fact that those are the easy ways to go.

I have no easy way.

Nothing is easy.

I'm straining myself to stay alive.

The others had it easy.

Ever been in a worst-case scenario?

Here I am, alone in the Nevada desert. My only ride took off two hours ago. I'm thirsty, sweating. It's early in the morning. The sun is now my enemy, glaring at me with its evil iris that just won't close. And, to top it all off, I'm standing on a landmine in the middle of nowhere. Or, I guess, I should say out in the middle of bum-fucked Egypt. Nevada is just the same, I guess.

So, again, ever been in a worst-case scenario?

I think not, pal.

Who am I even talking to?

Myself I guess, reassuring myself.

Heat's getting to me.

Why did this have to happen to me? I'm nobody. I'm just a simple Joe working for an up and coming car company. My life is a series of statistics. Now I'm one of them.

Christ. Did it have to be this way?

I can't die now.

No, I'm not one of those selfish men raping the land of all its resources. Certainly don't want to live forever. Would have liked it if I could have been out the door at age seventy. And now I'm going to die at the age of thirty. That's way ahead of schedule. Funny in a shitty way. I'm early for my own death.

If I ever, strike that, if I could have avoided this landmine, I'd hike all the way back to Vegas and personally take a brick to the heads of the crackpots who brought me here. Taking my time with those pricks would give me enough energy to grab a quick drink at the bar, wait in the lounge, read a book. A nice thick one. Can't have everything I guess.

If I had known they'd pull this prank, I would have given the four of them the double-gun middle finger specials and told them to screw off. Could have been in my bed in New York right now. Comfy. Spooning my wife as we get our rest because we have a barbeque to go to the next day.

Instead, I'm spooning my heart, trying to get it to calm the hell down. But my imagination is getting the best of me. I have to stay scared. Have to stay on the edge. Must dig my leg harder into the ground. The second I loosen up, my toes will be gone, followed by my leg which gets driven up into my ribcage by the awesome force of the blast. My glasses shattered. My head tilts back as I feel the flames tickle the whiskers of my blondish beard. My existence on this earth gone in a flash. I am the ashes, I am the dust. Just on delay, standing here like a dumbfounded statue for show and tell.

If I were a statue, I'd call myself *Screwed Indefinitely*. A new upcoming piece.

Pieces.

I'll be blown to pieces.

Oh God.

I'm doing it again - losing control.

Calm down, dammit!

No, don't calm down.

Be edgy.

Be heavy.

The leg is going numb, a phantom leg ready to be erased.

It was just supposed to be a weekend of gambling and drinks. In a gothic way, it is. I'm sweating so bad it's leaking into my mouth. It tastes sour and hard, much more than whiskey. I'm gambling with my own life.

No.

They did.

My supposed friends.

Bagged me up in the middle of the night, drove me all the way out here, then rolled me out like a fresh new carpet, then trailed off. The last image in my head of them is waving, smiling, mooning me through the black jeep windows as they head back. They knew I'd make it back. Couldn't be more than a short hike. An unexpected inconvenience that would have them laughing for hours.

I broke into a run, trying to catch the jeep. As I was slowing down, trying to catch my breath because I don't run regularly, I came to rest, to my surprise, on what I thought was the stump of a cactus. But then I heard the snap, the beep. Without removing my foot, I looked down. And it all became clear. I was dead meat standing, cooking in the sun. Can't move off this spot, no sir.

Somewhere on a map there is a red dot in Nevada that says just for me, 'You are here. And you are fucked.'

Maybe I'm dead already. And the hell of it is that I don't know what's going to happen when I lift my leg. It might blow, might be a dud. Might be the button to an underground trap door. How the hell should I know?

I'm going to find out sooner or later.

I can't die. Not now.

Putting my hands together, I pray. I pray that somehow I overcome this. That the lord could give me strength, courage and wisdom all at the same time. I may have well asked for gold, silver and bronze. That and all my parking tickets paid off. Regardless, I pray. I pray for an answer. I swear I will make each day last if I'm able to get out of this predicament. I hope for a way to find me. Am I supposed to die? Death is random so why not, huh?

No, the Lord is giving me strength to hold my ground. He's given me the privilege to think.

But what good could that do?

Nothing, I say.

Tools. There must be a way that I can deactivate this thing. Some way to turn it off, or at least in some small way delay the blast from coming. There must be. Well, one comical way of doing it would be to dig around the edges of it, pull it up with my leg until my knee is against my chest and try to kick it away. That's no good. Not only would I explode, but I would explode stupidly. Then there was the excruciating unreliable choice of holding it firmly to my foot as I shimmy on my back all the way to town. My back would get all tore up, so that was out. Plus, unlike a grenade, there was no telling what would happen once I got this thing out of the ground. I keep thinking of a wire from the bottom attached to a pin of a grenade underneath just in case the people who placed this knew I would get smart.

The people who placed this?

Who the shit was putting landmines out in the desert in the first place?

Of course, it could always be a dud. A lost relic of a forgotten age, an heirloom of destruction unused.

Keep your leg steady, dammit!

What can I use to diffuse it?

Diffuse it? That's a laugh. I work for a car company. I

don't have the foresight to assemble a bookcase let alone diffuse something that others need to be trained to do. I have nothing on me. Just my tan cargo pants, my black shirt, and my glasses. But I need those to see.

All I see is empty space.

Need to do something.

If my friends weren't such assholes, I could be at the hotel right now, watching them sleep as I mope. I would be at that dresser, writing to my wife, telling her how bored I am without her. Then, as always, work on some last-minute forms, plucking the paperclips out of each one.

As a little kid, I always had a particularly annoying habit. One time, long ago, when I was forced to sit in the corner of the classroom for dumping milk all over Penny, I'd confiscate paperclips. Those little things would be so fascinating when you were bored out of your wits. After bending them into various animal shapes, I'd move on to linking them. During a business meeting, I made a link of twelve then just snapped out of it and paid attention to the boring CEO giving the presentation. Some people collect rubber bands, stamps, coins. For me, there were always paperclips.

There were always paperclips?

That's pathetic.

I know. Had a good bunch of them at home too. Made a ball out of them in fact. 127 in all.

Wait. The dresser. I left some on it. Right before I went to bed. I was on the phone with my wife and I saw them there. But did I unconsciously pluck them off the paper and start fooling around with them? I never realize when I'm doing it. It's possible.

I reach into my pocket and find…

One.

Just one.

That might be it.

It might be the one.

It's cold.

I kiss it as if it were my wife.

If this works, I'll curl my lips around her head so fast and hard it would take the Jaws of Life to separate us.

But what about the others?

What others?

It could be two things I have to watch out for.

Two hours have passed since my friends left me here. Right around the time I made my discovery, after they were well out of sight, I heard something. Something faint, almost like a thump. Not quite an explosion. But then again, they were a good distance away. What if they encountered another mine? What if the back tire bumped it, exploded and sent them sailing through the air on wings of metal and fire?

Or that sound could have very well been inside my head, the sound of my world shattering around me.

Where are my friends?

Are there more mines?

First things first.

Deal with this and all your problems melt away.

Kneeling down, keeping the weight hard on my leg, I try to stay steady as I unwind the paperclip. I'm not sure what I can do with it, but I do know that the only thing that's keeping me on this earth is a tiny little mechanism that needs to connect with the trigger. Like any trigger, if it were blocked, the weapon cannot fire. Let's hope that it can't, anyway.

That's a good thing to hope for.

Curling it into a question mark shape, I crane my neck as low as it can go. Now, at eye level with this thing that can destroy my face, I see the tiny peg staying steady. All you need is a firm hand and an iron constitution.

My hand quivers a little.

I steady it.

I plunge the clip forward, curling it into the guts of the explosive. Once I find the peg, I wrap it hard around the clip. That should keep it down. But with the weight I was pressing on it, it was a risky guess.

Not going to die like this.

Absolutely not.

Until my fingers are bleeding, I twist the tiny metal rods together.

It's done.

Now comes the part that I was dreading. Pushing myself to stand, I close my eyes and say a final prayer. Everything comes to mind like a big bang. I want forgiveness. I want my wife. Can I overcome?

I open my eyes.

Now!

Run!

With great effort, I launch myself off the damn thing as if I were on my neighbor's trampoline. I land, but in a way, not really, because my feet are way ahead of me. They are taking off like God's lightning is coming for them. I grunt and scream, wailing into empty space as I pump myself forward. I hurt, but I keep moving, despite the fact that the leg I was exerting so much energy with asleep and somehow swinging itself wildly in the right direction. I hold my hip as I run harder. I am away. I am alive, damn it. I'm running faster than the fucking Flash. Faster than Superman on speed. I'm breaking the sound barrier.

Then comes the blast.

The sound barrier just decided to break me.

Again, I'm launched into the hot air, taking off on invisible wings. I'm suspended in midair. Can I reach the heavens?

Reality stabs my eyes as I look down; gravity decided to show up.

I tumble and fall to the dusty ground and roll for a while.

Duck and cover my ass.

I'm spitting blood as the immense heat simmers down. My hand raises all on it's own, shielding the sun. My glasses are gone but I can still see that I am alive - alive and kicking, so to speak. I still had my legs but my pant leg was completely ripped and gone. Must have gotten caught on the mine after I high-tailed it.

The smoke clears. I'm a good distance away from the little black Pandora's Box of pain.

My arm feels dislocated. I tell it to stay put, not to spoil my victory because it truly is a victorious day.

I lean my head back, laughing at the clouds. I'm laughing my happy ass off.

And with tears streaming down, I reach my fist into the air and shout, "Baby, I'm coming home!"

Lighter

How do you find your weapon of choice?

In my experience, you can't depend on complicated machinery. Bullets clog barrels, knives bend and break. When it comes right down to it, they can fail at any given moment. And that's just too risky for me.

As I stand in here, at a pawnshop that will remain unnamed, I am taken aback by the amount of space. The entrance is five feet by four, and that is all the space that the owner thinks you should have. In front of my eyes, a great big wire mesh and behind that a big, greasy man in overalls that is missing his right arm. Possibly a war wound?

Dangling from the counter on a chain is a wide booklet, reminding me of the phonebooks that used to dangle in phone booths. It seems like nobody bothers to glance at those anymore. But I do.

I pick it up, open it up, and inside is a brief listing of every item behind the wire mesh and behind the fat man watching the fuzzy reception on his portable TV. The ones that have been bought already have red marker cross-outs.

Weaponry is the top seller on the list. Guns, guns, guns. But more importantly, guns that have no papers. Guns that have… what is it?...fallen off the back of a truck? Guns, in a fashion, that are good for a point-blank robbery or a wide-open massacre.

I scratch the tiny scar above my eye and try to understand it all. This fascination with guns; are people really so dependant on them? Perhaps so.

Old, fat and ugly is now looking up from the scrambled screen. My guess is he's watching a porn movie, I could hear faint moans in between buzzes. What else could it be? He's staring at my hand. I take a look myself. It is unsettling to prying eyes because it has horrible burn scars and is yet somehow still intact.

I lower it routinely.

His eyes drool back to the poor man's excuse for a television set.

Why is it that some people are so quick to judge?

Burns are the hardest to hide. Can't glove it. Just looks silly and hurts like a bitch. It's still fresh, you know.

Burns are the one drawback to my sidearm, my weapon of choice - a lighter.

For those still scratching their heads, let me elaborate.

Lighters are common. Lighters can't be traced. You can pick them up at any gas station, bowling alley, pool joint - the list goes on. Lighters have it in for the smokers of the nation. Imagine a world without them; cigarettes gone to waste, wicks to bombs not being lit, secret documents never to been burned.

I suppose those things can still be done with matches, but matches are very unceremonious. Just like lottery tickets, you scratch a few, they might be duds, but every once in a while you get a strike. For a brief moment you are delighted with the little petal of flame on the tip of that dead head stick. But you must act quickly otherwise you get a reminder from the bitchy flame that your time is up.

Lighters, though, are like a constant friend. Two click-click's and the tall orange fellow is up and ready, ever burning and ever watchful; a hypnotizing lovechild of the devil in the palm of your hand. And with it, be my guest, have at the world. I know I have.

With my trusty Zippo, I've made card sharks squeal. I use it for torture.

In another instant, it helps me out of a jam. Just ask Norman the, laughable, tough shit who made the mistake of putting me in a headlock in '86. His cufflinks ended up melting into his own wrist.

I even one time lit a stick of dynamite in Jerry's mouth while he was taped to a chair. In order to make the information keep pouring and the time to keep running, I bought one of them nice long wicks, the ones I call 'two yards of truth'. I'd light it all the way down to the floor, pretend to leave, then he'd spill his guts. Then I'd bend down, stomp it out, snap the wick a few inches from the burnt tail and light it again. With squealers, there's always a chance that they left something out. I don't give them that chance. I'm not afraid to die, and they damn well know it.

There was never a chance for anyone to get the better of me. My little sidekick would fight all my battles, and the little tyke did it well.

"Decide yet?" came the croaky voice of the pawnshop owner.

This I practiced thoroughly. I masked my face with confusion, anchored my brows down to the bridge of my bulbous, fleshy nose. "Got any of these in stock?"

The print was small, which worked in my favor. The owner came forward, leaning closer and closer to the wire mesh as I turned the book towards his prying eyes. The suspenders to his overalls were dangling off the little narrow opening on the counter, enough for a hand to reach through and...

Now!

I grasp this jelly man so fast, I'm able to bang his face up against the mesh to where his surviving arm goes limp and his vision goes blurry.

"Imp," I breathe. "Tommy don't like welchers. And he

don't like no gluttonous freak shows eating into his money. That money was his bread, Imp, and you know damn well you couldn't live on it for long without someone noticing. Who drives to their work, a pawnshop no less, in a brand new '79 camaro?"

"Your name?"

"That doesn't matter."

"It does to me."

I looked him up and down, he was massive but in all the wrong places, a weakling that could barely breathe past his folds. I figured he was going nowhere. First I would start with his face. I'd bring my trusty friend up to his face, yes, and burn him till his eyelids curled shut. They can do that, you know. I'd circulate the flame around his face until it molded to the wire mesh he'd been accustomed to staring through. But first, I figured to let him have his name, and I decided not to lie for once.

"Willis Fry," I said. "And may I ask, what kind of a name is 'Imp'?"

"My brother gave it to me. One of the only two things he gave me before he died."

"Oh," I groaned with boredom. "That's so sad."

At this point, I reached into my back pocket and fetched my little friend. His shiny golden smile was irresistible as I flipped him open to see his stand out wick of a tongue. *Yes, my friend,* I thought. *You've licked me once before. Burned through those ropes that had me, and you helped me escape. You knew sooner or later I'd have to sacrifice myself to you - your burnt offering. And now, I'll feed you again, my unquenchable friend. I'll offer you this man.*

Then I looked up. Imp was blinking frantically. I realized that the whole time I had been mentally prepping my little tyke for his feast, I had been mouthing the words as well.

No matter.

I clicked his wick and he stood tall, wavering calmly, ready for the intimidation game.

"Meet 'Little Fry'. He's my accomplice. You could say a man's man."

Just then, there was a pain in my wrist that was holding his suspenders and a familiar chink of cold, piercing metal. My wrist was caught. And with the other, he clicked it to the wire mesh. But even with my wrist handcuffed, I did not loosen my grip. This tubby fool was quick with his one arm, but he would unlock these sooner or later.

After securing me, he reached his arm under the table and brought up the blackest, meanest, biggest contraption I'd ever seen. And it flickered to life with the help of the breathing tip touching my little tyke. My soul sunk down to my shoes as my friend left me to leap onto this machine.

"Meet my mistress!" Imp snarled. "The LPO-50 Flamethrower. Friend of the Soviets, used in the Vietnam War, a gift from my brother!"

Powerless

As a 'stay at home' mom, nobody would have guessed that this particular human being was infinitely special. She looked normal enough; fashionable glasses, auburn hair always done up in a bun, a heart-shaped face, and woodsy brown eyes. At age thirty-eight, Abigale Newell was still a knockout. Her husband, Douglas, only ever knew that she was the world's perfect wife and mother.

Perhaps *too* perfect.

When Douglas arrived home, always late in the evening, the house would always be immaculate. His dinner was always ready, his suit was always laid out for the next day, and, remarkable as it may seem, Abigale remained with a pep of energy every night. Throughout college, where he met her, she always had that little spark that never seemed to fizzle out.

Of course, Abigale, it seems, was never above her own eccentricities. She would cry over the morning newspaper sometimes. It was always the worst on Mondays. During her two pregnancies, four years apart, she was battling with, what Douglas thought, was very heavy postpartum depression. Needless to say, it was difficult counseling her through those troubled times. Douglas, the good husband that he was, was always there for her through those rocky moments.

Not only was the daily news always on her mind but it was apparent that Abigale was determined for her two girls to be well-mannered with good heads on their shoulders. Lyra, her youngest, was a good-standing girl who always did well in school and would one day be a successful photojournalist. Courtney, however, never stopped her shenanigans and had a deep affection for a boy that Abigale never approved of and always questioned.

On a day like every other, a Friday, in the month of June, Abigale pretended to look hurried and flustered. Just as she had countless times before.

"Courtney," she called to the top of the stairs, "get down here right now! This one woman standoff has got to stop!"

Courtney was always late for school. Abigale could have fixed that with a jerk of her neck, but she didn't want to. Teenage girls needed their reluctance in effort to maintain their normal life, or what was deemed a somewhat normal life to prying eyes. Yes, Abigale had a good secret or two. These were the same secrets she concealed from her family on a daily basis. But, every once in a while, the lovely Mrs. Newell couldn't help but flex her talents.

No one was in the kitchen.

She double-checked, splitting herself into two people. Her double walked to the doorway connecting the kitchen to the dining room, took a few looks around. When all was clear, her second self walked back to her, like a trained dog, and melted back into her.

Breakfast.

Her husband would be up soon and he would be hungry. Lyra was in the bathroom and, from what she could hear, Courtney had just hit the snooze button on her alarm clock. *Good girl*, Abigale thought.

The radio on the counter clicked on without anyone touching it. Radio static buzzed for a moment as Abigale squinted her eyes, trying to catch a perfect song in that great big cloudy mist. She found one and mentally tuned the radio into that particular station just in time to hear the beginning of a golden oldie. She really was a remarkable woman.

Marvin Gaye came alive lightly through the speakers and started chirping away with 'ain't that peculiar.' With Abigale in the kitchen every morning around this hour, it always was just that - peculiar.

Bread sailed out of the cabinet and both slices jumped into the toaster.

Eggs crashed against the pan and the stove set itself.

Fresh slices of ham took their familiar pathway to the second pan where the bacon and hash browns were arguing over which one would have the privilege of jumping into the pan as if it were a private swimming pool. Of course, bacon and hash browns don't have a personality. Abigale created personalities for them just to further amuse herself in her daily routines.

"Now both of you stop that right now," she whispered.

They both looked up at her, then, with an ounce of chivalry, bacon backed away so that hash browns could have their fun.

The newspaper exploded into the kitchen and several articles swirled around a controlled tornado of news. The toast popped out and she stole a slice to chew on as several articles zoomed up to her, begging to be read. Whatever she didn't find interest in, she said 'next' almost dreamily.

Her chair slid away for her, as usual.

"Why thank you."

Suddenly, she heard footsteps.

"Psst!" she said to the tornado of news, and soundlessly the articles gathered into the shape of a full newspaper and calmly came to rest in Abigale's outstretched hands.

Lyra peaked around the corner. Her dark brown hair was unkempt and her stuffed panda was in the nook of her right arm. Even as young as she was, she always seemed to be getting younger, almost shrinking.

"Thought I heard noises, Mom."

"Well, it's just me poking around."

"I could have sworn…"

Douglas entered, already a smile on his face.

He picked up Lyra and gave her a strong hug. "What? My

little baby swears. I don't think so!"

He tickled her playfully.

"No, Daddy," she said through fits of laughter. "I thought I heard noises."

"It was probably your sister." He put her down and she scurried to a seat next to her mother. "Speaking of which. Courtney! Get your butt outta bed! Join the ranks of the living!"

After he called up to the rooftops, he made his way to the coffee pot, where a nice fresh cup was ready for him. "Now that was fast. How do you do it, dear?"

"As quietly as possible." She chewed on her toast as she looked back to her paper.

Douglas had the charm and wit of any man but bore a striking resemblance to a young James Garner. And that was perfectly all right with Abigale.

Shortly after, Courtney, the bushy blond-haired wonder, appeared in the doorway, sneering at everyone as she sauntered over to the fridge, pulled out a canister of peanut butter and walked back to her room. She never ate breakfast with the family. Her attitude was, who would want to?

At 7:50 a.m., both little darlings were dressed and ready, backpacks packed. Abigale watched as they scurried onto the bus and set off for school. As she stood there, watching the bus leave, she was almost tempted to split herself into two again and have her double chaperone the kids to school. But if she was to be considered normal by the neighbors, she was just going to have to suck it up and worry along with the rest of the world's mothers. If they could do it, so could she.

She closed the door behind her and headed for the kitchen. Her husband was still there, sipping his coffee and staring out the back window. She snuck up behind him, wrapping her arms around his waist.

Peeking over his shoulder, she saw what he was staring at; a male painted bunting perched on their fence. It had a red breast and hints of blue, yellow and green on its backside. To anyone else, it was a simple colorful bird, nothing more. But for Abigale, it was a signal. A predestined signal that would only come along when it was that time again. Abigale, try as she might, tried to wish the bird away. Sadly, that was one little trick that wasn't in her bag. She hated that painted bunting about as passionately as she hated world war.

Although, she did feel fortunate to be able to get the signal to let her know it was time.

Her husband knew something was wrong.

"Abigale, you're hurting me," he said.

Forgetful, she unhooked herself from his waist. He started breathing in big puffs as if he'd just lost a wrestling match. He looked at her awkwardly then set his cup down on the counter.

"That's one grip you got there. Pilates teach you that?"

She giggled, a tear creeping out of her eye, then it oozed right back in. Of course she would tell him, she'd told him countless times before. Each time that she did, she'd wipe the memory out of his head. There was never a right way to put it, and so far, it had always met with hostility.

"I'm not normal, Doug."

"What's normal?"

"No, I mean, there's something in my genetic code. A defect that allows me to control things with my mind. If I will it, it happens."

He paused.

He moved closer to her, playing along with what he thought was a game. "How much power do you have in that beautiful little head of yours?"

"You know when every woman has her period, how she can say that she can just destroy the planet?"

"Sometimes one time too many," he chided playfully. "But yes."

"It's so dangerous. It works."

"Really?"

"Real as reality."

Douglas looked around, nodding in agreement. Obviously he was skeptical but still in a good enough mood to carry on with the game. "Then tell me, darling, how come the world is still spinning?"

"I enjoy it too much to want to destroy it."

"But you can literally destroy it?"

"Not here. Another one."

"Which one?"

"Pluto."

"Pluto? You've destroyed Pluto?"

"It's just a big rock of ice. Not really a planet when you think of it. Just a ball of ice in an orbit. No life there. Don't worry, I checked."

"Pardon me, but isn't that a tad farfetched?"

"I can prove it to you."

The phone rang.

Abigale clicked her tongue and the signal went on speakerphone. "Jerry, so good of you to call. Douglas will call you back. He hasn't found the fishing line yet but he promises he'll get to it. Say hi to Margot for me."

Douglas was staring at the speaker, utterly amazed that it came on without her pressing the button.

Then, like a delayed punch line to the end of a joke, Jerry said. "Oh. Yes. Fine. Um. Yeah. Bye."

Again, Abigale clicked her tongue and the call ended.

Douglas, blinked, his eyes were searching for something inside his own head, almost like he was thinking something over. Had this happened before, many different ways?

Somehow, his mind was telling him to believe rather than stray, that he had had far too much experience with powers beyond belief to be doubtful now.

"So instead of using your powers for evil, you've decided to live a life with me."

"Yes. It's calming."

"So why the long face?"

"Every time I am able, a painted bunting stops by our house to give me the signal. Mother Nature is my correspondence. She's telling me that it's time."

"Time for what?"

Abigale approached him, leaned forward and kissed him. The kiss was so passionate and ever so tasty. The sheer power of the kiss was so overwhelming that Douglas couldn't help but close his eyes tightly. When he opened them, they were standing in their bedroom. The door moved with the will of Abigale and closed behind them.

Downstairs, the radio came alive once more, this time it was squealing, then exploded in sparks.

Toast popped out of the toaster, windows banged open and shut. Electricity was surging through the house and the furniture trembled. After a while, everything was calm.

It was done.

And instead of being happy about the whole ordeal, Abigale was sad. Her husband was there to comfort her. "Did I hurt you?"

"No," she sniffled. "It's not that."

"Then what? What has you so upset?"

"I'm pregnant."

"Come on, it doesn't work that fast."

"It will though."

She stared at the clock on their nightstand and squinted hard to make it rise and levitate. It defiantly objected. To her, it was a blessing and a curse. Meant to trade one joy for another.

"My power is gone," she said softly.

Douglas felt ashamed. "How can that be?"

"It was supposed to be."

"How long will you be powerless?"

"Nine months."

I.F.

In the time before Christ, man discovered fire. Naturally, the discovery came with fear…then fascination. Fire served as a tool for beginning man.

In June 2023, a man with no prior history of accomplishments made a frightening discovery. Just like the early man, first came fear…then fascination.

A four-story apartment building became complete smoldering rubble in a matter of hours. Fifteen people were consumed and die, wailing in confusion as they expired. Onlookers stared at the building in disbelief and awe.

No one dialed for a fire truck.

After the investigation, it was determined that it was a fire. But the strangest discovery came from the witness statements. Each story sounding exactly the same - irregular. Every single one of them had said that the building wasn't on fire at all. That it just mysteriously disintegrated into thin air. The bricks and wood blackened and spread, almost like a plague spreading along the outline. Before they knew it, the building began disappearing. The smell was awful. There was no smoke, no flames.

The people inside clamped to their windows and screamed in agony as their rooms where decaying before their eyes, as their skin melted on the glass they were beating upon. Immense heat sucked all the life out of the building.

As a chief arson investigator, I've never come across a more unsettling case.

When you're dealing with fire, you're dealing with a fickle mistress. It's expected for her to ruin the lives of those she touches. But when the mistress turns into the mistress that never was…then you begin to question.

I was under the impression that nothing could change the elements surrounding us. Wind still blows, water flows, earth grows, fire shows. Nothing to it, really. It's basic common knowledge. That's what I thought.

Until I saw it firsthand.

A hobo, pushing his cart along Lineage Drive spots something he can't comprehend. He thinks he's going crazy. So, with the change he saved up from cans, he takes it upon himself to call somebody. Anybody. That one 'anybody' contacts the fire department. They arrive on the scene, bringing me along for some kind of explanation to this madness.

An abandoned factory near the bridge. Even as I see it, I still can't believe it. I could feel the heat, but there are no flames. There is no glow. The damn monstrosity of a worn building is disappearing right before my eyes, seemingly all by itself.

And instead of being greeted by loud, licking, roaring flames, I'm standing there in the dark hearing nothing but a slow sizzle.

I'm snapped out of my idiot trance as the boys felt that the tradition of rushing water would not let them down. They spray in a sweeping motion with the fire hose. It seems to be slowing down the process, but with black night being unforgivable, they aren't sure where to aim. They began testing patterns. It is remarkable. For centuries, man has been dealing with fire the old-fashioned way. But on that night, all the professionalism is drained out of these fine young men as quickly as the water rushing out of the once useful hose.

I come home beaten and battered, smelling like phantom smoke, feeling as if God decided to play a joke on me.

After twelve hours of firefighting, I go in to survey the scene. The chemical tests later confirm that it was indeed a fire. But there is a faint trace of something else. A scent that I picked up that the computer dubs UNKNOWN. Now isn't that the topsy-turvy way. What technology can't find, my nose can. And I don't even have that good of a sense of smell. I consider myself normal, not special at all.

I down some hard whiskey even though it's illegal now.

I don't care.

The phone rings and it's morning. I'm still wearing the clothes from the night before. There's drool on the collar of my overcoat. My breath tastes foul. I yank myself from my recliner.

Crunching? Hmmm.

I must have dropped the glass in the middle of the night.

I pick up the small, dime-sized receiver and stick it in my ear. After tapping it twice, the thing reads my fingerprint and connects me with the call.

"Hurst!" a voice cries.

"W…what? Who? Tone it down a bit."

"It's Danbarid. Where the fuck have you been? I've been calling you all morning!"

"I took a sedative, yeah, to help me sleep," I lied.

"There's no time! There's no time!"

"Time for what?"

"Hurst, I'm sorry! There was no way of knowing. It was another one of those disintegrators again!"

"Are you serious? Where the hell are all these coming from?"

"Hurst! Pay attention! There's more to this!"
"Spit it out, then! I sure as hell ain't stoppin' ya!"
"Jake and Maggie were in it."

Jake and Maggie Hurst. Brother and sister. Both married. Both have kids. Both very close. Both in the same hotel at the same time. What are the odds of that?

I am there when they open the body bags. My hands touch their flaky charred skin. My arms move all on their own, lifting them up and pressing both of their blackened faces into my chest, ruining my overcoat with two ink blot type smudges. My tears are no comfort to them. They drizzle over their foreheads and are lost.

My children.

Lost.

More whiskey. It's the only thing I live for now. The mistress is getting the better of me.

Ten more unexplained disintegrators proved that this was the work of a very determined arsonist. One who found a way to make flames invisible to the naked eye. Hell is hell and no one can change it. But if you can't see it coming for you…well…that's another hell all together.

The only thing I had to show for it was that strong pointed scent, invading my nostrils. I became ill, paranoid to be exact. I could smell the scent on me all the time and thought it would consume me from the nose down, just like fire. But it didn't. I wished it would though. The whiskey wasn't erasing the pain quick enough.

Nothing would. The only thing left for me was to face the bastard who burned my life down.

I had to find him.

For some reason, I stood to emphasize my determination. I

tripped over the two wobbly legs that God gave me and landed on my glass, breaking it. What a pathetic mess I was. Sure, I would catch him. But first, I would need to sober up.

Thirty-six more I.F.'s (short for invisible fires) popped up all over the city. Religious fanatics called it the end of the world. I called it the end of buildings. Never been much for superstitions. I've been more of the type that if I can see it, I know it exists. But I guess that changed over time too. Everything does.

I walked amidst the struggling chaos that this fair city had to offer. I saw men and women crying for salvation, crying for an answer. An answer. Anything. I needed one too.

For days, I shuffled around the city, wandering aimlessly, only stopping to eat and use public restrooms. My life was reduced to a choppy, sleep deprived existence.

One night, walking into an alley, puking from all the junk food I had eaten, I found something extraordinary. I found the greasy son of a bitch.

To this day, no arson investigator is permitted to see the accused under any circumstances, even in the case of being victimized by his previous crimes. Scumbags like these get to see their lawyer first before anything. Then again, times have been a changin'. I had to bribe four people with fifteen pounds of pure sugar. Can't get the stuff anyplace else other than my medicine cabinet. I think I may have been the last person to buy some before that got outlawed as well. Not good for you, the government said. Degenerate psychopaths aren't good for us either, Uncle Sam. Haven't you heard?

With a heavy heart, but a victorious will, I closed the door behind me and locked it. The room was cold and blue. Fitting.

Through hundreds of man-hours, we tried to find this chaos

man, this ghost. And I had to be the one to stumble across him. It was too easy. You can imagine, that didn't sit well with me.

Here was a man I could never imagine, not even in my most vivid nightmares.

The boots that dressed his feet were muddy and old, both held together by two different colors of lace. If I had to guess, I'd have to say that they came from as far back as the 90's. He wore charcoal slacks with an old-fashioned rope to hold them up. A white, grease-stained shirt was underneath his wrinkled long-sleeved navy blue dress shirt, with the sleeves rolled up to his elbows to expose his hairy arms. His arms were folded across his chest, unmoving. This guy didn't have the shakes as most arsonists do. That was a first. His dark hair looked as if it was infested with sewage. It was greasy, wet, full of dandruff. I thought saw something move within that mesh of a head. There were bags under his eyes, and they were bloodshot as well. There were only faint traces of stubble around his chin and his upper lip.

On the table in front of him was a mike.

I felt myself walking toward it…and I turned it off.

I sat down across from him, reached into my pocket and retrieved the small baggie with the personal effects we found on him. As I sighed, through my nose, I laid the three items on the scratched-up table as efficiently as if I was setting up chess pieces.

It wasn't much to go off of, to tell you the truth. Nothing but a blank cash strip, some cigarettes and two tinfoil sealed sticks of chewing gum.

I was expecting more.

I expected matches at least.

Looking down at the items, I found no comfort. There should be something more!

So I decided to add to the pile.

I pulled out my wallet and found two photos. One of Jake at five years old. The other of Maggie at seven. I slid them both across the table under his view, folded up my wallet and stared at him, maliciously.

After a long pause, I spoke first.

"You burned my babies."

He looked up at me on the last word, rolled his eyes, and scratched his head. "Funny, you should call them that. I figured them for adults."

My chair screeched as I stood fast and clobbered him across the jaw. His head made a sudden jerk, but he did not show pain. I didn't like the tone of his voice. That stupid voice. That bastard of a voice. That voice which was the sound of a smoker justifying his breath.

"Strike one," I grinned.

He licked his lips, looking bored.

"For the record, state your fuckin' name," I said.

"Riley Frears."

"Well, seeing as how you have no identification on your person, I'll take that as your alias. We'll see if we can get a match in our system, won't we?"

"I guess."

I blinked toward his pack.

"Have a cigarette every once in a while?"

"Sometimes."

"Like one now?"

"Wouldn't hurt."

Quickly, I raised my fist and smashed his stupid little cigarettes to grains. Using the same hand, I wiped them off of the table and out of the equation of items.

"Feels good, doesn't it? Fucking around with someone's head," Riley said.

From this, I didn't know how to respond. I admit, I was trying to scare him, but I guess this side-street bum was immune to intimidation no matter how far up the ladder you were.

Now I felt him, trying to run this game of mine. So I let him talk.

"Suppose you figured me for a raging psychopath. A man living on the edge. But the truth is, I'm not a psychopath. I'm not even a man with a plan. I'm just a man who stumbled into the discovery of the new century."

"Discovery? Enlighten me, Riley."

"Happy to. I don't have to tell you about Larson Industrials."

"Yeah, I know the company."

"But do you know of their chemicals?"

"What chemicals?"

"Two chemicals. On one side there is ZX13, a fine white powder used in common fertilizers. Then there is X12Z5, a green powder most commonly used as an acid for developing pictures. While running from the law, trying to look for a place to sleep, I wandered into one of Larson Industrials' factories. It was abandoned, rundown, waiting to be torn down.

"I was cold. Stupidly cold. So cold I was desperate to have heat. Sleeping on a rusted grated floor was my bottom low. So, I dragged over an empty barrel and loaded it with a quart of regular gasoline. Found the two chemicals, figured them for drugs, figured I'd burn those two, maybe get a high from the fumes, you know. Being high makes you forget who you are and just how poor you are.

"And wouldn't you know it, fifteen minutes later, I found that the flames that warmed me up were slowly disappearing. I figured myself baked, hallucinating it. But my senses told me otherwise. I felt the heat, could feel it. But I couldn't see it. And then, the heat got inside my head. Changed my way of thinking – yes, sir. Imagine what it would be like if the great Chicago fire went on for weeks simply because it was never seen."

I smashed my fist against his teeth again.

"Strike two," I said, sweating with impatience. "And you're on thin ice."

This time Riley drooped his lower lip out in order to catch the blood that was dripping from his nose. With his right index finger, he scooped up some of it and wiped it on the table.

"Sorry to disappoint you like this, Hurst, but I can't feel a damn thing that you've been dishing out. My nerves are numb. I can't feel anything. Is that clear?"

"Operation?" I asked.

"Birth defect. Aren't I lucky?"

"Oh I wouldn't think so. We caught you."

"Only because I wanted you to."

"I doubt that."

"You caught me in the alley starting a normal store fire. It was only after I admitted to the I.F.'s that you decided to bring me in."

"Think again, shithead. We have several people who could put you at the scene."

"Yeah. I'm a sucker for watching my own work."

"You're going to hell."

He jerked, his mouth frothed over so fast I had to remind myself mentally that I was the one who was supposed to scare *him*.

"I am the hell fire! I am the carnage of the streets! I brought the hell that surrounds all of us every waking moment to the surface! Is it so wrong to bring the fire that comes and devours the wicked?"

"You are nothing special. You're not even a footnote in the book of life, my friend."

I reached for one of the sticks of gum. Since I couldn't bring my whiskey in here, I figured on chewing something to calm my nerves. It's an oral fixation and one that I haven't been able to get over.

My nerves were a jumbled mess, nagging me to say something more. But it was hard to breathe when you were at the bottom.

Just as I was unwrapping the blue stick of gum, Frears moved forward, eyes wide, anxiously looking at the gum.

"Let's join our pieces!"

"What?"

"Is it all right for me to have my piece if I agree you can have that one?"

Normally, I would have cracked him across his stupid-ass chin, but this old dog was tired and could care less. People have their habits. It would show that I'm not all stone and could give him at least a chew of his own gum, giving him one last taste of freedom to accommodate his grim departure out of this world. I knew that he would get the death penalty.

I nodded briefly.

With his dirty hands, he unfoiled the gum and sniffed it enthusiastically.

I continued to hold mine in my hand, fixated on how this creep functioned. Truth be told, I forgot the piece was even in my hand.

Something didn't feel right.

"It's my duty to tell you," I said, "that you've made a lot of people angry. You've ruined lives, caused billions in property damage, may have caused a collapse in the government structure. I suppose an anarchist arsonist like you eats that up for breakfast. But you could have done something beautiful with this discovery. Can't you at least see that? Man always has a choice to take something rotten and breathe new life into it. Do you understand? You had a choice. Now you must live with the wrong one that you made."

With a smile that had the sharpness of thumbtacks, he lightly folded the piece of gum into his mouth. He breathed in, exotically, one could say.

"Strike three," he breathed heavily.

Then, with the horrified thought I had come to realize, I got up and backed myself into the wall, my hands in my pockets, my body shaking.

Before my eyes Frears was starting to change. Around his mouth I could see bubbles. They were blisters, they were popping, leaking fluids over his lips, which were sizzling like bacon as he chewed so vigorously.

He was chewing on the mistress herself.

He rose from his chair, the table blackened as he placed his hands on it. And now came the insane choking laughter that rose up in his throat as his hair began to shorten.

I don't remember scrambling for the door, but, within that instant, I kicked it open and closed it shut with a slam of my shoulder. My fumbling fingers found the lock and cranked it a good one. The man was now locked inside with his friendly invisible flames.

He came up to the glass, still laughing, eyes melting, slamming his fists up against the door.

The room blackened behind him, pulling the plague over the room. The sprinkler system kicked on, gushing its relief in the room as well as outside in the hallway. The running water ruined my hat. Through all the dripping, I could see him flail, still smiling and throwing things in the room.

In no time at all, people hurled themselves around the corner like a wave and met me at the door. The poor bastards believed that they could pry me away. I firmly clenched the handle and didn't budge. Not even when they threatened the end of my career, my pension, my life after my work life. Call me old-fashioned, but I wanted to watch the bad man burn, and no one was going to take that way from me without a fight.

The sprinkler system shut off suddenly. It surprised everyone. And as everyone was looking up, I drew my gun, aimed it in a sweeping motion and yelled, "Back!"

"Goddamn it, Hurst! You are going crazy! Put it down! Let us through!" they all said.

Not a chance.

The room was still burning, and the man was still moving fast, jumping around like a chicken with it's head cut off. I know that he could feel the pain, the heat. He was doing this song and dance for show. And what a show it was!

"What would you have done?" he shouted at the top of his screeching lungs. "WHAT WOULD YOU HAVE DONE? WHAT WOULD YOU HAVE DONE? WHA WO YOU HAV DON?! WHA HAV YO A DON? WHA HA YO DEN?"

Try as he might, he could not stop the invisible flames from burning up his lungs. Even as he kept thrashing around, giving me a new nightmare to get over, he was getting sluggish.

I turned back to my coworkers and supervisors. Their faces, all of them, like stone.

Shivering, I found the gum I had absently placed in my

pocket. To my astonishment, I wrapped it back in the tin foil before I left the room. Here she was, the slippery, sultry mistress. With all the lives she had consumed and all the hearts she had broken with the aid of this man who was misguided by her hot, loving charm.

I kept telling myself, throughout my career *only for good* is what you do. Turn something rotten into something productive.

Now I had the power.

But it was scary to comprehend.

Handle it with care.

Keep it safe.

Change it.

What would you have done? he said.

What *would I* have done?

We'll see.

Gun Control

On Glock Block, neighbors stayed in their homes, no matter what. The only thing they did properly was open the door to answer it and then close it. The entire block was a populace of shut-in's and yet, somehow, plants were watered, lawns were mowed, and papers were delivered. All outsiders tried to peek in.

So, on a Thursday, it came to be a puzzling forty-seven degrees. Adrian Kapp, A.K. as the neighbors called him, always predicted a whopping forty-seven degrees.

Two strangers trotted along the valley-like front lawns of the people they would visit. Both men wore sharp black suits, hair slicked back and toothpicks dangled from the corners of their sneers. Damian, the taller of the two, motioned for Dillon to pick up the pace. There was fresh dew on the grass which made it very difficult to walk on with dress shoes. Twice already he'd tripped, falling to his knee on the hand that carried the Uzi. He nearly dislocated his thumb the second time.

But Damian, with quick reflexes, saw that Dillon was about to go down a third time and caught his arm before he could slip.

Damian tapped his index finger a couple of times on the brow bone of his partner. "Got to keep up, bud. We ain't travelin' this far again."

This, for sure, Dillon knew. Damian was never a man to go back on his word.

Four houses wasn't much for a day's work.

The usual.

357...358...359, Dillon counted in his head.

They passed several house numbers.

Damian cleared his throat, clicking the safety back and forth on his silencer that he had anchored to his left hipbone. "Weather's been acting screwy."

"You think so?" Dillon asked.

"Course. Look at them clouds. Them ain't natural. Must be tornado season or something. Believe you me. Look at all that swirly shit."

No doubt, as Dillon stole a glance at the skies, the clouds were swirling here and there, crisscrossing the sky. Damian had an eye for these kinds of things. Some could say that noticing little nuisances such as these were Damian's daily bread, always noticing something out of the ordinary. There was always something underneath the surface.

First house.

Mr. Remington.

Late payments as usual.

Both men wiped their feet on the mat, brushing each other off. Dillon needed more brushing, grass blades sticking to his pant legs.

"Look at that," Damian complained. "It's all over your back as well. Just terrific. Here, turn around. I swear, if I haven't taught you nothin'..."

Dillon turned, arms outstretched. His boss curled the silencer under his armpit so he could use both hands at tidying up his protégé. When all was finished, he turned around and found a nod of approval from him.

Damian knocked once.

He only ever knocked once.

Both men stared down, with their friends made of polished steel snickering behind their backs. Their ears picked up some movement - a shuffling of steps as a person approached. Mr. Remington held the door wide open as the heat started to pour out into the outside air. His kitchen TV was on and glowing in the background. Coffee mug in hand, in his bathrobe and slippers, he nodded to both of them, eyes full of questions but he only uttered one. "May I help you two?"

Damian smiled at Dillon.

He knew that look.

"Excuse us, sir, but would you mind if we fuck up your day?"

Before the man could make the slightest frown with his eyebrows, sneaky silencer made an appearance and invited three marble-sized soldiers through the mug, cheek and heart of Mr. Remington. The blunt force of the blasts shifted the man's body in odd, almost hysterical ways, like a rain dance gone wrong, one could say.

The man fell on his back, his two fingers still holding onto the broken handle of the shattered, forgotten mug.

Damian spotted the TV, which sent sparks to the tile floor and breathed smoke from the middle of its cracked frame. "Damn it all. What luck. Did not mean to hit that thing? Oh well. Guess we can't all be so precise."

With a couple of nudges, he was able to shift Mr. Remington's legs back into the house and shut the door to hide the mess.

No one ever came out of their house.

Ever.

Second house.

This one was bigger than the last, very spoiled by the looks of it but with a terrible roof. Some shingles were missing.

As they walked up to the porch, Damian noticed this. "Now would you look at that? What a hack job. What with the weather changin' every fucking five seconds, you have to have sturdier roofs than that. My grandson could do a better job than these pricks. Oh, remind me that I have to put in a call for my nephew's house. Needs a good deal on a roof. Just got married."

"Congrats, to him."

"Shut up, Dillon."

One knock.

Somebody cursed inside, much noise. A flush. Somehow Dillon doubts that whoever was in the upstairs bathroom had the courtesy to wipe properly before opening the door and greeting strangers.

The man they call Mr. Ruger, a veteran of the war era, stumbled down the steps, cane firmly in hand, and eyed the two men through a passing glass window.

The door made creaking noises as three separate latches were either pulled back or unfastened.

Damian and Dillon tensed up, waiting for the sluggish man to open the door. Damian, Dillon noticed, continually clicked the safety on and off more rapidly than before.

Mr. Ruger pulled the door back, revealing his sullen, sunken green eyes, messy bedhead and a forest of uneven gray hairs that lined his beard.

With scrutinizing eyes, he sized them up to be salesmen from their suits, or possibly government. Even though he would never admit it out loud, he was hungry for the war again, but nowhere near as hungry as his next-door neighbor.

His shaky right hand eased the door wider, giving Dillon a partial few of Mr. Ruger's spotted, unsightly leg.

"May I help you?"

Damian cleared his throat, saying, "Just wanted to let you know that there's someone on your roof."

"Huh?"

Mr. Ruger craned his neck to the side and up to try and see over the storm gutters. All it took was one behind the ear and that was it.

The old man's eyes shut with a final, firm blink. Blood splattered the mailbox attached right next to him. And like a ton of bricks, he fell back and clattered to the carpeted entrance.

Damian couldn't help but smile. This one went easier than the last one. Sure, there were freckles of blood dripping from the doorframe, but Damian knew that it would be washed by the coming storm. Careful not to crush the old man's slippers, like before, he nudged the legs back into the house as he closed the door.

Dillon looked up as he heard the rumble-grumble of the clouds gloom.

Suddenly, he heard fingers snap.

"Pay attention, son." Damian lifted the smoking barrel up to his smile. "We're about ready to meet our quota. Just a couple more to go. If we're not tired, we'll do more."

The swirling blue smoke curled around his lips as a sly mustache would. Noticing this, he hooked his finger through it and rudely ushered Dillon on.

Third house.

An aging old thing.

The house of Mr. Wesson.

Excited, Damian toggled the safety catch even faster now. He practically hopped up the porch steps. Dillon was slow in his approach. Not once had he gotten the chance to flex his skills. It was always Damian who had all the fun. But, then again, he had been in the business a good long while, not to be outdone by someone who trips easily.

"Show some control," Dillon mumbled to himself.

Damian waved him over, agitated by his lack of enthusiasm.

"Are you ready?"

Dillon shrugged. "I guess."

"No guessing. Be on the ball, be presentable, be stable."

Damian huffed, puffed and knocked on the door.

On the other end, tires shuffled and squeaked.

A man answered the door, his face was long, his eyes foreboding, and as he ushered the door out of his way, his legs came into view, draped in a plaid red and green blanket. The metal wheelchair attached to him was old and rickety but served its purpose.

Old, crusty Mr. Wesson brought his arm back and set the brake so that he wouldn't roll right out of his own house.

"Well," he croaked, "what in the hell you fellows want?"

Damian took a deep breath.

"Free lead, sir!"

An exhilarating wave of euphoria washed over Damian as a few raindrops smacked against his already greasy hair. His arm came around his frame, introducing the man to a swollen panic that rose inside him. After the journey, the silencer presented itself with a deafening click.

Damian's face fell.

His arm frozen in time.

He forgot the safety catch.

Already, the old man was scrambling at the blanket that covered his loins.

Dillon, surprised by the sudden click, remembered that he himself had a gun, but he failed to use it.

The blanket rose, and the two men faced down a double barrel shotgun.

The shot that all three men waited for finally rang out, and it blew Damian across the lawn, catching him in his stomach and slamming him up against a parked car.

Dillon stumbled a few feet to the side, grabbing at the wall as his ears rang.

Mr. Wesson then aimed at him, noticed the grass stains on his pants, and gestured toward them with the shotgun.

Dillon looked down, thanked him, and brushed the few blades away. Then he stood upright and adjusted his tie. He lifted the Uzi and…

Bang!

Too slow.

The old man quietly breathed in a sigh of relief, gently bringing his shotgun to lay to rest across the armrests, the smoking barrels to his right, trigger end to his left.

His gray eyes marveled at the unmanageable sky. “Aw shoot,” he said, licking his lips. “We’re in for it, fellas. Just look at all that swirly shit.”

10 Days in the Extra Life

It was the middle of July, hot as hell, and all four of them would be down in Ronnie's cool basement. Drinking, playing games, having good times.

Ronnie pulled the shades to block the afternoon sun. He turned on all the lights, opened the fridge, pulled out a six-pack of buds and sat on the couch opposite the television. Paul, his best bud, would be over soon.

Ronnie was famous for keggar parties, but they were all bullshit. What he really loved was just hanging out in his basement drinking with his best buds. It was usually him, Mike and Paul, but Mike decided to bring in some new blood. Someone underage and stupid. At least, that's what Ronnie thought.

He took a beer from the stack and opened it. Quickly, he sucked in the suds. The fridge was stocked, the cable was set, the foosball was out (newly resurrected from the garage and had a few gouges in it), everything was set. There was a knock at the door. Let the party begin.

* * *

Paul spat out his beer, laughing hysterically. "There's no way," The suds gave him a white chin. He wiped them away. "There's no way, man."

Ronnie shook his head, laughing along with him. "I'm telling you. Ate his whole fist..."

Mike was busy watching the boob tube in the corner, building a pyramid of empty beer cans. He turned toward them, knocking his masterpiece down but chiming in himself, "Yeah. And his girlfriend walked right in on him and asked what he was doing."

"What happened then?" Paul asked.

"Well, he was trying to say 'Honey, I'm trying to break the world record here.' But all that came out was," He stuck his fist in his mouth, "'Oh no, I'm trying to fuck the waffle maker.' Or at least that's what she heard."

They all laughed, even the new guy, who was playing foosball with himself. He had blonde, muffled hair and mainly kept his thoughts and his hands buried deep within his hoody when he would sit. He could only stand two beers so far. Soon he would pass out, and all of them would plan to draw on his face in his sleep. It always happened to the new guy.

"Man," said Paul, "some guys are so stupid."

"Hey, we were put here to entertain the female of the species," said Ronnie.

"I can't believe it. Whatever happened to Jim?"

Ronnie spread his hands as if gazing into a crystal ball. "The legend says..."

Paul gave him a good jab in the arm. "Seriously, Ron."

"Okay, okay. The story, or at least the version I was told, is that after he said that, she ran out of the bathroom and started packing her stuff. She said that she would come back for the rest and that it would be unexpected. The guy, however, from shoving his massive fist in his mouth, because as you know, Jim has humongous hands, was taken totally by surprise. Anyway, he pulls it out of his mouth and his mouth is all rubbery. He can't spit out nothing but syllables. He was trying to ask her not to leave. He was practically blubbering his words together from the shock. You got to admit, it was a pretty weird predicament. The guy had his pants to his ankles."

"Why were his pants down to his ankles if he was pissin?"

"I…um…" said Mike, trying to interject but instead belched.

Ronnie continued, "Let me, *the Ron-myster* tell you. He's one of those aincy types. He feels that the pants constrict him while he's going so he pulls them all the way down. The bathroom, also you have to remember, was across from the door. So he was facing the wall when she barged in. The stupid-ass left the door unlocked."

"Yeah," Mike finally said. "And I admit it's pretty weird that he would choose right then and there to break a world record."

"Tell me he didn't use the trigger hand," Paul said.

"No, no, no," Ronnie assured. "Hell no. He was using his clean hand. But she didn't know that he had his hand in his mouth. He was trying to speak around it!"

Paul stifled a laugh. "So did she ever come back?"

Mike scraped all the cans off the table, watching them make muffled thumps against the red shag carpet. "Oh yeah. She came back all right." He stood up and put his hands on his knees for balance. "Took all her things and she took the waffle maker with her!"

They were clapping their hands, stomping their feet, enjoying their laughter.

From the laundry room, the new guy stepped out with another beer in his hand. "Whoa, what'd I miss?"

"You just missed the best part," Mike said through laughs.

Paul was having a fit, laughing uncontrollably. "Stop it, stop it. It hurts too much."

Ronnie waved a hand in front of Paul, eagerly trying to get his attention. "She left a note too. It read 'Jim. I know we've been having troubles, but that doesn't give you the right to grab the nearest household appliance. I'll never eat breakfast again.'"

Mike, at this time, fell onto the coffee table, rolling in his belly laughs.

The new guy pulled up a chair and took a seat between Paul

and Ronnie. He nursed his beer patiently. "What the hell are you guys talking about? Can't you start over?"

Ronnie, not even taking a break in his laughter, continued to joke with Paul. "Can you imagine trying to wrestle that thing away from him if it was true? What would he say?" Ronnie pretended to hold a waffle iron to his crouch, legs pointing east and west. "Hey! You Leggo my eggo!"

The new guy shook his head. He was completely lost and he hated it. "Why do you guys always do this? You always tell the juicy stories when I'm going to the bathroom. I'll never piss again."

Mike sat up from the coffee table faster than anyone anticipated. They all turned to him as he pointed at the new guy. "Now that would be a world record."

"I wouldn't hold it that long," said the new guy. "I'm not that brave."

"Maybe that's stating the obvious."

"How long do you think you could hold it?" Ronnie asked.

The new guy took another sip. Sighing overdramatically he said, "Welp, if it's a long car ride...oh...about ten hours."

Ronnie swatted the air. "Nah, I've held it longer than that."

"What were you doing?" Paul asked.

Ronnie looked at him to see he was now doing an impression of a cowboy riding a bull, but everyone knew it was something else he was referring to. "Very funny, Paul."

"I'm just saying, man. I'm just saying."

Mike looked at his watch. "Friggin' time. I gotta wake up early for a morning shift." He yawned as if to confirm his point.

"Hey," Ronnie said. "Didn't you stay up all day? Why are you going into work in the morning? Why don't you take the day off? You need sleep, man."

"No, no." Mike firmly shook his head. "I need the money. Besides, *The Guinness Book of World Records* says that the only guy ever to even feel the haziness effects was around the third day."

Paul whistled. "Third day? How long did he stay awake

for?"

"A full ten days." Mike said.

They all whistled.

"Impressive." Paul said.

"Crazy," the new guy said.

"Bull!" Ronnie spat.

"Hey, I kid you not," Mike said. "He never made it to the eleventh day. I think you'd start to lose your mind then."

Paul thought about this for a while as he sipped his beer. When he looked up, he noticed all the others were thinking about it too. "I wouldn't. I do it all the time. I stay up here and there. It's no problem. I bet I could make it to the eleventh."

"Now *that* I would pay to see," Ronnie said.

"Hold up!" Mike stood. He came over to his friends, plucked a new beer out of the pile and sat on the opposite side between Paul and Ronnie. He directed his question to Ronnie, a glint in his eye. "Did you by chance mention greenbacks?"

"Yes, Sir Galahad, I did."

"How much?"

"I'm willing to bet fifty bucks that he can do it. He looks like the sturdy type."

"I bet you one hundred that he doesn't."

"No bullshit?"

"No bullshit.'

"Hey, hey, hey," Paul said. "I hope I'm not going to be the only one doing this, here."

Ronnie nodded. He set down his beer, sat up and disappeared into the office next to the laundry room. He called it an office because that's where he wrote his songs and kept fresh stacks of musical sheets and pencils. But it was really just a closet. He came back with one blank musical sheet and a pencil. He sat down and began writing. "Well, we'll split it up into different bets."

Mike put up his hand in protest. "I can't do the sleeping thing. I've already got problems with that. I got work. I'm not lazy like you bums."

Ronnie grumbled. "Why don't you shut the hell up for ten days? That's something I've been wishing for for a long time now."

Mike smiled and raised his beer like he was about to give a toast. "Easy as pickety-pie." Then he gulped the last of his beer.

"God, I hate it when you say that. Believe me, I won't miss it. All right, we'll do a hundred a bet. Whoever drops out forfeits their dough. Whoever is left standing wins the pot."

"I thought we were betting money," Mike laughed.

"Of course we're betting money."

"Just checkin'."

"Let's see. For Paul: no sleeping, For you, Mike: no talking, and…"

"I bet I can hold it longer than ten hours," the new guy said quietly. "I'll try it."

"No, no," Ronnie waved a pencil at him. "We've got to be on the safe side here. Try and hold it for three days."

"Got to piss or crap?"

"Well, I'm not going to do neither till I get up."

"No, which one do I hold, I mean."

"I don't know. Pick one. You could maybe hold in crap for at least ten days. But stick with it."

"What about me and Mike?" Paul asked. "What's our limit?"

"Ten days a piece. It's too risky to try to reach the eleventh day, Paul."

"You just let me worry abo..."

"No! I'm betting on you. I call the limit."

"Right, whatever."

"What about you?" Mike asked, pointing his beer at Ronnie. "What're you gonna do?"

Ronnie thought about this. He was never one to take risks, never the one to stick his neck out even for the sake of others. But if he had to give these boys an answer, he would. "I dunno. I'll…I'll…um. Fingernails, right? There's something in that book about a woman with the longest fingernails. I bet I can..."

Paul and Mike were both shaking their heads now. Paul sat forward for once. "Not that. It has to be something risky."

Ronnie thought again. He lifted his eyes, serious was never his strong suit, but he faked it brilliantly. "I won't drink water for ten days straight."

"What?" the new guy couldn't believe it.

"I'll just drink pop or something, but I won't touch water at all."

"Guys, come on. This is getting serious."

Paul patted him on the shoulder. Poor kid. "A hundred dollars each is serious, junior. There ain't no way I'm dropping out."

Ronnie put the pencil down after he finished scribbling one more thing. "So it's set. We all start tomorrow morning."

"Piece of cake," Mike said.

"It'll be a snap," Paul said.

"I dunno," the new guy murmured.

Ronnie folded the bit of paper and stuck it in his pocket. It was a bit of insurance. He had their numbers and their friend's numbers. He'd set up a network of people to watch them, make sure they stuck to their guns, to be kept on their toes. And if any of them gave out, he would collect. Lord knew he needed four hundred bucks for a new amp and maybe a new guitar. He could burn a CD and send it off to record companies, maybe make his start, all off a whim of a stupid bet. *Rolling Stone* would love that. "So what do you think your girlfriend will say about it, Paul?"

"Hey," Paul said, holding his chin high, "Paul Roven makes his own destiny."

Game start. Begin level. That's all it is, Paul thought *Just a game. And I'm going to take those suckers for all they're worth.*

~

It was midnight when Paul woke up on Saturday. He wasn't going to risk losing this bet. He got ten good hours of sleep that he figured would last him two days top. The third day would be brutal, no doubt. But if he could make it over that hump, everything would be golden.

He shut off his alarm and sat up. In the dark he found a clean shirt and threw it on. He was wearing his shorts and walked to his fridge. Once there, he filled a popcorn bowel with ice cubes and then walked across the apartment to the bathroom. Leaving the door open, he poured the ice cubes into the sink as he got out one last yawn. Everything was still a little bit hazy.

He turned on the sink with cold water for about five seconds and turned it off. For five minutes he looked at his watch, waiting for that sink to get frost cold.

He stood up and hovered over the sink, hands gripping the edges. He looked at his watch. First day. 12:35 a.m. He could do it. "Paully Roven on the rocks, it is," he mumbled.

He didn't move.

"C'mon. Just do it, you wimp."

He felt himself dozing a little, then shook his head and plunged his face into the frosty glacial puddle.

~

Ronnie never believed in pedestrians having the right of way. *They need to get out of the way. C'mon get,* he thought. *I have a car. I will hurt you badly. Thanks for taking forever, jag off. Sheesh, if I ever have to see that tomato head again, I swear.*

He parked in front of his apartment complex, getting out of his truck to the warm afternoon air.

An elegant, but powerful, black hand pulled him away from the door and slammed him up against the driver's side window. The woman was not strong but caught Ronnie in mid hop and by surprise, which put him off balance. He stared into her furious eyes but couldn't get those angelic lips out of his mind, even if she was shouting at him.

"Sheena, I…"

"What gave you the right?" she screamed.

"What? C'mon, I gotta go…"

"No!" She shoved him back, keeping her weight on him, not caring if she was crushing him. "I wanna know! No! I wanna know! Who do you think you are gambling with my boyfriend's life?"

"He agreed." He shoved her away. "We all did."

"Oh I bet you're sitting pretty right now, aren't you? Do you realize what I have to go through?" She was on the brink of tears, sniffling. "He's completely shutting me out! He never shuts me out! It's been seven days already, and you've turned him into something else! That *thing* who locked himself up in his own place is not my boyfriend."

"I told him to quit."

She gave him two good slaps across the face which he did not block. Instinctively he raised his hand but carefully lowered it and put it behind his back. He was ashamed, but he would listen to her. "You told him at the wrong damn time! You're his friend! You were supposed to tell him not to get in it from the start!"

"I'm just following what he said."

She was in hysterics now. "What? What? What did he tell you? What did *he* tell you?"

"Paul Roven makes his own destiny."

"He said *what*?"

"Paul Roven makes his own destiny. That's what he said to me. I almost didn't want to look into his eyes when he said it. It's just…those eyes. Well, I don't have to tell you. You seen 'em, haven't you?"

She held herself tightly and shivered.

This scared Ronnie, but he wouldn't show it. Not for her. Not for anybody.

"I didn't see *him*."

"I have to go." Ronnie opened his car door again, realizing he still had his keys in his hand. "I have to get to work. If you want, you can go and talk to Mike and see if he can…"

Sheena laughed manically. Ronnie kept his back turned. He knew what was coming next. He knew exactly what she would say.

"Well, we all know what happened to Mike now, don't

we?"

~

From Ronnie's network of spies, friends he did favors for and gave beer to, to his knowledge, this is what he knew. Mike, after spending nine days in silence, but staying active, frequently jogging, decided to give up the contest and talk to some girl sitting on a bench. He couldn't. Panicked he rushed to the hospital where, after evaluation, they found that his vocal chords had atrophied. The doctors said that he was born with naturally weak vocal chords and his hectic lifestyle mixed with this recent vow of silence had errantly damaged his vocal ability. He later quit his job and moved back in with his parents where he was currently trying hard to learn sign language from his mother.

The new guy, whose name was really Leonard, was currently at the same hospital, going through emergency surgery for a bowel blockage. He was currently recovering.

Ronnie, unknown to all, was a cheater at anything, especially when it came to bets. This one was no different. He carried on in his apartment as usual, drinking water whenever he felt like it. No one was the wiser.

But Paul Roven was a special case. Paul, to the amazement of the spies, only had activity during the first three days of his bet. He kept his lights on at all hours of the night, read magazines by the basket, kept his apartment and himself tidy. But on the third day, sometime between 7:30 and 7:45 at night, one of Ronnie's spies walked by to see Paul sitting outside in a lawn chair rapidly talking to someone on his left and his right - even though there was no one there. After that peculiar night, Paul confined himself to his apartment, convinced that the outside world had a breakable frame and was a level he could not cross. Ronnie very much doubted he would get any money out of the bet now.

~

The apartment was an absolute wreck. Paul, the man who chose his own destiny, was truly convinced that he was going mad. It was now the tenth day in his no-sleeping cycle, but that didn't matter now. Collecting on the bet didn't matter now. He wanted, he needed, to reach the eleventh day. There was something hidden. Hidden in time, he knew it. He felt a tear occur in time. He realized that being awake for two days offered only a marginal buzz.

But that third day.

That day he met the others.

Two of them just showed up, practically mirror images of himself. For the first few hours of their arrival, they acted like newborns; mouthing words, eating mud, asking where they came from. They found some crayons in the park and brought them home, in adorable handwriting, they etched 'Day One' and 'Day Two' on their white shirts. Like something out of a twisted Dr. Sues tale, they wrecked his apartment, looking for something. Perhaps their sanity.

No nine-foot cat arrived in a striped hat, thank God. Instead, every day that passed brought another of the Paul Roven duplicates. With each day passing, slower and slower, Paul noticed that the duplicates were getting smarter. They taunted him at night, kept him awake: afraid that they would disappear when there was five of them.

Paul sheltered himself in the bathroom where it was cold. It was the only room in his apartment that he could stand. Every time he walked out into his once spacious apartment, his senses would go into overdrive. The colors of his world were now distant greens and yellows. He saw every speck of dust inside the apartment and gave them names like planets in a solar system.

He only had one food group when he decided to retire to the bathroom indefinitely - applesauce. He drank his water from the sink, he took cold showers frequently. He never changed his clothes.

There was a point where he was certain that he could penetrate walls, the others could not.

Paul pondered whether he was Martin Luther King Jr, John

Lennon, Jack Lemon, Walter Mathieu, Mama Cass, Abraham Lincoln, and Edgar Allan Poe. While he was going through this identity crisis he found that his watch told him he was debating this for thirty seconds. But to him, it felt as if a month had passed by.

Letters would slip under the door, the phone would ring like crazy until he unplugged it, occasionally there was a knock or two but no more, or he just didn't hear them anymore on the ninth day. All sounds were now harmonic and echoed until they eventually became one screeching sound. Except for the others' voices, they were always different.

The bathroom door opened a creak, to Paul's surprise.

"Someone's in here!" he shouted instinctively.

The person who looked exactly like Paul in every way came in and smirked at him, sitting next to the bowel of the toilet, slurping his applesauce from a cup.

"I figured," said the teen.

"Who are you?" Paul asked. "You're not from around here, are you?"

"I'm Ten. I would have hoped that you were expecting me." Ten sat on the edge of the tub, folding his arms across his lap. "We need to have a talk, Paul."

"I'm listening."

"You need to stop this. Look what it's doing to you. Look what it's doing to *them*." He gestured out the door where Paul could see from where he was sitting that all of his duplicates were horsing around with each other. Three were in the kitchen discussing philosophy, which was no big surprise. Days Four, Five and Six were wrestling with each other. Then Paul spotted one of them holding what looked like an arm, feeding itself on the muscles of the fallen Day Nine.

Paul laughed then muttered, "Seven ate nine."

"Look at you. All this for more money. Now you don't even care about that." Day Ten shook his head. "What are you after?"

Paul tried to focus on Ten. "There is something, isn't there? I'm sure as hell not playing this game for nothing."

Day Ten sighed. Paul knew that Ten was not one to give up the goods, but he also detected a hint of sympathy in his eyes. "You're messing with time. And time is starting to lose track of you."

"Losing track?"

"Time, like all things, has its place. Everyone follows it, adheres to it, accepts it. Your body and your mind do not. You're lost to time. You may not know it, but time is a living, breathing thing. Once you start fooling with that, you're off the radar. You are in time out."

"I've lost my place?"

"Not permanently. If you decided to stop now, you can go back. You'll be granted the fabled extra life."

"Extra life?"

"Paul, stay with me. You sound stupid when you repeat your elders."

"Sorry."

"It's fine. The extra life is what you will be granted. All you have to do is blink and it will happen."

"But…there has to be something more. Isn't there something that happens on the eleventh day?"

"Yes, but I doubt you would enjoy it. You, me, all your friends in the next room disappear."

"You're lying."

"You can't risk testing me, young man." Ten pointed a finger at him. His voice was ragged and cold. "Here you are dealing with the fabric of life in time's place. To upset that flow is to flood a dam. You. Will. Burst. Paul. I'm merely giving you an escape hatch. To be nothing or your original. That's it."

Paul whimpered. He was tired, his sturdy reserve was gone. He felt the crumbling sensation of defeat. This humbling experience showed Paul that you cannot conquer time; it will catch up with you.

"What's the matter?" Day Ten taunted. "Little boy, are you afraid? Well, don't just sob yourself into a corner. Choose your destiny, tough guy."

Paul wanted to say something.

"Will it..."

Paul blinked.

~

Paul found himself laughing. When he opened his eyes, he saw Ronnie laughing in front of him. The new guy, Leonard, was also laughing to his right. Mike was equally lost in laughter to his left. Paul, dazed, wiped the beer suds from his chin. He had received the easy way out. Paul chose.

He got the joke, but would not delight in it. He set down his beer, went into Ronnie's closet and took with him all the music sheets and all the pencils to write with. Before he could climb up the stairs, Ronnie stood, spilling his beer on the carpet. "Hey! What the hell are you doing?"

Paul turned to them. He gave a wise and wistful nod. "Just making sure you guys don't do something stupid."

Regenerhate

It all began with a severed finger. The finger in question used to belong to a man named Mel Larkin. Mel Larkin, as you may already know, was a very pompous celebrity. Like many young hopefuls, he began by doing commercials and worked his way through various studio pictures. By the time he did his first sex scene at the age of twenty-one, he was sipping champagne every day and living in a mansion five times larger than a normal dwelling, isolated from the world except when he had an appointment with his agent.

On his way to his agent, never bothering to invite him to his mansion, in his eye-catching silver Rolls-Royce, he marveled at how he was all over the city. Posters, magazine stands, billboards. His Romanesque features were stunning even to him. He was amazed that he was where he was rather than in that deli that his father owned, making a measly 5.25 an hour.

For some reason, he ran to the elevator. He could have easily waited for the next one, but, as with all rising stars, they needed to have everything now. It was instinctual.

Coffee! Now.

Massage! Now.

Paper! Now.

Makeup! Now.

And at that point in time, due to his feverish greed, he wanted in the elevator right now.

Now!

Slam!

The crunch wasn't loud, but to Mel, it was ungodly. Compared to the shrieks he was making, the crunch spoke volumes. Bystanders stopped their nonsocial sleepwalking routine, arching their necks in unison at the young, devilishly good-looking, young man flailing his arms, kicking his feet, and pounding his good fist against the slick elevator door.

"Somebody! Fuck! Help, You fucks! Help, you fucks!" was all Mel could scream.

Something insane crawled within him. The pain was too great to stay with.

He pulled. Pain.

He jerked from side to side. That made the bone snap.

Three people came forward, leaping into action as if a phantom director had given them their cue. One woman tapped furiously at the call button, while the two men let their briefcases clatter to the floor as they tried, and failed, to pry the steel doors open with their baby-soft fingers.

To no gain, or release, Mel continued to jerk, only inviting more pain jolting up his arm.

Then, to everyone's horror, the box was rising, and Mel's hand with it.

As he was getting closer to the elevator, he snatched the handkerchief out of the man's pocket to his left, then bit down onto his own tie. In his mind, Mel could already see the inescapable pain coming. It was only fair to brace himself for it.

With a crack, and a snap, and a slush, away it went. A quick spray of blood covered the bald man with glasses to the right. Like a child, he ran away screaming. Some people giggled in shock at how ridiculous he looked.

Mel clamped the blood off by tying the handkerchief around his hand. That was it. His pinky was gone.

===

Instead of going to the hospital, like any normal person would, a very determined Mel marched into his agent's office, a disgruntled look etched on his face.

"What did you want me down here for?"

Mel's agent looked up, he was in the middle of stuffing papers into his desk. His usual fake smile was prepared but dissolved quickly on seeing Mel's left hand wrapped in, what looked like, a bloody rag.

"I…hey…you're dripping all over my carpet! What happened?"

"What did you want me here for?" Mel said, loudly this time.

"A commercial. What happened?"

"A commercial! Well, I'll be damned. That's what I rolled myself out of bed this morning for? Is that what your telling me?"

"I'm calling an ambulance."

"No need. I ain't *in no hurry*!" On the last three words he jerked his blood-draped hand at his agent, flicking small droplets of blood on the nice clean white walls.

"What the hell is the matter with you?"

"What kind of a commercial, pal? Get to the meat and potatoes, dammit!"

"Dear God, man. Just a watch commercial. That's all."

At this, Mel curled his lip into a disbelieving smile. Clicking his tongue and shaking his head, he held his clenched fist, the cloth still sticking to it. "That would be a hoot, wouldn't it, Dick?"

"Don't wave that thing anymore. My office is going to look like a slaughterhouse now!"

"It's only a couple of drops, you pansy."

"What happened?"

"My pinky! You fool! My pinky! My pinky got caught in your faulty elevator doors!"

"Dear Lord."

"Was running for the elevator, shoved may hand out to make it stop! Didn't work! As you can tell! God, I'll sue. Oh yes, I will sue."

"Mel, You shoved your hand into the door? What would possess you to do such a thing?"

"I didn't want to miss it! Ended up missing something else now. Snapped my finger clean off. Ran up ten flights to catch up with the box. Thought I could pull the whole ice cube tray shit, you know."

"Why didn't you?"

"By the time I caught up with that stupid thing, I found a lady cringing in the corner, wearing the ugliest dress I've ever seen on a woman. She didn't look half-bad, but still, that didn't make up for it. 'Where is it?' I shouted. I know, I know. I must have looked like a maniac with both arms blocking the door, but I would not let her leave until she told me where it was."

Mel took a heavy breath and rubbed sweat away from his forehead with his good hand.

"And," Dick asked, hanging on the edge of the story, "where was it?"

"This bitch was afraid! You believe that? Afraid, she said! She thought it was disgusting, she kicked it to the crease of the door."

"Dear Lord almighty."

"And that little thing went *wee wee wee* all the way down that damn shaft. Lost. Lost, I tell you!"

"Well, she didn't know."

"Didn't know what? It's a finger! Be a Good Samaritan, find a fridge, flag some help, press the stop button, ask around, that's all she had to do! It ain't hard to help!"

"I hope to God you didn't do anything to her."

"No!" Mel shouted. "Of course not! She gave me some painkillers to make up for it! I can't feel a thing in this hand."

"My goodness." Dick looked befuddled, checking his pockets, grabbing pens. "Have to find out how long this will affect me."

"Affect you! What about me?"

"Mel, I'm sorry, but without your finger attached our clients will pull out. They need all of you, they won't settle for a fraction less. You should have checked the basement for that finger."

Mel began to laugh involuntarily. "Dick, it's gone! What you so worried about! Wouldn't do that crummy commercial anyway. I mean, it's stupid. This whole thing is stupid."

Mel unwrapped his hand and wiggled the four fingers he had left. A pathetic, bleeding stump tried to catch up to its brothers. "Take a look at this ridiculous shit."

"Mel! Good God! Be civil for crying out loud, people are looking." Dick made a rush for the blinds and closed them.

Right there, Mel knew that he'd be out of commercials for a while. But what if it didn't stop there? What if the entire world regarded him as a freak just because he didn't have one more dainty digit? What then?

===

"I mean, c'mon, Doc, it's not like I'll be out of work for life, right? Scrambling to find my due, that's not me. I want something, I get it. So how do we do this?"

Doctor Moore, not even hiding his bored, flat expression, examined the hand and jotted down some notes. He was a studio doctor, a man who had worked with hundreds of Hollywood stars and starlets.

"You were lucky. It was a clean break and the painkillers slowed the bleeding. We'll stitch you up."

"Stitch me up? What about my five percent of me? Don't I

get a replacement or something or other?"

"If we had something to work with, yes. You should have found the finger and put it on ice. That does the trick until you have it sewn back on."

Mel took in a breath, searing. "Well, I guess I just didn't think of that!"

"Quite few people do. Relax, look on the bright side. At least it was your pinky and not your pecker."

"What on earth?"

"Oh yes, you'd be surprised. Hardly anybody remembers to bring those in on ice. They just get so panic stricken, the wives usually, that they come running in with it dangling between their dainty fingers."

Mel stiffened, blinked even. "Look, Doc, I didn't go running for the elevator with my fly undone and my pecker out. I'm trying to have a serious conversation about this issue."

Doctor Moore, still off in his own little world, set the pad down and swiveled in his chair, craning his eyes toward the ceiling as he recollected in his mind. "Glory be, I've seen some weird cases. Twenty plus years and it never ceases to amaze me. Think of it, Mel. All those wasted peckers. People chop 'em off, dip them in soup, lose them while car blowing…"

"What the hell?"

"Ornament accidents, screwing animals, screwing dead animals…"

"Doc!" Mel shouted. "Enough with the pecker punch lines! Can't you just fix me?"

The doctor stared, offended by the sudden outburst. With some time reserved for silence, he contemplated, shook his head and swiveled back to his notepad. "'Fraid not, son. Most I can do is recommend you get one of those plastic-rubber replacements. Frankly, in this day an age, it will fool no one and there's a little matter of it slipping off at awkward moments."

:"But. My. Hands. My hands are my fifth best feature. The women love them. I can't give them up, man. There's got to be something. Think, damn you! You degree-totting peckerologist!"

The doctor took no offense to this. He had seen his share of actors coming loose at the seams because of a gash, cut, balding, etc. They all reacted similarly when it came to lost limbs. And even though it went against his better judgment to refer Mr. Larkin to take experimental action, Doctor Moore still kept a card or two from the actual HM facilities.

As Mel was looking at his dangling feet, sulking on the doctor's table, he heard Doctor Moore search some cabinets until he finally eased a white business card into Mel's view.

"Contact them. They might be able to grow it back."

Mel, confused, took the card gently. On the one side, it had the letters 'HM', and on the other it had an address that Mel wasn't familiar with.

"You mean…to tell me that all I needed to do was pout in order to get my way?"

"Hardly. One request: memorize the address. If you must have their services again, hide the card away. Some of my patients put it in a safety deposit box, if that suits you. But this…facility is highly secretive and exclusive. Only the crème de la crème, if you get my meaning."

"They really can grow it back, then?"

"They just might there, tiger."

===

"Seriously, I'll give you anything you want! Just let me go!" The black bag was chaffing his cheeks, but, more importantly, his ankles and arms were bound to a chair. He had no idea where he was. And that was exactly the way they wanted it.

Mel felt a hand approaching his face.

His first instinct was to bite it.

That's what his character did in that spy movie he made two years before. It did well. Not your standard box office net, but enough to make three sequels following it.

Instead, much to his surprise, the hand smelled delightful and mystically fruitful.

The blackness rose and the woman folded the black bag in her delicate soft hands. From her black stilettos to her sexual eyes and eyebrows, she gave Mel a certain tingle that he hadn't felt since *The Dame Parted* - his first sex scene.

Judging by her pointed nose, sharp eyebrows, and intense cheekbone structure she was surely a vixen who you did not cross. But, on the inside, she was hiding something luxurious and yet vicious, and Mel wasn't just thinking about if that was under her skirt or not. Not to mention, she could have blown the original leading lady away.

Her blonde, yet dark-rooted, hair was fashioned in a swirl atop her head, held together by black chopsticks.

"Whew," Mel breathed. "You can bag me anytime."

She made no hint of regarding the comment with distaste, but she also did not deny his charm. He was, after all, a well-known movie actor. Twelve pictures and running…if he ever escaped this.

The area that surrounded them felt cavernous, locked away, some unknown factory.

Mel shifted in the seat, trying to ignore the uncomfortable hole that was right in the middle of it.

"Mr. Larkin," Her foot rose and it came to rest forcefully on the chair in the space between his reluctantly open legs. Mel shuddered a bit. Just a little closer and Mel would have agreed that his private parts were, in fact, her stomping ground. He looked up, fully attentive, sweating, and couldn't wait for more. "We appreciate your business. We don't tell this to all the boys. And we don't shy away when it comes to customer satisfaction."

"Point taken."

"If you'll allow me to speak freely, I have to admit that I'm a true fan of your work."

"Good to know."

"Pardon the precautionary measures but we can't afford outside spectators. You understand the risk, don't you? Nothing is more special, more exclusive than our services."

"Is that why you snatched me up in the park?"

"The very one we told you to meet us at."

"Who's we?"

"Come, Mr. Larkin, don't try to figure us out. Your characters could, maybe. But you're not really concerned with how we'll help you…"

She curled her fingers around his wrist, releasing the strap as she lifted the bandaged hand to her face, like some secondhand Christmas present waiting to be opened.

"…you're just interested in how much it will cost. May I?"

Before Mel could nod, the woman peeled the bandage away, revealing the stump and its thread, giving a closed eye look.

"Tsk. They stitched it. Well, now it's going to be that much harder. We'll have to open them, you understand?"

This he did.

Then he nodded slowly.

It helped that her voice was sultry sweet; otherwise no one could convince him to abide to that graphic nightmare.

Out of the shadows, a hand came with a needle and quickly poked Mel's right arm. It shocked him, but it was over in an instant.

Then, from the left, another arm, this one much fuzzier, came and poked him with another needle. And while this madness was going on, a third carefully plucked a long strand of hair out of his head.

"Sheesh. Wait a damn minute! Is this the treatment?"

"Part of our many tests."

"Look, toots, all I want is a spare. Not a tune-up."

"Witty, Mr. Larkin. But you know how this song and dance works like any other. There will be contracts, fees and a percentage of the next three pictures you are involved in. That is our standard rate. Still with us?"

"As long as I get my five percent of me, I'm good."

She smiled. It didn't suit her. It felt like a business smile. And, with Mel being a celebrity, he found shame in not being able to wiggle a genuine smirk out of her. As his character Danny DeLomantes would have said, '*This broad means broad business.*

Ain't no talking her outta nothin'.

"Beauty always comes at a price, Mr. Larkin."

"Cut it, babe. You can call me by my first name."

"Oh. Your first name or your real first name?"

He sighed. "It's irritating. You wouldn't like it."

"Try me."

Mel licked his lips. "Wish I could."

Now it was her who felt the shudder, giving Mel the added bonus he wanted, and now he felt the other five percent of himself starting to rise in triumph. But if the ladies really knew him, it was really the three percent of his little mischief maker.

She took her heel off the chair and lowered it, rubbing her two fingers along her neckline.

Elevated heart rate, she could be swayed. Mel still had it.

"Look at you. Strapped to a chair, bound, pinkyless and yet you still have enough guts to try and *talk me out of my own undies*."

"Claire Redford's line. My second picture. You know your movies."

He shifted again.

"Problem?"

"I've got to use the bathroom."

"There's a bucket underneath your chair. My associates took the liberty."

"What a place."

"We'll take care of you. So, marvelous Mel, let's have it."

"Not a chance. No one knows it."

Behind him he smelled a chemical, it made him a little woozy. There was also a bottle top being screwed back on. Mel guessed that this was the part where they knocked him out and fixed him up. "All right. Beam me up."

"Wait." The woman held her hand out, warding off the hand that was about to come around and douse him. "Just...just wait."

She breathed in a bit, composing herself as she flattened her clothes down, wiping the sweat off her palms and blinking for a brief second.

"You're a lucky man, Mr. Larkin, you're getting two of what you want today."

She leaned forward; Mel could only imagine her well-rounded ass rubbing against the darkness behind her, convincing Mel that the darkness would get so excited that it would turn into light all of a sudden.

Her rosy red lipstick looked juicy as it glistened off her pouty large lips. "Consider this my treat."

Her lips thrust forward and their mouths got tangled up in a passionate bobbing. And it was worth losing a pinky over to come here, to Mel. One of the most mysterious, most seductive creatures he had ever met, and she would be gone in a second. Perhaps that was what turned him on the most. The woman breathed hard as she held his cheek, lingering with him. He took the kiss like a hero would.

Sadly, as they parted, she traced his lips once more with the tip of her tongue and gently pecked him to put a stamp on it.

By now, the heated kiss showed all over Mel's goofy smiling face. The marks of red swirled around his lips in an uneven circle.

Heart racing, eyes dancing, Mel breathed in the last bit of scent from her. Was that her fruity perfume, or did he awaken the hormones?

Mel smiled again, shaking his head as she slowly leaned away. "My name's Melward."

She stiffened. Her smile faded. "Ugh."

"Told you you wouldn't like it."

And then the cloth went over his mouth.

===

Three days later, Mel, really Melward, awoke in his mansion. A clean suit was laid out for him. His blue one. A note was taped to his hand, his perfect hand now complete with his small digit. The note, after he sat up on his bed to read, had nothing but a lipstick mark. Someone had smooched the paper. That would be blonde bombshell who knew his real name. Behind the kiss mark was a phone number. Mel laughed.

It was odd that they left him in his house like that, from the way they dropped him off, you'd have thought he hadn't invited anyone over. There was no trace of these people. All the carpets were vacuumed, and not with his own vacuum, he checked. These people didn't miss a trick.

"What service," he said, holding his pinky out to his gold-framed bathroom mirror. The pinky had no visible scars, was on straight and looked better.

===

Four weeks passed. His agent, not often surprised by his unscrupulous client, was astounded to find that his cash cow had grown back its udder. When asked how, Mel just gave him a smile and wink. Like he always did.

While on the set of the big budget beach movie *The Sun don't Smile for You,* Mel had to retire to his trailer. It wasn't really an end to the day's filming but Mel ran off the set in a hurry. So, when Mel booked it, it was pretty much a wrap for the day. Even the director couldn't argue with that.

But Mel only ran to escape the looks. He was panicked. He locked the door, took off his Hawaiian shirt and shorts and jumped into the small shower. He grabbed a bar of soap and scrubbed furiously at his pinky. There was a mark. After all this time, a mark. A big purple blotch. Of course, to any other person it would appear to be a birthmark. But Mel had no birthmarks of any kind. Whatever this foreign purple blotch was, he despised it. It made him sick. Sick to the point that right there he vomited his high-priced meal into the shower drain.

===

A horrible thing occurred two and half weeks later. While still on the set of the hot action thriller *The Sun don't Smile for You,* nicknamed *Sunspot* by some of the extras, Mel injured himself. It was during a shooting break, when he and the other stars were sharing drinks, that a section of wall came down from the building beside them. As all of the others dashed away, bikinis and all, Mel went back for his drink, even though he could afford to buy another one, that is, if he wanted to drive five blocks out of his way for it.

When the dust settled, Mel rose. His hand, the one he paid much for with the pinky problem, was now gone; severed and smashed into the sand somewhere in the wreckage. But Mel stared, amazed by the fact that the blood around the stump was bubbling and a new finger was rising out of his wrist.

Covering the miracle with a towel he took off for his car and drove away.

===

A month had passed and Mel Larkin wasn't any richer. He regretfully had to turn down two commercial spots and three picture deals, two of them being sequels. The director who called him the most was the one from that old *Sunspot* feature. He'd tell him, threaten him, which was a thing this director wasn't famous for, that if he didn't come to the set within the week, he'd finish the picture without him. CGI was currently the big buzz and, after all, the face mapping with the technology wasn't all that difficult.

The last time the director called, Mel yanked the phone out of the wall with his deformed hand. Yes, deformed. It was nothing like the original Mel Larkin hand now. No, now it was something of a charity case. Mel felt as if he were one part elephant man.

The digits that were on his hand were bulky, misshapen and there were eight of them. All with purple and brown splotches. Whatever miracle drug they had given him had failed and was now turning the rest of his arm into a mess.

In his bathroom he cried, when he wasn't vomiting. At one point he dialed Miss Blonde's number. Even with his career folding, he would not accept defeat. He wanted to keep his charm. He wanted to hear a lovely voice. He wanted to see a lovely ass. But while he couldn't stop staring at his monstrous appendage he thought, *Yeah, I guess I'll have to settle for a lovely voice.*

"Melward."

He grimaced. It was her all right. "Miss Blonde. Tell me what is happening. I'm no fool. I'm staring at a breach of contract right in front of me."

"There's no point fussing about side effects. We've been paid in full. You can check your accounts. We've emptied all of them. We no longer hold you as a client."

Mel's face boiled. Of course he didn't believe her, but he was dumbfounded how a weak woman like her could think that she had the balls to do this.

"You're not getting away with anything, honey. I could bring down the shit storm right now if I wanted to. I've got…why…I've got…" He searched his mind, and then the bathroom for incriminating evidence against her or this secret healers' club. He eyed the kiss mark. "I've got your DNA, someone will trace it."

"Not my shade, not even my lips, I'm afraid Mister Melward."

"I've got the card that my doctor gave me."

"All it says on there is HM. That could mean anything. Knock yourself out."

Mel stamped his foot.

"I'LL KNOCK YOU OUT, YOU BITCH! I'LL COME FOR YOU PEOPLE! AND WHEN I DO I'M GONNA RIP YOUR FUCKING TITS OFF! YOU HEAR ME?"

He heard her sigh.

"How can you, Mel? You don't even know where we are."

She hung up.

===

For days Mel sizzled and boiled and transformed, ever fixated on the phone that he left in the bathroom. It was still off the hook. Nothing mattered anymore. The stuff inside him moved to his right leg and deformed it to an unimaginable size, complete with browns, purples and hot reds. Every so often, Mel stroked his own cheek, where Miss Blonde had stroked him. Now, his cheek was protruding, hair would not grow on that portion of his face anymore. He cried, but only one eye was strong enough to emit tears. The other was now as small as a marble.

He'd rip this city apart to find them. Especially to find her. That's just what he intended to do.

===

In the event that rocked the small Californian town, several people were still affected by it. Many left to go back home to their mothers. Teenagers and children were sent to psychologist to work out their fears, the most prominent being a fifteen-foot monster attacking the city. The foul naked beast was male, having multicolored skin and veins that protruded everywhere.

A group of construction workers improvised a plan that night where they successfully pinned the beast with two cars. It was then showered by bullets from a Gatling gun by the arriving SWAT Team, seeing as how that was the only weapon that worked.

Even with the horrific episode terrifying the lives of the once beautiful city, there were still many unanswered questions. Too big to be covered up, too gruesome to walk away from. Only seventeen people were injured, three were dead, crushed as the beast trampled them.

One such man, Enrico Gonzales, heroically helped the construction workers with pushing the car that pinned the monster. The beast took a failing swipe at them, but only made contact with Enrico.

After the beast was killed, someone noticed Enrico's hand. This college boy, Danny Nichols, who would later write the screenplay of the event which would go into production two decades later as a monster effects movie, pointed the wound out to Enrico.

"Dude, you're missin' a finger, man."

Enrico looked up, smiling as he patted the young man's shoulder. "Fear not, my friend. I have found the finger. She is in an icebox."

The Aches

The word. The word is here. The word is now. Must go. Very dark. No sight. Keep moving. Here. Go through. Go through even with crunch crunch. Buzz buzz. Must stop. Crunch crunch. Taste stings. Find box. Find Box. Found. Pull. Harder. Rip wall. It curls. Have box. Get out. Out here. Out there. Here I am. Hand over. Walk away. Find bench. Bench near. Here. Rest here. Rest stop. Stop. Pain. Nothing.

* * *

Five hours later, which wasn't a very long time, a bank manager exited her car without knowing the wild event that had happened earlier. Her hair was put up in a dirty blonde bun. Her olive skin sweated in the curiously hot air. She adjusted her rimless glasses as she closed the door and pressed the button to put the safety alarm on it.

And then she looked down.

Right in front of her were two small, bloody footprints. Much smaller than her shoe size. From the look of it, there were also glass pieces revolving around them. She pivoted on one foot as she turned to find that the trail ended twenty paces across the street and on to the sidewalk where they faded miserably.

Right away, something horrible crawled inside her. She thought she was going to be sick, never feeling like this before. It was almost as if she felt like she was drowning. She coughed violently and turned back to the back. Now she could see, the glass doors were shattered completely. Taking quick steps in her high heels, she entered through the opening and looked around. To her right, on the wall, the alarm was smashed. And all she could think of was to call the police right away.

* * *

Carl Fens was a disgusting man. A homeless man who lived off of the people he hounded night and day on the street corner. He wasn't your typical bum that would tote a cart along; no, he was special. He had with him a battered suitcase which he had stolen off of a businessman on the subway. The documents inside were boring and most likely divorce papers. Carl found these as sufficient toilet paper even though the documents scratched him up something good in the rear. Now the only thing kept in that suitcase of his was a couple of cans, a bottle of hooch, three half-eaten chicken wings, and his own hat along with a mountain of change - dimes and quarters.

The suit that he wore was a pale blue and used to belong to the owner of the briefcase but was now as useless as its owner. It was missing three buttons, had a rip above the right shoulder and reeked of tuna. Ordinarily, Carl wouldn't choose to bath properly. He mostly cleansed himself whenever it rained, which was brief at that and what gave the suit that *unique* smell.

He scratched at his beard as he walked down the sidewalk, hoping to make the early bus. From the look of it, there was already a person sitting at the bus stop, protected by the three glass walls that surrounded her.

Now, Carl was never one to admit this, but he liked people, even when they disliked him. He found comfort in having company and just yakking their ear away with his adventures.

But this was a special case - a special case indeed. For the women who was sitting upright, with her back facing him, was a curvy vixen who, for some reason unknown to him, had decided to wait for the bus in her silky nightgown.

Now this *did* need an introduction.

Carl licked his dirty palm and tried to slick some loose strands out of his eyes, preparing what to say to the young woman even though she would no doubt be repulsed by him.

As he came near, he twirled around the pole only to be repulsed by her. He dropped his suitcase which opened on impact and tumbled his life-worth into the gutter. He fell back on the street as the bus approached him. He shielded himself from the coming blow of the tire, but instead, the bus driver saw him just in time and slammed on the brakes. The tire appeared inches away from the frightened man's face.

The driver cursed the man through the windshield and eight passengers cursed at him for stopping so abruptly. But their yelling ceased when Carl pointed a bony finger at the woman sitting on the bus stop bench. Then, the bus driver, as well as the passengers, screamed in unison at the sight of her.

* * *

Tom Wile arrived on the scene, coffee in hand. When the police had contacted him, he knew that whatever happened had happened with a clear and logical reason behind it — the cops just couldn't find one.

He yawned and groaned as he usually did when being woken up on the weekend. What a perfect beginning to his day.

He sipped the scorching hot coffee and was delighted to find that it was a really good roast. The surprise that he got from his coffee was about the only thing that was on his mind as some of the men guided him to the tapped-off scene. The bus was still parked at the bus stop and all of the passengers were sitting a couple of paces away, giving their statements to the local officials.

Tom walked up to his friend, who was behind the tape and tapped him on the shoulder.

"Mornin' Jacob," Tom said.

"Tom Wile," his friend said, wasting no time at all to lift the tape for him. "I heard that they called you back this way. I almost gave up on hearing from you. How's the biz?"

"Biz? Is that what you call it nowadays? I assumed you would be out of the game earlier than I would."

His friend smirked. "And let these hogs have all the fun? Never."

Then his friend noticed something new. Something that Tom didn't want to talk about at all. His collar was opened up two buttons from the heat, which he always did, and a banana-shaped scar was smiling at him. It ran from the collarbone straight to the center of Tom's chest. It was jagged and still looked horrible.

"Whoa. That's new."

Tom saw his gaze and buttoned up.

"Yeah," Tom said. "You're wife kept me up last night."

His friend snickered a bit and then gave him a shove which almost spilled the only good coffee that Tom had had in months. "Whoa! Careful, man. This roast is hard to come by."

"What? That the French shit."

"That's the *exquisite* French shit, thank you very much."

Some of the other officers watched as Officer Jacob led Tom Wile to the frozen women on the bench. Now, they didn't know it, But Tom was no stranger to the weird. In the ten months that he was on the force, he uncovered more mysterious circumstances that you can ever imagine involving the occult, which was something they liked to keep a distance from as much as possible. Ever since his wife died of an accidental overdose, some of the men had been talking. Thought that he quit the biz and thought he was dried up altogether. But Tom still had a level head and these types of things kept him busy, which was always a good thing when you were a widower. The best prescription was to keep your mind busy, which he did now more than ever and was sharp in his perceptions.

Carl was still wrapped in a blanket as Tom approached.

Tom pointed to the treads on the humongous front tire of the bus.

"See that? That could have been you wedged in there. Feel like talking now?"

"Mmm-mmmehm-mmmem," was all the man could utter, still shaken.

"That's all right," Tom said. "We'll come back to you. Sit tight, buddy."

Tom, along with his friend, stepped onto the sidewalk and finally came up to the body. It was wrapped in a white sheet which made it look like a poorly dressed Halloween ghost.

"Now, I must warn you, Tom, prepare for a bit of a shock here. Remember, this woman was found this way and hasn't been touched."

Tom gave him a glare. Sometimes it annoyed him how these men treated him like a novice to the profession rather than a skilled individual. "I'll try and be careful."

With his free hand, he curled his fingers along the edge of the sheet and brought it up to his eye line, making a thin triangle of space to look through.

The victim was a mid-twenties woman with a killer night gown but with a sorry mess of a body that was deformed from its previous state. Her small feet were covered in dry blood and a couple pieces of glass were still sticking to them. Past the legs were two hands which were, hard to believe, but completely pulverized. The knuckles were bruised and the fingers were almost like jelly, the bones that used to be inside them collected in dust at the tips of her fingers. Her arms were swelled, which made her look bigger in size. Her face was a blank stare, her pupils gone white. Her nose was as equally crushed as her fingers and her mouth was a gaping hole of lacerations and broken teeth, like a mistreated shredder that was given a tack hammer to destroy. It looked as if someone *had* gone at her mouth with a tack hammer, poor girl.

Tom lowered the sheet. His face never turned, never folded

under the pressure. To some this scene would activate the gag reflex. For Tom Wile, the scene just made him thirstier. He sipped at his black coffee with his eyes closed.

When he opened his eyes, his friend had a somewhat puzzled expression on his face. "That must be some good coffee right there."

"Oh, the best."

"Any ideas?"

Tom scratched at his hairline. "She hasn't been moved, you say?"

"Not at all."

"Well, she certainly looks beaten. I'm not sure what this is but I'd rule out suicide. Someone must have taken her, either brought her here or attacked her here is my guess."

"Some of them men have been saying that she might be a prostitute."

"Not likely. She looks like a levelheaded girl to me. I dunno, something about that nightgown says 'good girl' to me."

"Then why would she be out and about in a nightgown?"

"She wanted to impress you."

Again, Tom felt a whap against his shoulder as the officer grimaced at him. All jokes aside, Tom didn't tell his friend what he was really thinking. It was a fact that even though Tom said a couple of sentences, his mind was racing with activities, theories. And he was running through every single one of them, like decoding a password.

His friend told him that she lived no more than a block away and was discovered around 8:30.

To Tom, this seemed a little bit familiar, like this event had happened to him once before. Instantly, a horrible feeling was tugging at his gut. He belched a bit and it felt acidic. It was a horrible feeling, but apparently one that would not make him lose his coffee. Tom and his friend put their hands on their stomachs at the exact same time. Tom looked over at him and could tell right away that his friend had that same acidic taste in his mouth.

"You feel that?" Tom asked.

His friend agreed.

Tom turned, looking at the onlookers, the officers, the passengers, even the bum, who was sitting on the curb. All of them seemed to have their hands meet their stomachs as if they were carrying a child. The looks on their faces were similar to his. This event was strange, to say the least. There must have been a logical explanation for it. Not everyone could have stomach pains at the same time, could they?

* * *

When Tom and the boys in blue finally answered the call, it was well past 11:00. Tom got a refill for his Styrofoam cup as always.

"Don't you ever throw that thing away?" his friend asked as they were riding in the backseat of the squad car.

Tom looked puzzled, damn near insulted. "Why? It's just a cup. It bother you that much?"

"No. It's just that that thing always seems to be connected to your hand - constantly. Ever thought of getting a new cup?"

"I don't find it necessary."

"A slave to tradition?"

"If you wanna call it that."

Already they could see the disgruntled woman, her hair completely out of her bun now and wavering in the unrelenting heat.

"Let's get this over with," Officer Jacob remarked.

Tom opened his door and put a foot on the crunching road.

Crunching?

He looked down.

Yes, crunching. He lifted his foot and saw a bloody foot print with three or four flakes of glass still clinging to the dried blood.

"Connected," he whispered.

In his mind, a nuclear bomb went off. After all the theories and possible scenarios that ran through his head, Tom knew…

"These are both connected!"

And then he spilled his coffee.

* * *

The rest of the day went on like a blur. Tom went home after the investigation and sat in his recliner. He was sweating profusely and on the brink of a breakdown.

"Margaret," he whispered.

He closed his hands over his eyes as tears swelled in his lids.

He knew who did this.

He went by many names but Tom only knew him by one - Will Shaker.

Here was what Tom knew. Sometime around three o'clock, Lisa Boyle received a call. All that was on the answering machine was one simple word - Bitch. After hearing that word, Lisa stood up from her chair and left her house, barefoot and in her nightgown. Her eyes were lost, lost in nothingness. And her heart was beating so fast, it hummed. She made the journey across the street where she arrived at the Plympton Bank. Once there, she put both fists through the glass, wasting no time to walk across the glass and into the vault. Alarms sounded but she deactivated them in time and chewed them to bits. She entered a room where a safety deposit box marked 665 was awaiting her. The person controlling her did not know where the key was, so he commanded her to pry the box out with her finger tips, convinced her that she had strength that she was beyond normal women. And in her mind, she solely believed him. But in reality, she was putting her body through extremes. By the time she got the box out, which was roughly the size of a briefcase and wider than one, all her fingers were broken. Whatever happened to that safety deposit, Tom did not know. The contents of that box were unknown even to the bank.

After the man was done with her, he guided her to the bus stop where he let her rest. And then, after a billion times of beating, her heart stopped abruptly, which made her crunch what was left of her teeth and die.

Hypnotism.

That was his game.

The man had done it before.

Will Shaker had done it to Margaret, Tom's late wife. Made her wake up in the middle of the night with a phone call. Tom was almost out of bed when she decided to get it. Margaret picked it up, heard one word and dropped the phone. Her heart raced to unbelievable heights and the next thing she knew, she was in the bathroom choking on an overdose of pills. She had taken them all.

Tom awoke when he heard the sounds and cradled her in his arms. She was frothing at the mouth and on the brink of dying. Tom heard laughter. Not a homely, jokey laughter, more of an evil cackle. There, dangling from the table outside the bathroom was the phone, and the bastard at the other end cackling hysterically, and then the line went dead. Margaret died in his arms.

The call was meant for him. Tom had gotten too close to Will before, and now he had paid for it. Ever since, the force had always been puzzled by Margaret's supposed suicide and thought that eventually Tom would quit playing detective. But he never did.

* * *

Tom sat across from his foe. Will Shaker had been waiting for him, setting tea out as he greeted him in his olive green robe and his bathroom slippers. On the table was a partially eaten chicken salad with no dressing. Will's cold blue eyes gave Tom a formative stare. "You should have known better. It was mine, and you had no right to steal it from the crime scene."

Tom regarded Will's dry accusation. To him, it was a foul deed that he did, but how could he know? It originated from the first crime that Will had ever committed, forcing a man to beat himself up in the alley of a bar, Will made his getaway through the front, still controlling the punches of the man bruising his own features. Tom knew it was foul play. Will directed Linda, his wife, into the cab. She was still in the dark about his powers of mind manipulation. And after that rude man had come on to his on his wife, Will couldn't help but teach this man a lesson in self-evaluation. "Beat it," Will had said. In those two words, the power of his mind played with the man, enough to where the man's eyes set off a panicked look, as if he had stepped over a freshly dug grave, and he walked stiffly out the back to be beaten against a brick wall with his own hands.

"I planned to give it to her." Tom unscrewed the cap of his flask. "Was going to give it to her on our anniversary. Ten years, never apart. Not even a wink apart."

"But it didn't belong to you, did it? That was my wife's necklace. She dropped it right as we drove off."

"By the time I got to the crime scene, you were busy giving your wife mouth to mouth resuscitation, and I was searching the front. The necklace was too precious and special to leave there on the curb."

"Taking it in your care, that wasn't enough. You had to lock it up in a safety deposit box. Left it sitting there, waiting."

"Had it personalized before I did."

"Hoooow sweet," Will seethed.

"My colleagues told me someone was there desperately searching for a necklace. I was not inclined to give it back."

"I knew you wouldn't. And for that, you're wife is dead, and I have the necklace."

"Did you have to use some random girl as your gopher? She was just a girl, for God's sake."

"That girl had no future. I followed her, saw that her mind was weak enough. For that, I took advantage. She served her purpose. No more."

Tom sat a while, playing with the cap of his flask. Then he looked back up, grief dripping from his face. "Had I known that the necklace was the only way your wife could survive in our world, I never would have stolen it. Not for the harm it's caused me and others. You've made me mentally ready to wilt and die."

"Just what I've always wanted."

"You could have hypnotized me to kill myself."

"I was halfway there, while you were in your bathroom, shaving."

Tom blinked, the horror firmly realized in his eyes. "The day I blacked out…"

"…Margaret thought you had a lapse, no doubt. She took care of you, yes?"

"Yes. I remember waking up in her arms. She was dabbing my chest with a whole roll of paper towels. My chest was aching, the razor was still in my hand." His eyes left the table, somewhere in a dream. When he looked back to his nemesis he whispered, "Suicide?"

"That's what it was meant to look like. But my plan was going through changes in mid act. I phoned you, told you to *cut it out*. I wanted you to cut out your own heart, but, to your reprieve, my ulcer was acting up. I lost concentration."

"Wanted me to stick around."

"Of course, there were ways of making you break. And *starting* with you would hardly have a palpable effect."

"Your one weakness, that damn stomach. When you lose that concentration of yours, everyone gets the aches."

"Aches?"

"You didn't know? A phantom pain is left behind. We feel your ulcer."

Will was puzzled, but only for a moment. "We all have our pains to bear. Are you finally accepting of your fate? Or shall we play a game of chess?"

"What makes you think we aren't playing now?"

Tom took a good swig from the flask with a tilt of his head. He breathed in deep. "Ahhhhh."

"Refreshing?"

"Like you wouldn't believe."

"What's it loaded with?"

"Rum. All I ever drink is rum."

"Goes down smooth?"

"Slicker than shit."

Will considered the flask for a moment. To Will, it was only a brief moment. However, Tom picked up on this immediately. "Care for some?"

"I shouldn't. It's your last drink on this earth."

"Now, Will, please, is it wrong to tempt the devil, even in the hour of the damned?"

Will looked at his sullen face with suspicious eyes. But in the game of mind breakers, Will was at the very peak. Not only had he made Detective Tom Wile shed first blood, give his wife worries, turn the wife against herself and made him guilty of a complete stranger's death; but he would finish the last of the man's drink with a tasty relish for Tom's disdain just before killing him.

"Just a short one," Will said. He gently slid the flask out of Tom's thumb and forefinger and beamed. "To your health."

"May I be so lucky?"

Will swallowed the contents whole and slammed the flask down against the wooden table, much like slamming a shot glass down after having a dare. The half a second before he joyfully slammed the flask down, Will felt burning.

He coughed some.

A few coughs became louder and with much more force behind them, enough to warrant the assistance of his own hand. Seconds passed as his face grew a distinct shade of amber and his forehead began sweating. Violently he gagged and coughed, his hand wrapped around his pulsating throat.

Tom smiled, holding up a hand. He was calm, collected, more than happy to shed some light on the subject. He held up a hand. "Now, I know what you're thinking, what have I gotten myself into? My insides are on fire. I did not lie when I said there was rum in that there drink. But not just that. It's a combination of rum and a few selected favorite hot sauces of mine. Now, I've always been a man with a cast iron stomach. Never knew why I was privy to such, what I thought to be, a useless gift. But, as you can see, I've been well suited for this event. I swallow spices you could not imagine. All while staying relatively cool. All I get is a tingle in the back of my throat. Yes, I may not have much of a life to live, but I'll pay for it by making it up to that poor girl's family. As for you, well, I can see you're busy. I should leave. Is all that bubbling to the surface, Will?"

During Tom's speech, Will's torso was slowly moving down, along with his veiny face, like being lulled to sleep. A silent sleep. A permanent sleep. A sleep that burned its way into hell. Finally, Will was dead, bleeding from the inside, head rested on the table, hand crushed between the table and his own torso.

Tom stood and patted the man on the head.

The Subtle Teachings of Mr. Rifa

I woke up, sun in my eyes, drowsy as hell, and see my wife sitting by the foot of my bed reading a magazine, the top of her curly red hair peeking over the spine of it. Well, from the looks of the base, the bed isn't mine. Got my socks on but, oh, dear God. My right leg is in a cast. I look at my wife, Angela. She sets down her magazine and looks up at me. She's not mad at me, I'd be able to tell. Oh, the crookedness of that smile. I know that one. I had a slip.

But where the hell did I have it?

"It was the fly?" I cringe. "Did I really fall in the classroom in front of all of them?"

"What did you expect, Harry?"

I had almost forgotten how marvelous she looked, even when she would lightly scorn me. She's wearing that flower dress I like with the faded blue hoody. Must be Tuesday. I slept through the weekend?

God, my head hurts.

"It was…a matter of principle."

"Principle? You had them all freaked out."

"I was proving a point. You always have to finish what you start. Where would we be if Mark Twain hadn't finished Tom sawyer, if Melville never finished Moby Dick?"

"Speaking of dicks…"

"Walked right into that one, didn't I?"

"Yes, dear. How's your head?"

"Another dick joke?"

"No, jerk, your *cra-ni-um.*"

"Feels like silly putty, I feel a knot."

"Lucky that thing didn't crack in two. The linoleum split."

"Angie, who brought me here?"

"Mark Tory."

"Mark Tory? Gave him a C minus. He's been holding back. That kid can't write cursive to save his life."

"Willing to jump back into work already?"

"Not so much. That's not like him. Thought he hated me."

"He was worried about you, Harry. He called me on your cell, said that all the other kids picked you up, stuffed you into his car and carted you to the hospital down the street."

Need to sit up, ow, my back.

"OOOOOooohhh."

"Here, let me help."

Mmmmmm, her hair smells like raspberries. Last time I made love to her was four weeks ago. Been through some rocky stuff ever since the miscarriage.

Oh, look at those gigantic blue eyes. I remember those all right.

"Now will you stop trying to do everything by yourself? Will you try not to fix everything all the time?"

"It's my nature," I grunt.

"Your nature is up for review, genius. I mean, c'mon, Harry, why the hell would you spend all that trouble trying to kill one damn fly?"

Chap 2

I've tried teaching first graders, yikes. Can't handle those rugrats.

Hated the idea of teaching college, the variety of ages throws me off. So many damn adults coming back to school, middle-aged too. Feels like I need to split myself into three people; one for the fresh kids, one for the rising artists and one for the hard of hearing. No thank you. Been there and done that.

High school's better.

Less shit I have to take.

Of course, teaching these teens how to write has been the best thing for me really. My class, room 303, isn't a hard class. An easy credit down to the letter. But because so many think they can take it and slack off, my drive to teach disappears.

I found a much better way to deal with my seventeen lucky students; be unpredictable, they won't know what hit 'em.

On the first day of class, I didn't say a word. I posted signs all over the classroom that said 'No talking'. Each kid, tall, short, black, white, male, female were instantly confused. Nevertheless, they shrugged and sat down. For the entire hour, I was combing through pages of my favorite book *To Kill a Mockingbird.* I'd sneak a peek at them now and again. Out of seventeen, thirteen were reading novels, one was sound asleep and the other three were carving stuff in their desks.

When the bell rang, I closed the book and came to the front of my desk.

They stopped gathering their things and sat back down. An involuntary reflex, I love it.

"Class," I said, as if I was beginning the lesson. "Think of this as a social experiment. I know now that thirteen of you are serious about writing, the rest of you I'll just have to work on. This will be the only time that the class is silent. I just wanted to give you one bad day. Now that you've seen it, a bit of discipline, I trust you won't want to give me a reason to do it again."

"Fine with me!" came a voice from the back. Mark Tory, the first day.

"That's a minus ten," I said as I pulled a pencil from my ear and marked it in my notepad.

"For what?" Mark again.

"Another minus ten. You now have a B for the first day. Because, Mark, I expressed a rule for today that there will be no talking. A simple rule. You don't follow the rules, you don't pass this class. Clear?"

"That's bogus," Mark said.

"No, that's a minus ten," I said.

Chap 3

"Harry Rifa, the fly was not your great white whale. It was a fly. Like many things, you could have just let it go." Angela is closer, trying to play mother, feeding me applesauce. It's Wednesday.

"I'm not a quitter."

"Harry, you've quit plenty of times. Harry, it's human nature. Harry, it's just ridiculous."

"Call me Ishmael," I smirk.

She slaps me on the knee, a good one. I'm startled as hell. Thought she was going for my bad leg.

Character doubts. Sheesh. I should know better. She is a strong woman, but not cruel. From the beginning of that beautiful moment when we thought we were having a baby to the bloody mess that followed, on my writing chair no less, she cried for only a few days, then toughened up. I was right there with her, and we've found sex unneeded for fear of another phantom baby.

"Edwin," I whisper.

She spills a gob of applesauce on my gown. I knew that was coming.

"W...what?"

"That's what I was going to name him. Edwin. Not Michael. Maybe it was a bad omen just thinking it."

She sets the applesauce down on the chair next to her, wiping up the mess she made on me. "Why would you think that?"

"Charles Dickens was a brilliant man, great writer - one of my favorite writers. But that brilliance only carried him so far. Not far enough. Had a storke before he could finish his supposedly great opus *The Mystery of Edwin Drood*. Poor bastard. I thought, if I named our son that, he'd become curious and eventually want to know why I picked that name. I'd read and give him my entire Dicken's collection. Now our son…well…you'd believe that name was a curse if it was you who picked it. Our son, like that book, is a mystery…lost. I hate it. If I hadn't been silently thinking that name to myself, would our boy still be alive?"

"If you wanted to name him that, why didn't you say so? Names don't carry curses. They're not inherited or genetic, you know this. You're just being stupid."

"Perhaps even…an *Idiot*? Worthy of Dostoevsky?"

"Can you think of anything else but writing?"

"Hard not to. All the greats started sober, ended either drunk or dead. I'm still struggling with the great American novel. Five years for fifty pages of garbage that I can't continue. Hmph. What a writer I turned out to be."

She's eating some of my applesauce now.

"Hey," I say, "That's mine."

"Sorry, got hungry while you were pining away for your lost art. 'Oh muse, how dreadful you are to leave me. Come hither.' Give me a break." She stirs the last bit of sauce into the spoon as she holds it up to her mouth. "You're already a writer. The point is not to write but to have written."

She notices my pause.

"Didn't Dorothy Parker say that?"

She smiles. "I don't know, did she?"

She shovels it in, the sauce as well as her wisdom.

Chap 4

"Today, we'll start with Thomas Jefferson."

"This ain't no history class," Charles says.

I place my glasses carefully over a copy of Charles Dickens' immortal classic *A Christmas Carol*. It's the middle of

May. They notice.

I stand.

"On the contrary, this is about writers who changed history. Jefferson wrote the Declaration of Independence. A declaration which clearly spat on the nefarious King George. Thomas was angry, driven, inspired to write that piece. Now it sits treasured and untouched."

"Bor-ing," Mag says.

That did it.

"All right, Mag, stick this in your pipe and smoke it; Jefferson wrote 1500 letters throughout his life. And those are only the ones they found. He created the first copy machine, fastening two quills together. Young lady, he even donated his lifetime collection of books to the Library of Congress. A man of many words? I'd say so."

"Fifteen hundred letters, huh?" Mike asks. He's all the way in the back of the class, so naturally he has to be loud. "They hear of carpel tunnel syndrome back then?"

That gets a laugh.

"All right, all right. Settle down."

I catch a glimpse of Jonah scribbling something.

The piece of paper is out of his hand and into mine faster than Bruce Lee going for your jugular.

I'm walking slowly as I bring it with me to the front of the class.

I push my glasses on as I read the paper.

"Mr. Rifa needs to jump his ass out the window and..."

The class tightens up. Jonah cringes a bit and starts biting his nails.

I fold the paper into an airplane and toss it out the open window at the back of the classroom. Sitting down for a moment, I set my glasses back on the desk. These little pissants are trying to anger me. Well, the hell if I'm going to let them do that.

"Jonah?"

"Ye...yes, sir?"

He's quivering.

"Y'know, that sounds like a pretty good idea right now." I slap my knees, purse my lips and march to the open window. I get one leg over and I clasp the top of the window frame by the time some of the students are trying to stand up in protest and are gasping at my attempt. But no one advances forward. They are frozen in disbelief.

I turn to them with a smile.

"Hark, I say!" I use my stage voice. "If young Jonah see fit a mutiny, I must walk the plank!"

I hear a few uncomfortable laughs.

I start rocking back and forth on the window ledge, stirring up conversations on the soccer field below where gym has started for a class of students. "But what next, Jonah? You only have one sentence here. Not even a complete one at that. You've got me and your audience on edge. Good. What's the next move?"

He looks around, puzzled.

"Once I'm out, will I fly? Possibly make it to an uncharted land hidden between a dimension of stars like J.M. Barrie's *Peter Pan*? Will I contemplate suicide? Didn't Hamlet do that? Or shall I save myself by confessing that I, and only I, my lad, know of a hidden chest of gold?"

I stare out the window, for effect.

"Is there a *Treasure Island* somewhere out there?"

"Jump!" I hear someone say from below.

"Jump! Jump! Jump!"

Turning back to my class I see that Jonah is considering the alternatives. Have to press him.

"Welp, the I's have it. Jump it is!" I point my finger at him, as if it were a sword. "Written of royal decree by Jonah Macintyre."

"No!" he stands up and shouts.

I pretend to lose my balance and latch onto the window frame for dear life. "What sayth you, good sir? A twist, an honest to God turnaround?"

"Yes! Yes!" he shouts.

"You know the rules, lad. Only by royal decree."

He quickly takes a pencil and scribbles something onto a piece of paper.

"Hand it to me, lad. For mine eyes need to seeth this for mine…ah, whatever, just give."

He walks slowly and sets the folded piece of notebook paper in my hand.

I step off the ledge. People are clapping inside the class as well as outside. I only hear a few groans from below. I hold the piece of paper like a torch in the air, the light of freedom. I embrace Jonah with my right hand. "By royal decree, I am free to live another day!"

We both take a bow.

"Son," I tell him, "you've just changed history."

Jonah nervously smiles, trying to pretend that we had this prearranged act.

You have to understand.

This was the week of the miscarriage.

I had to invigorate myself with new life.

God, I love teaching.

Chap 5

It's Thursday. Angie's reading *A Midsummer Night's Dream* to me. That Shakespeare. He can be a nasty devil when it comes to sex comedies.

She's doing all the voices, which livens me up.

She smiles, I smile. Just like before.

I never told her this, but the reason for my writer's block was mainly due to her episode. She was having problems with her back that day, the happy mom-to-be. She asked to use my chair, the one I get the majority of my writing done in. Well, I was a dick about it for fifteen minutes or so then grumpily carried it into the living room for her. So unlike me.

When I came back with the popcorn, she was lying on the floor, clutching her stomach; a smear of blood was on my seat. I feared for the baby, I didn't know what to say. But my mouth murmured, "My baby. My chair."

While in the hospital, I interrupted her reading that day to apologize to her. She grasped my chest hard as she hugged me.

The weight lifted.

Had to let the ghost of little Edwin go. For the both of us.

To my students, I guess seeing a grown man trying to kill a fly was odd and a bit overdoing it. Shouldn't have climbed up onto that damn desk, that's for sure.

But I do believe I had to fall in order to rise.

Hmmmm, not bad.

My students, the ones I called my 'lucky seventeen' tolerated my antics and even encouraged them, except for this last little bit about killing a fly. They didn't know what the hell I was trying to prove.

Some visited.

Some sent their short stories to me in the hospital. Seven short stories from seven different genres of my tumble. Meg typed up the episode as a romance tale, the misunderstood Mr. Rifa falling in love with a fly, not knowing what to do but catch it to become a fly myself. It was cute. From every different angle they analyze my fall: The horror of it, the comedy, the romance, the mystery.

I'm happy to announce that Jonah has published two short stories, edited by me.

Mark Tory became a paramedic, but still admits to me, through e-mail, that he writes at night, always during his lunch breaks.

As for me, I wrote this on my last night in the hospital. It's just for me. A chance to realize the things I had trouble to understand. You know, why shouldn't I be happy?

I have a darling of a wife, students who not only write to their hearts' content, but stay in contact with me, and a child on the way. I should accept the way things are and be content as well. In the words of my wife, the great muse, it is not important to write but to have written.

…Dammit, there's a fly in here.

End?

Notes

On Pennies:

When the story was first conceived I only had two basic things to work with: a title and a main character who wasn't fully formed. At first I didn't know how I would write it or why in the hell I gave it such a vague title.

I was terrified to write this story because I didn't want to screw it up. Then, after one paragraph, the story took on a life of it's own. My mind, I realized was combining all the stuff that I wanted to write about the 1950's era: Tough guys, loan sharks, contract hits and a little bit of mystery. I've read a good mystery here and there but I was always puzzled as to why someone would want to figure out a crime when the person who did it is much more puzzling and interesting to analyze. While I wrote this, I put in some trait elements of my father into the character of Horace Grant. No, my father is not a hot-headed sonofabitch. I just put a dash of my father's undying ability to be fascinating into him. You could say that the story is extremely, loosely based on him. This a story for anyone who has ever been worked over, cheated, scammed and wanting their due.

On The Letters:

I'm sure that as you're reading this, you're determined to find an explanation of why I wrote such a God awful story. And here's my answer: It was an exercise of limitations. Sometimes during writing I hold a lot of stuff back. It is a simple fact that when you write a story, you backtrack and erase, leaving a phantom trail of what could have been. One day, while daydreaming, I was reminded of Chuck Palahniuk's extreme vision of *Choke*. This guy, surprisingly, doesn't hold back. I can't imagine him ever deleting anything. Even after the editors, I'm sure, took a stab at it, the finished product is widely extreme and controversial in nature. Welp, I guess you could say I was trying to top Chuck Palahniuk when he wrote *Choke* and his short story *Guts*. If you weren't able to finish the story, it means that I've done my job and the material was either too real or you didn't want to open that door in your imagination. If you were able to finish it all the way through, I should be asking you what your problem might be.

On Your Escape plan Now:

I have always wanted to write a story in which an important document would be the basis for imagination. Yes, it would have been easier to write out all the details, to construct the lab and scientists and all that junk. But I felt that when reading what was written from one point of view and to imagine the character accomplishing this journey, it would spark something different. Or maybe you imagined that the character just sat there, not moving, just reading. Did he accomplish all of these tasks as he read them one by one? Did he make it? Would he make it? I wanted to toy around with these questions.

Here was the other task that I felt I needed to do: I had to write the story in one sitting. And I did. I felt that if I was able to write in one continuous stream, which for any writer is impossible at times, the urgency of the document would show through.

On Failing upwards:

This story I would love to tell over and over again to a group of friends. It was basically a collision of ideas. I was lying on my bed, trying not to sweat from the heat wave, watching a movie that I had always wondered about: *Barton Fink*. In a nutshell, that story is about a playwright who tries to write a melodramatic script to a b-movie wrestling picture as he sits in his hotel room. It was more awkward than funny. I didn't really get it. Maybe I'm not supposed to.

So there I was, watching *Barton Fink*, thinking about the movie *1408*, which was another movie I really wanted to see about another man trapped in a hotel room of haunted doom. That story, weaved by the master Stephen King, intrigued me. I was drawn to it. I haven't seen a good haunted house-type movie in a very long time.

While ignoring *Barton Fink*, caught in a daydream, my mind started to replay the instrumental masterpiece that is *In the Hall of The Mountain King*. For some reason, I was obsessed with this song and still am. Then, like a note slipped under my door, it occurred to me; why can't there be one hotel story that is funny and wild?

That's how *Failing Upwards* was birthed. A hotel story that incorporates music, elaborate dance numbers, stunts, slapstick all wrapped up in a sympathetic character who tries hard not to be pathetic. Like I said, or suggest, sometimes a collision of ideas is the best way to find a new story waiting to be told.

On Alex Dujima's Book Code:

Put simply, I wanted, for once, the bad guy to be as dumb and as brutal as he possibly could be.

On I.F.:

This one is simple enough. While walking around the corner of a mall, just nearing a parking structure, me, my girl and our two friends Tandra and Latia all smelled smoke. We all thought fire, became paranoid and looked around. After a few minutes, the inquiry died down but I was still a bit paranoid. I felt, smelled, knew there was a fire somewhere but couldn't see it. And that's when, as my friends will tell you, I froze up and felt the idea hit me square in the head. To this day, I never knew where that fire was coming from.

On The Aches:

It began as a collaborative story experiment. I had always been fascinated by the story of how Mary Shelly developed the idea for *Frankenstein*. For those of you who don't know, she began a scary story contest with her friends and that's how it all came about. I was curious to find out if my girlfriend and I could do something similar to that. I thought, wouldn't it be exciting to jump back and forth, letting each one write a different segment of a short story? In the end, I jumped into crazy hour with my segment and it branched out into a totally different story. But it was really fun, the whole thing. And when my girlfriend and I looked back on the stories, we were both amazed at what we had accomplished. Like I told her, we are all hidden writers.

On The Subtle teachings of Mr. Rifa:

To their credit, I have had some pretty interesting teachers. All of them lent to the character of Harry Rifa. Mr. Zambole, my math teacher in grade school was a funny guy. Helped me a lot. Mr. Biba was my earth science teacher in high school. I borrowed a bit of his unpredictability. Mr. Kosina, my English teacher is the man who holds the mighty tag of the "Minus Ten." For the look, I used a bit of Mr. Mendelsohn, my film humanities teacher. And of course, there is Mr. Nedrow, the guy who didn't take shit, had a fun class and got us interested in literature. This was in college. I honestly couldn't write this story without a bit of inspiration from all of them.

On Powerless

This tale I've held onto for a long time. Can't remember how it came about but I'm finally glad that I get to tell it. When I started working on the first draft of the story, the bird was originally just a robin. But I needed something more than that. I wanted a bird that was unique, rare, and gorgeous to look at. A red robin would not do. So I searched up what birds I could find and came across the multicolored Painted Bunting. Now *that* is a bird. And it encompasses everything in the world. Sometimes, when writing short stories, it's the little things that need to be adjusted.

On 10 days in the extra life

When I was really big into filmmaking, I would outline screenplays of ideas I wanted to experiment with. One of them dealt with sleep deprivation and how it affects our minds. I can personally say that staying awake for extended periods can alter your perception. Like Paul, I stayed awake for three days straight before I finally gave up and slept for 14 hours after that. It wasn't due to a bet, like in the story. This was due to the fact that I thought my nightmares were too vivid to revisit. One of them even spawned the ever watchful creation of *Mr. Dead Eyes.*

Turn the page for a preview of Roberto Scarlato's upcoming book

Mr. Dead Eyes

Prologue

Kenora, Canada
2001

The sun was setting at the base of the woods, the endless woods from which nature howled. The gleam of the arc sent a luminous glow upon the shining glass doors. A shadow of a man in his late forties stepped toward the window with a glass in his hand. He drank the orange juice. Licking his lips, his eyes gazed outward along the woods. The trees aligned down the hill like a green stream. The woods were his favorite part of being on vacation. They were calm and the activities of certain crawly creatures were always in motion. He could always watch. Watching the birds, the winds through the trees, the silent shaping and growing of the leaves themselves; the earth being born in a slow, but constant pattern.

His eyes stretched across to the now dipping ball of light left. Inside, his house was as warm as the sun, hollow and slightly faded. The hallways were long and narrow. Henry's pupils began to expand with the distant fading of the sunset. He felt relaxed and calm with his place in life.

His house was empty all except for his thought winding and his presence. It seemed as if he was the last known person alive. *If you're the last; aren't you lonely, old boy?* his mind commented. True, he was a single man all these years and he would like to forget, but he couldn't.

He turned his gaze away from the fevering glass double doors. His two tropical plants were at each corner of the double doors, wavering in their calm growth. The ceiling slanted upward at a triangular point, connecting to the skylight. Soon, it would be glowing with stars. His hot day inside the house would be swallowed up by a cool and moist night of dreaming.

He crossed over to his living room, his bare feet taking muffled steps against the blood-red carpet. The living room had three steps down into a slight square decline surrounding the couch, the table with medical books and his big screen television. The wall around the fireplace (which was a burning blaze) was covered in ancient-like stones bricked and cemented close together. Behind this sturdy wall was a grassy covered hill that reached upward.

He set his glass upon the table, condensing as it slicked against the polished wood. He sat carefully across his tan couch and flipped the channels while searching for nothing. *No use. Nothing good on anyway.* His mind was a long time friend who a long time ago had worn out his welcome.

"I know that," he replied to himself. "I didn't come all the way out here in the middle of nowhere to watch television, you know."

A simple click ended the reception.

He carried his drink with him as he made his way to the bedroom. Brown wavy hair was brushing Henry's forehead. It was wiping the moisture away. He wiped a hand across to have temporary dryness for the moment. It was his own fault for cranking the thermostat up to a melting temperature, but in this weather, you had to have it.

Crossing the kitchen, he noticed a few letters on the table that he hadn't opened yet. He waved a hand dismissing the chore immediately. He would read them when he felt like it. Couldn't be anything more than bills.

On his way, he closed all doors that were left ajar in his carelessness of wandering around. The closet, bathroom and finally the bedroom. Inside the closet were some old clothes he wore for pride of his own wealth. Clean suits and shirts. His doctor's coat was among these, still with the stethoscope hung across the collar in the back of the closet. "Trying to forget about work, if I can," he grumbled as he closed the closet door.

The sun shined no more. Only a blanket of orange was seen through the window of the bathroom. It painted the bathroom door with a cube-shaped window frame. The bathroom was a bit bigger than the closet. The blueness of the tiles against the wall gleamed a shiny smile. The white marble floor was always slippery when he just got done taking a shower. He would kill himself on a whimsical accident someday if he wasn't always so careful. The thought was a ridiculous one: dying amongst your own wealth by slipping on your own expensive floors.

Another door closed and only a few steps away to his goal. The walls were a peach color, but it had faded along with the darkness that was coming. He opened his bedroom door and walked in tiredly. His bedroom was darker than the entire household, echoing his loneliness as he closed the door behind him. The wallpaper was a black and gloomy purple. The carpeted green bedroom floor looked a sickly vomit color as he made his way to the enormous king-sized bed. He wanted this kind of bed because it lessened his annoying tossing and turning habits, of which he had many, not to mention it cradled his pudgy spare tire belly, through those long nights when bad dreams plagued him. His bed was his sanctuary. The red covers looked inviting and almost hypnotizing to his tired eyes. Under his enormous bed was a shoebox containing an instrument used only in emergencies.

Setting down the glass, like the sun that set in front of his eyes, against the nightstand, he yawned painfully. He began to slip under the covers, pulling them up to his chin. He began to unwind from his day of research. He didn't bother to take his clothes off. It would only be a short nap. The warmth of his darkened house comforted his slowly slipping sleep. The whole house was covered in gray. It moved with the force of the skies, drooping a blackness of the woods.

Night had come.

The last man alive was sleeping, unaware of things to come.

* * *

His eyes bulged, and he let out a frightened gasp. *I heard it, I heard it.* His mind raced excitedly. He birthed his way out of the safety of his covers as he went for his gun, which was still under his bed, like it was a present he couldn't wait to open. He opened the shoebox and grabbed out his Smith and Wesson .38 revolver. He thumbed six bullets in the cylinder. He had argued that the gun was for his protection, but he couldn't deny the excitement that built when he handled it. The thought that he could take another life sent a thrill down his spine.

He kicked the shoebox under his bed, cautiously crawling like an animal defending its domain. He opened the door, just a crack, to see. Peering across the hall to the glass doors, which he couldn't see very well, he could hear rapid crunching somewhere in the house. Pulse racing, he anchored his gun on his hip. The sweat was starting at the top of his forehead and led down in a stream.

He didn't want to move but knew that he had to if he wanted to get the drop on this guy. As he opened the door, as if it were in flames and scared to touch it, he noticed that this would be a lot easier if the heat wasn't an issue, his fault to begin with. His arm was seen exiting the bedroom doorframe, aiming for an intruder. Making his way slowly, he moved to the glass doors that were at the end of the narrow hallway. His legs were spread through his steps, almost resembling a duck waddle; only this duck would not have long to live. He knew it as soon as he woke up with a start. He knew that something awful was going to happen.

The draft had surprised him as he found where it was coming from: the glass doors were shattered all over the living room rug. Light snow was drifting in. You would think a bull had charged its way in by the disarray of the glass sparkling moonlight across the floor. At this point, Henry knew that this night would end in an unpleasant way.

"I know you're in here," he said, holding his gun tighter in his grip. *Well, obviously, Sherlock!* His mind was mocking him. "I know you're here," he repeated, making his way back down the hallway. He whispered a pathetic "somewhere" as he proceeded with caution. His curiosity was getting the best of him.

He crept towards the closet doorknob with one arm outstretched, a flesh-toned claw shape, ready to grasp the knob and shoot the vandal. Standing still at the door, he debated on whether he should open it or not . . . and whether or not someone was in there. He coiled like a viper and summoned his strength. With a great shout, he lunged through the door. The door slammed against the wall so hard, it made an indent. His gun was positioned straight and narrow. From what he saw; nothing was in there. Henry lowered the gun and stopped his heavy breathing. He took his right arm and wiped the sweat clean from his forehead.

"Where the fuck are you?" he whispered.

If there ever once was a high-strung moment; this was it. Henry knew someone was here. He could feel it. The bastard was close and he was here for something. Henry could feel eyes watching him. His face was beet red and he could feel the choking heat of his anticipation. All of a sudden, as if making things worse for Henry, the bathroom door slammed behind him. He whipped around and fired without thinking.

The bullets ripped through the wooden white door like water droplets through tissues. Henry, dazed from how fast he had reacted, fell on his ass right against the wall.

That gun had quite a kick to it.

The once solid door was now painted with three brown-colored holes. The moonlight poured through, creating hypnotizing beams that made the hallway brighter. Light blue beams, which barred the hallway, shining like slanted bars on a jail cell, framed Henry against the wall.

Because of the door moving, he knew for certain that someone was there now. He tried to decide quickly what to do next. Most of all, he wanted to worry his enemy. He gave out a nervous chuckle and said, “I got you now, you fucking twerp.”

He kicked the door open and jumped in. The force of the kick sent the doorknob flying through the air, after making a divot in the wall, and then finally clanked on the marble floor.

Almost immediately, the door was shut behind him at alarming speed by an arm clothed in black. A person dressed in black jumped on Henry Stolley’s back out of the tub. This unknown phantom all dressed in black knocked the gun out of Henry’s weak hands. He bent Henry down to his knees as he pulled out a black nylon chord and wrapped it around the poor man’s throat.

Henry struggled vigorously for his life. The harder he tried, the more the madman would tighten the chord. Henry dug his fingernails into his neck, desperately trying to loosen the chord. His fighting was frail and useless as he mutilated his own neck by scratching desperately to loosen the chord. The pain was long drawn out, lasting almost forever. Each death yank was crushing his Adam’s apple. His mouth was making sounds that yelped pleas of begging for his life.

Henry didn’t want to die. His body started to prove that fact when a large, almost insane, rush of adrenaline rushed through his veins as he forced his back against the wall, instantly crushing his predator against the tiles.

Tiles clattered and rained down on both men.

The man in black grunted in pain.

Another courtesy yank brought Henry down to his knees again. He grasped for the gun and fired aimlessly in panic at the ceiling. The bright blasts shined through the bathroom window, letting all manner of wildlife see this predator's method of killing. They had seen him enter and now they heard this middle-aged man struggle like a fly caught in a web.

Henry couldn't hold out much longer. His face turned purple, his eyes growing huge with death breathing down his neck. The next few yanks did it. It cut off his air supply until he could breathe no more. His arms fell, pieces of meat dangling from a corpse. His lifeless body fell on its back to the cold bathroom floor. Drool was dripping out the sides of his mouth. His neck was laced with scratches and gouges from his own hands. Even though he was dead; his vision was quite clear.

The tall, dark, nameless man stood towering over his fallen prey. It was then, that he decided, to pull off his ridiculous ski mask because he was in the clear. It was also chaffing his cheeks.

Henry's blue fading vision caught sight of a familiar face. He had seen that bald head once before. Now, after it was undeniably too late, Henry realized that this was the man that was following him this whole time.

The man held his mask in his hands as he kicked Dr. Stolley's body. The blow could have killed him, had he not been dead already. The man, bending down over Henry's dead stare, spoke with eerie calmness as he was cleaning up after his mess. He crept out of the tub from which he strangled this man and said to his dead face, "Sore throat?"

The question was asked with a sick grin.

He retrieved some pills from his pocket and threw them at Henry's face. "Take two of these and call me in the morning . . ."

Made in the USA
Charleston, SC
15 May 2010